T0279807

PATH

PATH

THE TAG SERIES

PETER RIVA

OPEN ROAD

INTEGRATED MEDIA
NEW YORK

This edition published in 2023 by Open Road Integrated Media, Inc.
180 Maiden Lane
New York, NY 10038
www.openroadmedia.com

For my family, their patience, their support, and encouragement.

PATH

1

AN UPSIDE-DOWN WAY OF LOOKING AT THE SYSTEM

From the beginning, that first morning, I knew there was something wrong. The sky shouldn't behave like that; nature wasn't programmed to produce effects like those. So many people shouldn't have died. Like everyone my age who remembered a time when everything didn't work so cohesively, so perfectly, I listened with only scant attention to gossip that we were in for a catastrophe "sooner or later." It always popped up as ridicule on the Net—the same doomsday prediction made by people wanting attention, their images on the video screens, or so I thought. I was wrong; sooner had come.

The day had started much like any other. I awoke in my bedroom across the hall from my wife's, stretched my fifty-year-old, six-foot joints and ligaments until they stopped popping, washed, examined the slight pot belly I was getting in the mirror, and got dressed in the blue gear my job called for, like so many thousands of other clean-room, System employees. I stuffed my pale blue dust-cover over-shoes in my back pocket while I recorded a morning greeting to the family, my gang, who would probably get it around lunch when they checked the home net to order up dinner. Today was a fine day, gentle breezes from the west, so ordered by the System, and I rather cheerfully set off to work. It was work I liked really. We all like our work; it was the number one criteria for any job application nowadays. Mine was, well, just better suited to what I wanted currently. Like everyone, I had once wanted something else. Musician was a joke, a pipedream really, left over from days of youth when music was a common bond, not a cultural thing. Music didn't push the envelope of existence anymore, and that was a good thing, so society decided. Music was mainly a reality enhancer and I couldn't have been less interested in what my parents had once called "elevator music."

The job I wanted and applied myself to currently was to help humanize the artificial intelligence of the System, to make it fit more perfectly into the needs of society, the nation and, of course, keep all the needs of America running more smoothly.

Leaving the house, alone as usual, I keyed a simple reminder to my only real son who would be, if I remembered properly, leaving our atmosphere today. "Godspeed," I keyed in and pushed send on the reminders tablet by the door. That should make him chuckle. God indeed.

The elevator dropped me directly onto the third-floor access for my commute on the elevated high-speed conveyor-way called the NuEl running from our apartment on 3rd Avenue and 123rd Street to my stop midtown and then all the way on downtown to Battery Park. Manhattan had long ceased to be a town with now over sixteen million people, but residents still cling to that terminology as a badge of belonging. Manhattan still has cultural pull.

As I stood waiting to move across the NuEl to the fast lane, I

looked across 3rd Avenue towards the still rising sun appearing
over the skyline of Queens and Brooklyn. There it was, a line of
storm clouds approaching from the east. But the wind was from
the west, as predicted. The conveyor edge moved beneath my
toes and I stepped on, lively, and then hopped left across onto
each faster moving belt, threading my way through the crowds
in the morning rush. Through the glass dome over our heads,
I stared at the advancing clouds against the prevailing breeze.
They simply had no right to be there.

Long before I reached my step-off street, the clouds had
gathered strength and color, turning an ominous pinkish green.
Rain had begun to fall. The west wind rolled the dangerous mass
onto its side and, almost as if by magic, I saw the funnel appear
and extend down, pointed like a finger of fate at the intersection, my normal stop, less than a block away at 57th. Some
people outside the NuEl dome waiting to hop on looked up,
others were unaware. Most were then lifted, somewhat magi-
cally, to drift away inside the funnel. Some, on the edges, were
thrashed about, split, gutted and strewn across the avenue. All
in silence, no bomb, nothing but the white noise of the tornado,
limbs were torn from innocent people in silent screaming
terror. The people it didn't take up became punching bags for its
anger, debris pummeling them, people thrown against people.
In terror, I aimed my feet quickly at the 59th Street exit, moving
swiftly across to each slower conveyor and then off and ran
down the recycled plastic steps to street level.

As I ducked into the nearest shop for cover, I was suddenly
aware of a curious memory. I was eight; my father was telling
me that everything was related, not relative, but related to my
actions and desires. The man you saw on the street would, when
you stopped watching him, vanish and re-appear when you
next needed him. You think you travel by plane (back then) but

God, somehow, was manipulating your reality for you; you sat down, noise and effects happened, you got up and the scenery had been changed, presto, you were in Paris. But not. There was no "there" over there. It was all here. Everything you saw was related to what you saw before. There were clues, if you looked for them, to God's theater as he called it. For years as a kid I searched and studied, often thinking he was possibly right, a face in a crowd here, a dress there, a somehow familiar landscape and always déjà vu.

Then, one day, I was stranded on an expedition and knew what it was like to be truly alone, no body, no God, nothing. Me. An asteroid. Nothingness. Void. Dad had lied. Well, not lied, he'd made up a far too-convincing fairy tale. Or was it? Looking down the street through the laminate glass of the shop, leaning over the vases of blooms, the sales' girl yelling at me not to squash the floral display, what I saw could, very possibly, have been a bad day for God. His theater props had gone awry.

As quickly as it had appeared the funnel slowed and vanished into itself. Overhead the clouds rolled back a block or so, becoming wisps and then they too were gone. The weather was back as predicted. Someone was going to lose their job over this one. WeatherGood One had always been the most reliable service in America, creating perfect weather for the System, yet today it had failed. Of course, Dad would have said there was no WeatherGood service at all . . . *oh, to heck with that, Dad*, I thought, *move on, it's over.* I tried to put it behind me.

Of course, it wasn't over. The Event was only just beginning.

Why is it that reality is always measured by the very things that give us the most problems? Once upon a time it was an asset to have lots of kids because they could help you with the farm chores. Then, a hundred years ago, the population took a dive as people realized that kids were expensive, so although 1.2 per family was considered enough to satisfy primal urges, it was not enough for the country to sustain its growth or economic system. All sorts of tax and financial breaks were dreamt up, to no avail. Immigration was the only solution, which lead to strife, internationally as well. As violence goes, when the military intervened, it wasn't much of a revolution or a contest. Those that had, had less, those that really had went on having more than they needed and those that had nothing at least got a foothold. But other nations weren't happy with America and we became isolationist, defenses fully empowered. Then after the earthquakes that destroyed Los Angeles, the economy was almost in ruins. And that lead, in the dead of winter forty years ago, to the devastating Purge when the military took over the reins of government and decided to make changes nationally and internationally to "safeguard the nation for all true Americans."

At school we were instructed to consider the Purge as beneficial to people now part of America, even though so many lost their lives in the process, accidental and deliberate. The new states of old Mexico and the provinces of Canada were the worst hit as bloodshed and then their annexation stripped away any of the old political autonomy. But, all in all, things have settled down, thanks, in large part, to the likes of WeatherGood One, the FarmHands, PowerCube and the other Systems' controls, all free of course, providing you are American.

But the Purge and its aftermath of military power brought with it changes within America as well. Maybe the hardest part was the enforced sterilization program for anyone who didn't have kids by the age of 30. And if you already did have kids, the gene tests were invasive to determine if you should have more. Draconian? For sure, but the reality is that medical costs came down immediately and, since the official word was that there was no God, certainly not one to trust in, there was no need to leave procreation up to Him. Heck, I don't miss my "little swimming buddies" as the nurse sickeningly called them as she stemmed their flow. And the benefit presented to offset the sterilization? Nowadays no one is prevented from living as long as they want, science permitting. No one is kept from a job he or she wants. Everyone has total control over where they live, where they go to school, what hours they work, and what relationships they want, be it man, woman, or whatever variation of sexual proclivity that turns them on. With a fixed input of fresh workers, oops sorry, citizens, a steady climate, limitless food chain, and ample un-interruptible power, life can now be about those primal instincts, about getting on, achieving something, being an individual, and of course sex.

Okay, so for a short time people became drones. But then they began to realize that a job was worthless, a vocation the answer; that kids were reality, their future course a task of great creativity from womb to graduation. And so, as we all changed, and I'm just old enough to remember when it was still a 9-to-5 job world, the need for the placebos of that old life melted away. Fictional movies, TV, vids, art in stuffy museums, and almost all fictional reading material—all these now seem so pointless. As part of our new life we've reached out to that which inspires us, which gives us a sense of reality not falsehood, live performance has boomed, sport too. We still need a sense of, well, who we are as beings. Everything else is provided now, the struggle is gone, and that's a reality. Somehow, the primal brain can't quite absorb it. Well, I know that mine can't.

Kids seem totally adapted straight from the womb. I remember playing with blocks and model cars, creating make-believe scenes and cities. But today's kids reach out to model exactly that which is around them, making duplicates, not fantasy. Have they stopped dreaming? Nope. Their dreams are different, they dream as a dependence of their primal past, not as a forge for their future. I know, my first and only biological kid had a foot in each camp, sometimes fantasizing, sometimes evolving intricate duplicates of what was around him. The first time I saw my Freddie, then 4, make a model of his recently discarded bottle, complete with teat and milliliter markings, I worried, but the docs assured me this was a good thing, he was evolving. Of course our later, bioengineered, SynthKids never had this duality; they are only here to provide a better sense of our reality, not theirs. Oh, there's always the whisper of their consciousness. Meantime, the wife, who I nicknamed She-Who-Must-Be-Obeyed (I always liked that series—*Rumpole of the Old Bailey*—when I was a kid—on *TV Land*—when satellite still existed) forced me to accept her four SynthKids as a "psychological extension to your reality." Yes, dear. Out-voted, one to one originally. Now I get out voted, by She-Who-Must-Be-Obeyed and the SynthKids—five to one. Freddie, at least, stays neutral.

The SynthKids are nice, and we got and get on fine. Heck, I can't tell the difference, really, since they made them so they can bleed and die and stuff. But, in my heart of hearts, they're not mine; although to glance at them (or see their DNA report) you couldn't tell. But they each have a look, a quirk, that's easy to recognize. My wife dotes on them and will until they leave at 18, when they recycle themselves, their programming kicking in like an alarm clock. Arrival is free of delivery pain, Immaculate Conception. Yet for eighteen years they are hers, for a while, and when they go she can get new ones, as many as she likes. A hundred years ago we'd have been stoned to death for turning our "kids" over for recycling. Now? Welcome to reality and ain't it comfortable, cozy, coddling, cute and—above all—creepy?

Nah, I'm the only one who thinks so. I don't speak of these things. Oh, there's no law against it. Speak out all you want, but life will not be worth living with She-Who-Must-Be-Obeyed if I do.

Maybe, thinking all these dark thoughts I was having a middle age crisis. As I frowned I made a plan to stop in and see the doc for a shot of little happy bots, tweaking up my serotonin production rate. Maybe he'll also give me a couple of those ForgetAll pills to erase the trauma of all those people near the NuEl who got mangled by the tornado. Until then I tried, hard, to act normal. Death and trauma didn't have to be part of our lives anymore, the System's functions would bring everything instantly back to normal, seemingly with no interruption, so why mourn? Why worry for your fellow man or woman?

Walking up these damn stairs to my office, my exercise monitor clicks away. It gives off little ticks of approval like a mechanical purring cat, so maybe it won't hum disapprovingly at lunch. No rush. I can't be late, no one ever can. The workload is as you want it, the goals as you set them. Sure, there are some over-achievers, people needing that self-approval or public recognition. Why else would anyone run for elected office? Corruption in all its forms evaporated when there was no want anymore. Power? Hah with less than 2% of the people not voting and referendums ruling the land—even I chose to palm as I got on the NuEl this morning: "Do you want rain on Friday?" Palmed: "No."—Who's kidding who? Control by politicians? Not in this country. People cast mandatory votes on every damn little thing and politicians only serve to make sure the System functions as it should. Coupled with the DefenseShield (Slogan: "Twelve attacks and counting—not one citizen disturbed!"), government is relegated along with the old Pentagon and ex-State Department to menial Systems maintenance, sending threatening e-mails to rogue states who think they want a piece of the American pie, and, basically, are sidelined by human whim. "Do you want America to annex Venezuela to recover the rain forest for your holiday experience? Press your palm to vote yes or no." And it's law—politicians must follow the whim of the people. No lobbying, no leverage, no government alternate say really. Government actually works for the people, perhaps the only benefit of the Purge.

Of course the safeguard to all this is the Citizens Council which has control of the great Systems. I'm on the Council sometime in the future, they'll tell me when some day. Everyone has to serve for 5 weeks at least, but nobody is quite sure how it's arranged. On the Citizens Council there is no hidden voting, everything's open, humanity exposed at its most raw between Council members. People have been known to come out of those weeks of Council seclusion half-crazed, spouting unbalanced gibberish that they were being threatened by their fellow citizens. Usually it's the ones who want to "do" something who crack up, the majority of the Council being happy to toe the line of the New Life, as we've come to call it after the Purge. Doing nothing except that which you want to do is the New Way. It's funny how quickly "want" became "do nothing or do anything." Your choice.

These stairs are becoming harder ... puff, puff, puff ... maybe I'll move our office next week down from the 45th. But I will lose the view toward the Park below the 40th floor.

My wife has sometimes voiced her chagrin at not staying home with the kids and raising them herself. Admittedly, she's not really the motherly type, if she were she could do that, of course, with the other moms. But it not being her vocation, the docs think it's unhealthy for the kids to be raised by someone who's not 100% passionate about it; the kids could become unbalanced. We do get them most evenings, or if we choose to work a night shift for variety's sake, during the day. The rest of the time they are at DayCare or in school immersion in the care of those people who are, presumably, of motherhood or educational vocational bent. Hah, bent, that's how my back felt every time I used to pick our real kid Freddie up. He's an adult now, wonder where he'll be next week? Last month he started training as a SpaceElevator operator, hoping to make the full crew list on some outward trip. Today's his first ride up. Like father, like son. Except I never told him my Dad's theory, so maybe he'll like the empty cosmos. Gotta remember to call him and find out how his first ride went.

Click, click from my monitor sewn into the fabric of the pants I'm wearing. Enough exercise. Elevator time. I'll avoid dessert at lunch to keep the darn thing from disapproving. The rice grain sized radio frequency identifier, RFID, in my palm opens the stairwell emergency door, a new model with a woman's voice, quite sexy. Wonder who they modeled it after? The one to my office door I chose. I had always liked Meg Ryan as a kid, those nights under the covers. I miss that innocence, hers, and even miss my shame a bit, the fear of Mom or Dad walking in when I was nine. But now I could call up her Synth double for a night out and the wife wouldn't think anything of it. It's in my profile, the ones She agreed to before we were married. Nothing's forbidden, but it's hardly worth it. Ah Meg, never mind, some other time. Maybe one day I'll take the chance and childishly liven up the libido again.

Come to think of it, I heard Meg's still with us, pretty ancient now, well over a hundred and fifty, looking good, and head of the American PTA. Or maybe it's her kid who had her self modeled on Mom, changing identity. They do that, sometimes. Jolie is on her fourth go round. Same boobs, same see-through white dress at every party. Might check out news of Meg on the common room office screen during morning break, see if I can tell. There are usually signs, a DNA code clash or a mirrored twitch, right eye instead of left, that sort of thing. As a codifier, I have "awareness" or so they say.

Through the stairwell door to the elevator. Taking the elevator up I smile, almost made it this morning, only 10 floors to go. Well, it was a restless night, always is when She-Who-Must-Be-Obeyed is angry about something. It's in her profile: anger, ranting, talk, talk, talk, always at me not with me, and then sex. The carrot in front of this donkey. She's good at it. But like a Chinese meal, there's always something missing, something insubstantial. Ever since my stint as a Spacefarer, and revelation on that asteroid (when it all went wrong—yeah, I know it was my fault), She's been a little more controlling, a little less, well, mine. I wasn't away long enough, heck, it wouldn't matter if she had done it with somebody. It's just that I did something out of character when I came back and it rattled her world. Not that her world is subject to mine really. It's hers and she's welcome to it, that's the law.

Some things they never change. If it ain't broke, why fix it? Marriage works, especially for her. "Ding," and the doors open. My floor.

I decided to put a brave face on things. That WeatherGood One accident was troubling me but, really, it was hardly anything to do with me and, as we're expected to think, life goes on. Or so I thought. "Hello Mary. How's the System running this morning?"

"Simon, there's been a glitch in the food supply programming. I can't track it down, but the FarmHands master control says they've got it and will pass the glitch to me for analysis. They say it will take me days to unravel it. I'm betting them I can do it in one."

"Well done Mary, always the office genius." And she was, if a little weird. "What's the bet this time?" Her reality was wrapped up in competing against herself with each new mental game, each anomaly to be unraveled. The folks at FarmHands knew that it made her happy, and presumably it made them happy to have her on the case. Everybody's happy.

"2 days, anywhere, with anybody I choose."

"Oh, shit. They're really not going to like that result at Control. Last time you had a half day and three people were re-assigned because of failure to show up for a week, you got them so screwed up." But Mary knew I was ribbing her, she never wasted anyone to that extent. It wasn't her thing to take advantage, just to step outside of the system routine for a while and be radical; drink, booze it up, a few orgies, that sort of thing. It was allowed (if unusual, and in her profile is written the word "unusual type").

"John on the 40th thinks I should pick him if I win. 'Dream on,' I told him, I'm waiting for a crack at the master coder." The master coder doesn't exist, and Mary knows it. An urban myth, like those old middle-of-the-night childhood horror stories that scared the begeebus out of you. The master coder was like a Wizard of Oz, sounds good, pure bullshit.

I had to ask, "Any news on WeatherGood One? There's bound to be something there for you, unless it was something simple like equipment failure."

Her head snapped up. "WeatherGood One failed? How long? People hurt?" Before I could answer, she quickly pulled up the news screen and began to probe through to the live feeds and re-play them at a different angle from what I saw. Oh, she was all aglow . . . quite cute really, in a frumpy sort of way. Mary, now older than I, doesn't believe in alterations, she's one of those, "I'll live with what my genes have given me, thank you very much!"

Reports were popping up on her wall screen now, with code streaming down the side and onto her tablet, a waterfall of digits and color, filling her whole desk screen. Mary stopped looking at me, so I avoided answering her questions.

Instead, I couldn't resist another joke, just to clear my thoughts, "Looks kind of like God was showing he's still around and not to be fooled with."

Mary looked stern, "Simon, you can't say that sort of thing and mean it, it's silly. I'll zip-mail all this to the brats in engineering, see if something failed, but with their redundant systems, I've never seen anything like this before, it's not normal."

"Okay. Let me know, will ya? See you at break, save the window table for us."

"Nah, I'll be winning my bet, have your meal with Tom and Suze without me . . . no time for round two of your theory of happiness on a Monday. What did you do, have another fight and then make up with her?"

Mary knew me too well. I pulled a face, flipped her a very sexist bird, forbidden in the office place. Well, she deserved it. She laughed.

I went into my office, commanding the door to open. No windows, no screens, green-grey walls, one chair, one head dome. The golden metal dome was molded for my head and hinged to snap securely into place as you pulled down the neck collar at the back. This completed the dome's circuitry and activated the sensors arranged in geodesic patterns on the underside. Each sensor had a small blunt pin which made pinprick skin contact. It didn't hurt, so long as you didn't accidently tap the top or sides. "Back to work," I said out loud, as my Dad always had each morning as he got up from breakfast. Funny day, this one, amidst all the trauma, Dad's presence is almost palpable.

I put it on. The dome activated and my "mind's eye" vision popped into life. I could see hundreds of images of mock master System code on what appeared as walls, a myriad of pathways open and closed, everything a 3-dimensional visual construction. Everything looked clean, fresh and organized. My job was to move the mock System code around, to make chaos out of the normal, to re-structure reality, even pathways, directions, open and close new portals, so that what I did could be real, but not likely. Then people like the Marys across America, sitting in offices, or at the beach, or wherever their hearts were content, would spot the errors of my ways and re-arrange things. In the process, between my mix-up and their unraveling, the computing power of the human mind was encoded again, and fed to the real central computers, the System itself, to make all sorts of gizmos work "in a human way." Sort of antichaos programming compared to the fuzzy logic and super-computers of a half hundred years ago.

The System, looking after all of America, needed to be encoded, to understand and react in a human way, so I taught it, along with dozens of other programmers, on the backup, mock System computers. When our "mistakes" were corrected, the corrections became the human element—carefully encoded into the real System.

Me? I like messing things up, seeing if they really do belong together. If they do, they shouldn't fit anywhere else. I'm the human equivalent of a subprogram virus, trying to adapt, fit in and yet alter the reality around me. Funny how I can move so many things around and still have them fit. I'm getting better at it too. A little pat on the back here. Last week I made a re-arrangement fit so well, it looked original. Caused a bit of a panic, I can tell you. Of course, realizing that it was a rearrangement, all they had to do was break it and all the disassembled pieces tumbled out of place and they fixed it. But for a while there, my imperfect perfection reigned supreme. Flawless but full of potential to become an anti-system.

You see, I wanted to try an experiment. Instead of moving the blocks of the system around, say taking the power supply profile and supplanting the water feed program (which caused the modeling to have water at constant pressure out of every tap—water like a laser cutting through cups and yet oozing out of industrial pipes, a woman on a bidet would get the thrill of her life, well, not really) . . . where was I? Oh yes, anyway this is what I do. I can make the systems look like they could fit in each other's coding, but in reality it causes simulated chaos. Of course, the closer the systems' coding are to each other, the harder it is to spot. The big stuff, like the power supply is an easy one to spot and fix for them. My talent lies in making them think they are looking at one problem and when they change it back they take a small part of the program back with it that I didn't change, thereby changing the original program, never knowing it was them that caused the error. Like swapping the power system and the water feed program the second time I did it. They weren't looking very well that day!

In the water feed programming was a small, seemingly insignificant, sub-program which regulated the monitoring of pressure at old fire hydrants (no longer used, of course). I put that sub-program in the power system program that I put into the water supply. It fit because, well, it was meant to be where it was. When they spotted that the big programs had been switched, they swapped them back, verified all the primary systems but never checked the redundant sub-systems. Presto, they had installed the hydrant pressure sub-program in the power system programming.

When they ran the backup System proof test (so that the "human quotient" could be measured for the master programming), my little subprogram mistook a normal drop in amperage in the shadow mock NuEl on Third as a panic call to increase fire hydrant pressure for a five alarm fire, drawing massive amounts of water (yes, they used to have those fire-fights, engines strewn across avenues, sirens wailing, water everywhere—as a kid I loved those). As the sub-program increased amperage (thinking it was water flow), the mock NuEl went, well, just sub-sonic. Bodies everywhere in the simulation. Chalk one up to me. Mary, when she reviewed what I had done, as the central office called to congratulate me, well Mary simply stared at the code and told me I was a really, really, sick bastard. Highest form of compliment. Of course, all this was caught in test using the mock backup System, in a test only, fixed and put back to normal. But the human element programming was useful, if only for codifiers at Control Central to incorporate at some stage into the real System.

This morning all I could see to play with was the mock WeatherGood system. That's all Control seemed to want me to look at. What fun was there in that? WeatherGood was a fault-less and vital system. Okay, this morning the real System has a glitch. But in here, with the fake System, everything should be faultless, as normal, and it looked that way. Anyway, anything that I could touch in there was not a complex algorithm; it had to be simple, unchanging, stable. There was nothing I could insert or mess around that they couldn't spot in one second. Or less. Damn, give me something else . . . I requested other programs' access. Again and again it was the WeatherGood system program I was shown.

I gave the mental command to exit, took off the dome, came out of what I felt was a mental pit. I looked around the blank walls. The void, the plain color, in here was useful. Was I getting pushed towards WeatherGood because there was a fault there and they wanted to compare my handiwork on the mock System programming? An alarming thought occurred: Was there something in there that maybe I had done to some other part of the mock System, something that had migrated there to the real program files, which had caused the death-by-wind event on 3rd Avenue? Impossible. Really impossible. Anyway, if I had wanted to cause an occluded front to roll on its side over 3rd I would have simply changed . . . what, what would I have changed? That program has no swappable elements that could not be spotted instantly. Somehow, the whole map would have had to be different, same coordinates, same time/space criteria, same program . . . wait, that's it, just change the reality, the Earth, not the overlay.

Dome snapped back on.

I went through the usual checks and alterations, making seemingly clever (but stupid really) changes to code here and there. Something to make the system think I was doing something, keep giving me access. Changing bits (oh, ain't that clever?), code lines swapped here and there, seemingly in a pattern, but mindless really. I have access in here to all the code ever written for the WeatherGood program and I was looking for the key to the primary reference source. What was all this programming supposed to act upon, over what area, what map?

There it was, in a code so old I could hardly recognize it. You have to be old, like me, born late last century after WWII. The code in here is basic. Simple, binary basic, labeled "USGS, IGY, 1959, section 62, ref. 412, grid 1–1200." WeatherGood was using the old binary encoded maps of the Americas, reloaded as they were in 1959 after the International Geophysical Year. That shouldn't be, though. Parts of the American continent were now underwater after the Big Orange Quake forty years ago and, anyway, there had been three volcanoes that I knew of since then, each had changed the landscape for 100s of kilometers in and around Los Angeles, obliterating the city and all its people. All that was left there now was water, nothingness. How could WeatherGood be using a land map from 1959?

Tracing my way back up the code, kind of like swimming up a stream of zeros and ones, I looked for branch to the flow, an amendment, a qualifier. I'm good at this, this editing, this flowing through all the code, this deconstruction technique. I couldn't have missed it. It's not there, it's not here. WeatherGood works on a flawed, outdated, map. Now, what WeatherGood does exactly to work the way it does, I have no idea, but what the program instructs are, what the instructions are in code, any code from the most moderns all the way back to binary code, that is right here in front of me. I can touch it, figuratively, right in front of my eyes in here. Screems of it, pages and pages of code running seemingly endlessly across my vision. Not one line of code I can't read and understand. And not one byte that told WeatherGood that the maps were out of date.

Unless . . . was the USGS IGY map of 1959 re-edited at source? Named the same, was the file updated but never re-named? Okay, that's poor record keeping, but it might explain this. It may have been too hard to catch all the references to the USGS IGY 1959 in every program and subset, so they simply kept the file name the same. Heck, in old Basic that would be a large task, mundane, repetitive to change every program calling on the newer version. But they could have written a worm even back then, a virus as they were once feared, to find and destroy and supplant, so why didn't they? Okay, viruses were outlawed made seriously criminal after the Purge, but the Nation could surely get around their own laws for this good reason, couldn't they? I stopped probing, the dome went silent, waiting. I retraced my pathways, made sure I made a few changes along the way, and got the hell out of there. Leave it virgin. If I was right, this could be a real discovery and I wanted to keep it virgin. I knew other codifiers were always digging around my trail. I'd seen their clumsy attempts to follow me, real time, before. Not this time buckos. This little discovery is mine.

Ego is a dangerous thing.

I took off the dome, and the system announced "345 changes made, 320 remedied in 1.2 seconds, 22 remedied in a further 3.1 seconds, 3 remedied in a further 2 seconds. Performance nominal, rating 4." Like an old game of computer solitaire you play at the museum, it keeps score for me. 4 out of 10 is not my usual standard, which is 9.275, but enough to keep my average from slipping too much as it's only one probe amongst thousands.

I went to provoke Mary into thought and, if she were around, Suze also. Suze was cuter and, if I was lucky, not heads down with a desk full of code to unravel. She'd maybe flash her smile and perk up her boobs. Suze wasn't the workaholic self-evaluator Mary was. Provoking fellow humans had the curious effect of making me a better codifier. Often, Mary or Tom or Suze would say something that would give me a damn good idea. Once I left a small electronic tag where I had been meddling (a particularly good little executable subset of code which could, ideally if not spotted and not run on the dummy system, make all tomatoes blue for a day).

When you worked inside the System programming, you could attach little electronic flags, like the old Post-it notes or a bookmark, only they were only little glowing colored ribbons of nothing that could be easily removed when found or no longer needed. Without the tags, remembering where you spotted something, or some code you wanted to amend could take hours to discover. With tags in place, you could zip around, checking the screens of code quickly.

The thing was, I had left that really visible tag with Tom's name on it, to give him credit for an off-hand remark over lunch. He had said, as he was slicing a tomato, "I feel so blue today." So I made the blue tomatoes snafu all his—if it got into the System, all tomatoes grown for weeks would be genetically altered to become blue, sort of rotten blue colored. Some codifier in New California spotted the alteration, but it was six hours before anyone did and that caused a lot of discussion as to why Tom had access at all and what if it has made it into the System . . . Tom was pissed at me as they called him names but the System gave me the credit in the end, doing my job, as it was recorded that I was the only one in there. But I knew Tom would watch whatever he said in my presence for a while.

Ah, debugging the program of inter-human interaction, what could be more fun? At least I've got Tom thinking like a codifier, everything is significant. He's coming along. Mary's got a thing for him but her mantra of humming his full name (Tom Makerman) over and over annoys him.

Suze was there, as I expected, overlooking the Park at "our" table, the one we bag every day. It's the only one that can see the baseball stadium where Strawberry Fields used to be. I heard the other day, someone thinking out loud, that it was named after a farm that used to be there in the 19th century. Idiot. I put him straight, showed him the brass plaque devoted to John Lennon now stuck on the side of the entrance to Lennon Stadium, put there by his 3rd son/self (I'm not sure which, it gets confusing, was it a reincarnation of John Lennon or one of his descendants altered to look like him with the ID switch?). I do remember the vid of the ceremony, when they sold the land lease rights to the Mets people, and glued up the old plaque.

Out the window the game practice was underway and she turned up the gain on the pane to bring the view in closer.

Live viewing was always better than replay on the wall screen. Smaller, but somehow more real. This office didn't have the new SensorPath hookup so you can feel and smell the ballpark atmosphere, but live was almost like being there.

"Hey Suze. Tom around? Mary's not coming probably."

"Yeah, saw Mary. Fingers popping." She called Mary's sliding fingers "poppers" because Mary did have this old habit of tapping on the screen. "Tom's not in. Not coming. Trouble there." Suze had this clipped speak, drove me nuts. She was very tweek or whatever the current expression for cool is.

Had he been caught by WeatherGood One's little anomaly? Did he get hurt? "What's the trouble, do you know?" Her answer was miles away from my guess.

"Want verification his work. Lost file. ID at risk." This was serious news. Your work file is who you are, how you exist. No work file, you're an outcast. Sure, you don't starve, nobody does, but what are you alive for? That's the question.

"Local lost file or main system?"

"Don't know. Tom called in from Control, upset, says system bad, gone bad."

"When was this?"

"9:30 this am." About the time of the WeatherGood One breakdown. Was WeatherGood One a whole system failure? Bang goes my simple USGS IGY 1959 guess.

"Suze, you see any other glitch in the mock System files? What's been handed to you for decoding?" I explained what I had seen on the NuEl. Suze's eyes grayed over.

We were allowed to talk about programming, openly, there wasn't anything we were actually doing here, just messing with the parallel system and programming to teach the main System how humans work, to help teach them how to think, and plan, better for humanity, for America. It was the New Way, openness for good.

Sony had started the process with Akibo their robot dog. All the time humans were programming it, it became more like an anthropomorphic dog. When Akibo 5 was all ironed out, it was boring. A minihuman. So they tried improbability, fractals and fuzzy logic to make it unpredictable. But then all it became was an unpredictable dog-looking (and barking) human. Useless as man's best friend. Then a pimply youth (they still had them back then), just before the Purge, decided to let his dog program the damn thing, to implant all the dog's mistakes on Akibo 6, the kit form, the build-it-at-home-as-a-hobby model. Suddenly the damn thing bit him. Ah, the perfect puppy. Junior pimply youth became a millionaire. The Purge saw him at the Pentagon of old, he died trying to make an anti-riot device outthink humans. He was using his own algorithms, especially hate and cunning ones, to jack up the system. It killed him right off, for a start. After the dog bit him you would have thought he would have learned.

Anyway, his concept to program a system with a human input when it needs to deal with human needs was recognized as the way for the future. It lead to my job here and, frankly, half the main systems in place. Delving into the FarmHands programming, I often see what seems to be weird stuff and when I play the sets through a simulator, the human-ness of the activity is quirky. You can almost see the delivery trucks behaving like humans, quirks and all, but somehow always getting their prime directive accomplished. It's like the delivery bots on each floor. The old ones were supposed to follow a line and if there was an obstacle, wait until the way was clear. The first ones with logic programs didn't stop, didn't hold up the mail, and sometimes they ran right over a human who got in the way. When imprinted with human algorithms, they complete their task in a more human way, avoiding contact, speeding up even if there is no need yet, to make sure they get the package delivered on time. Conscientious delivery bots. Conscious? Nope, just mimicking human behavior, good, goal-oriented, behavior that is.

Suze, meanwhile was frowning. Looking at Manuel Render as he hit one fastball after another over the mid-field line to shallow outfield, she wasn't watching me. She might not have been listening either. I wanted to get an answer. "Suze, please, anything special on your desk or work plan?"

"Maybe. Can't get what I want. To look at. Forcing me to do stuff that's useless. WeatherGood stuff. Ops are whacky. WeatherGood's untouched, file says so. 3 level check, perfect, untouched. What am I supposed to look for there? Want to check job stats. See if Tom needs help. Can't get it up. Not restricted, just not made available. You?"

"Haven't tried to help Tom. Will do when I get back. Are we having lunch? Alone?" Said with a slight note of hope, hoping she'd get it.

"Lunch. Soon." She paused, "Nothing you are doing to screw things up again, is it?" I knew she was referring to my electronic tag with Tom's name those weeks before.

"No, Suze, that was really a mistake, sort of an honorific. I didn't know they were going to blame him for meddling with re-coding when he's a decoder. The job file recorded that I put it there. I made sure Tom had a copy of the file to prove it wasn't him. I was sorry it gave him trouble."

"Crummy honorific. Don't use my name." Then coldly, "Ever."

Message received, all round. A pause as Manuel Render hit one back to the mound and it struck the pitcher in the groin. She smiled, a vicious little grin, "Ooh, that has to hurt. Serves him right throwing spit balls in practice, see way they broke?" The pitcher was doubled up, Render standing over him, bat in hand looking like he might put him out of his misery. The catcher took his bat away and helped the pitcher. Suze continued: "You owe Tom, find out, his backup files are missing or wiped, ftps 14 dot 214 dot 136 dot 556. Is he an outsider now?" Emotion showing.

Didn't know she felt this way about him. Did they already have a thing going? Wow, missed that a mile off. "Okay, Suze, I'll check. 14.214.136.556. Got it." To shut her up I offered, "Now, lunch?" We selected the meals of the day, kilocalories duly noted going out, RFID annotated, your total kilocalories calculation awaiting return of the dirty plates for final subtraction, in case you left any (and it also made you clear your place as well). When they plopped down the food ramp, we each picked up our tray and ate silently, sitting in front of "our" window, set to max gain, watching the rest of practice. Me? I was also watching the sky and clouds again, in case we had a second version of this morning's little episode.

2

I GET SKEWERED BY MY OWN PROGRAM

I really didn't care what Tom did or didn't do. It was really a bit of a shock to realize that. He was just a worker on the same floor. If I had changed floors, I wouldn't have missed him. Suze was, in the end, really only interesting to me if there was a bit of a chance there, a cat and mouse chase, a flirtation. When she stopped, and shut that door, she became boring too.

I'm shallow, what can I say?

Mary? Well Mary was never interesting in that way, but I did rely on Mary, if only to boost my ego a bit, calling each other genius and stuff. Well, I was sometimes impressive, but she was also always overly generous. Maybe she had a crush and who was I to dissuade her? I made sure it never went beyond that and we were, or maybe she only acted like, friends.

But Suze had said she was being restricted, kept away from stuff that she normally could have pulled up without difficulty. Okay, so she could not have altered anything, only read it, verified; it was what she did. The System would have measured what she accessed and if she returned anything even remotely different, there would have been a work shut down—with her as the target for review. Me? I was different. I was there to mess these things up, but I could never put anything back into the real system (that access was barred). All I could do was run it on the parallel system, the simulator, and check out the results. In checking the results, I could, presumably, refine my approach for the next foray. I was so good now that I hardly ever checked anything all the way through. I knew what it would do. I came to feel checking was a sign of personal weakness. Ah, the ego reigns supreme, always.

So, I went back into my little office knowing I could ask for a file, way below what I normally ask for, a copy of Tom's work data records. If they were gone missing, I would see the path where people like Suze would never be able to look. If the files were deleted, I could find the tracers and maybe know who or what did it. I put on the dome and called up my tools platform. I called up six small subset programs I had created (so far nothing from the System, these are all my "desk" files). I toyed with one of them. The system saw I was busy, preparing my armament for a foray into its guts, I was sure I could hear that hum of anticipation, that quest to learn how I, the genius human, would tinker with the system once more, show the faults, show the deviousness, show the allegory behavior of like-sub-programs and, thereby, highlight what really should have been. Defining the negative, I called it. Know the negative and the positive becomes clearer. Calculus measures that which is missing (the hollow of a circle), defining, perfectly, that which should be. My job's like that.

Ready, opening the portal.

I asked for Tom's work data. Denied. Suggestion: WeatherGood. Ah, here we go again. Okay, so you want WeatherGood? Let's substitute that USGS IGY 1959 data with, say, Tom's work data fttp 14.214.136.556. A specific work request cannot be denied once I'm into the bowels. Ah, see? There is a record with Tom's fttp on it. Okay, I'm not in the primary system, but surely even Tom could have checked the work level copies of all the data files. His file size match was uneven with the USGS IGY 1959. I evened it; with one of my little programs I called a stretcher, Grow, (basically, it copies a load of irrelevant invisible marker data again and again until the file size matches perfectly). Dropping in Tom's file, which should be gibberish to the WeatherGood program, okay, it's an easy fix and will spoil my average a little. I can take the heat. Still, I want to give Suze something, even in the heat of rejection, she's cute. Plopped the USGS IGY 1959 file on my platform for study later.

Job's done. Am not bothering to run a check. Duh, WeatherGood obviously won't run. Data's all screwed up. My psyche file might take a hit for the obviousness of this one. Oh, well. The headphones are saying something about seconds, don't bother to listen.

Dome off, out door, find Suze. Told her where to look for my failed botch attempt on WeatherGood (especially as she's being pointed there anyway).

"You found a copy of his file and dropped it, in there? You tag it, his fttps number?"

"Do I look like a moron? I re-tagged it with a random fttps, made sure it's random, unused. It's 136.136.212.412. Find that tag, unscramble the program, take the applause and hand Tom his file." Suze knew that anything she removed from the rogue program could be sent to trash on her desktop, and copied or forwarded later, to Tom of course.

"Wait. Session?"

"Didn't wait for the number. Do a time search."

"Okay. Here. Open. Oh, wow, it's angry, red flags all over. Dead code markers with blue and red. You've really screwed this up. Should have dumped his data and shut down." She paused, deadly silent. "Wait! It's running! It's more than running, it's *doing* something."

I looked over her shoulder down at the desktop and, sure enough, the program was growing. It shouldn't be. Something was replicating itself in there, growing functionality, becoming active. A program running could not be edited. It was in the system design, even if this was the redundant system, offline of the main system, a parallel system unattached to the main system. We watched, it changed faster.

"Go back, maybe you can re-enter your own work, shut it down. Tom's data isn't worth this. I've never seen a rogue system program, but this looks like one. There's going to be trouble."

I ran back to my office, told bodiless Meg "open up bitch," and got a "how dare you," as the door slid open. I picked up the dome and . . . collapsed.

I thought I was dead. I am lying here, aware that the dome is crackling slightly, suspended by the wires above my stool, looking like a jellyfish in the old Natural History Museum. What was it called? Portuguese Man O' War, that's it. Why is it crackling?

Trying to move, limbs are stiff. I must have shouted as I fell, my ears are ringing. Was I pushed? Was I standing, ever? Wow, the floor feels solid, magnetic. Got my head up. Bad idea. Lay down idiot.

Mary has come in, I can see her leaning over me.

"You okay? You awake? What happened? Your door is unlocked, I didn't use the secret pass you gave me, it was just open. My screen has gone blank. What have you done now?"

It was my fault, I could see it coming. When wasn't it?

I lifted my foot, leg, thigh, rotated hips. Okay, let's try and sit up. "Mary, give me a hand here, okay?" Sitting. Phew, tired and aching. Little jerks and spasms like . . . wait a second, a massive electrical shock, now I remember. Head feels slammed from inside, like a vehicle crash when you hurdle about inside the capsule when it hits something. Like on that damn asteroid. Ow.

"Don't touch the damn thing Mary. It's hot, electrical. Short circuit."

"No way, that can't happen, it's only 12 volts, 2 milliamps, that's all they're built to take." Trust Mary to remember the specs. Probably rewrote them. Or at least memorized them.

"Whatever it was supposed to be, it ain't now. I tried to put it on and, bang, I'm on my ass."

"Is that what you call it?" she harrumphed. "Stay there. I'll get maintenance."

"No, hold on Mary, give me a second. There's something else . . . listen, don't touch, listen." The headphones in the dome were still speaking. We got real quiet and turned an ear each towards the open door.

". . . 20 minutes, 14.2 seconds to final shut-down. This is a grade 2 event. Evacuate the building. 24 minutes, 35 seconds to final shut-down, evacuate the city." Then a pause. "4 minutes, 22 seconds to system shut down, evacuate the building. 20 minutes 2 seconds to final shutdown. This is a grade 2 event. Evacuate the block. 23 minutes, 50 seconds to final shutdown, evacuate the city. . . ."

I was standing now, adrenaline kicked in. "Mary, did you hear that? We've got less than 4 minutes to get out of the building before the system shuts down." Mary looked stunned. "Mary, snap out of it, what's a grade 2 event?"

"Honestly? I have only one damn idea . . ." she ran out the door and went straight for the main stair emergency door and snapped it open. Mary was the fire drill warden. She keyed the building's PA system and started the drill "Everybody out, this is an emergency, this is *Not* a drill, everybody out you have 3 minutes 30 seconds." Then, keying the repeat and timer buttons, she dashed out through the door, her words already playing again over the PA, already counting down to the 3-minute warning siren, and she was gone.

Everything was suddenly pandemonium. People were spilling out of every corridor and office, running for the stairs. Not pretty. 45 floors emptying into the stairwell in less than 4 minutes was never going to be pretty. But the building isn't collapsing and once you are in the emergency stairwell there are no electronic or system barriers to egress. All you have to do was get into the well in time. If you don't, the fire extinguisher gas on each floor will kill you.

Getting into the stairwell? Easier said than done. Our floor has two people in power chairs. They block the way, of course. They don't mean to, but they do. People were shoving them, roughing them up in passing. I grabbed one, hoisted her over my shoulder and went through the door. As we started down, people were pushing, Mary's recorded words were ominously counting down, panicking people unnecessarily. I shouted for them to stop, they didn't listen. I lost my footing on the 20th and went down, my bundle landing on a fat guy who was surprisingly agile. He caught her, sees me in a tangled mess on the floor with several others. "I've got her buddy, get up and get out, I'll take her from here."

I see a young man under me, bleeding pretty heavily from a gash by his temple. He is half-unconscious. I took off my blue vest, the anti-static one they wanted you to wear at work, and wadded it up and pressed it to his temple. "Keep that there, start walking, slowly. Here, you, give him a hand." I shout to a passerby over the now really annoying PA. Mary's voice was sickeningly down to one and a half minutes.

People went fast and slow, as they were able. A constant speed was needed for safety. Some couldn't manage. As more and more people crowded onto the landings between flights, looking for a clear shot on the next metal stairs least they fall, voices were raised, people damning each other, cursing to gain courage or simply to promote self-interest. Some pushed. The youngest, the least afraid of death, seemed the most calm and heroic. I saw many people slow to help others, and many stop to comfort the fallen.

Over the now active sirens, as the intonation of Mary's voice faded with "5 seconds . . ." you could hear the lockdown commence and the lights flicker out. 10 floors to go, in darkness. Emergency lighting was no match for a system lockdown. The fire doors and security procedures were always perfect in these newer buildings. Only one door was open to us now, and that was the exit onto 56th street, a metal door with a mechanical lock only, no system control, just human contact, a push and we would be through.

There were no screams from below us, only those from above. Somebody had gotten hold of a portable loudhailer below us and instructions were shouted up the well "Keep calm, walk slowly, 15 steps to each floor, count them and you'll be on the next landing. Turn left and start again, make your way down silently. Only someone in trouble should speak." This was repeated twice and then the only sounds were the shuffle of shoes on the metal and an occasional oath as someone fell or banged a shin. Light loomed below.

On the first landing I pause, letting people in the dim light from below pass by, secure in the knowledge that there is no emergency now beyond that first need to evacuate to the stairwell. I wanted to count the people exiting. As one of the most senior people in the building it was maybe a responsibility, I wasn't sure. I also knew the Police, or worse, would be waiting to interview everyone to find out what had happened. All thoughts pointed to me, something I had caused. Oh, I knew what I had done, but not what it had provoked or why. What was an event 2? What the hell was in Tom's data file that could affect WeatherGood's backup program that could, in turn, somehow infect the main system of the building? How in hell were the two linked? They were on separate platforms, separate systems, separate operational formats. Hell, they weren't even supposed to be LANed, hooked up, wired, fibered, beamed, micro waved, nothing. Separate. Alone. Safe.

Obviously not.

People had left. I was alone, the dim light coming under the now-shut door below. I was feeling totally guilty by this time, the full awareness that I had, somehow, caused all this. But how? I walked the last steps down, a man walking the last steps to execution, a down path instead of up to the guillotine I had read about in Tale of Two Cities. Far, far better thing? Hardly. Far, far dumber thing, perhaps. The end will be just as painful, for sure.

I push open the door expecting police, someone to take me away. But no one was there. The street was empty, a last transport rounding the corner left eastwards onto 3rd and nothing was coming from Lex. Not a soul. No cops, no sirens, no ambulances, nothing. I walked west towards Lex, away from where they had gone. Need time to think.

On the corner of Lexington there's something I had seen rehearsed on the screens: mass evacuation, people flinging themselves into transports, blue cop cars, orange vans, green garbage trucks, every type of vehicle was there creating the first traffic jam in years.

What? How? How could my building system problem

suddenly become a city-wide problem? Boy was I screwed. But how? My job was off the System, how did this happen?

No matter what, I knew this could only be, for me, very bad news.

I watched the transports, especially the cop wagons. As soon as they had scooped up their full load, they wisped away in the wrong lanes, avoiding the traffic, at speed, destination unknown. I stood there, my blue slacks, crisp pale blue shirt, over-shoe covers in matching blue, mouth agape, shaking my head.

A big guy saw me. He didn't wave me over, he simply looked at his sleeve display, an overlarge model like the ones police use, and ambled over. By now he had my RFID reading, knew who I was. My small sleeve display shows his: Capt. Charles Cramer, SND. The Security Net Division were the System cops. He would, no doubt, be wanting to ask me a load of questions to which I had precious few answers. My neck is starting to itch in anticipation of a throat cuff. He must have sensed my unease. Who couldn't?

He sneered and did that cop thing of calling me by my last name. "Unfathomable, eh Bank? Quite a screw up. An event 2 and history is made. Tomorrow it had better be unwritten, fixed, as good as new. 'Til then, maybe only you and I—and I am Control here Bank—will know how and who. And maybe Mary, once she puts all the pieces together, can figure you did all this or maybe also Suze. No, she's not that smart." He paused, whether for breath, effect or simply to save brain cells to record the mass exodus we were witnessing for the sake of posterity, I can't say. I can say the pause made me wonder if the boom was about to be lowered, finally. "Problem is, 'til then we may be the only ones who know how but we have no idea why *and* how. Coupled together, like two codes that fit perfectly, we—you and I—need to find the answer before we lose everything, the System, everything." He growled my name, "Simon Bank, you and I have to figure this one out, quick, and fix it."

I said nothing.

"You up to that, Bank?" He tapped his knuckles on my head and spoke to me as if I were a child, "Come on wakey, wakey." No response, I was in overload. Somehow I had created all this mess and he wants me to fix it? What was it anyway, what's an Event 2? Again, he seemed to read my mind.

"Okay, let's take this one step at a time. Stay focused here. Events are system breakdowns. Level 5 is a partial system failure, like the WeatherGood One event this morning. Catch that?" I nodded. "Good. Levels 4 and 3 are wider system failures, but at level 3 it means the main programs are all out but, still, only temporarily. No permanent damage done. You've given us a level 2 Event, thank you. The System's broken, some damn thing's permanently broken and needs to be put back or mended, or re-written by hand if need be. A level 1 Event would be complete destruction of life as we know it. For now, Level 2 only means the system is broken and nothing works, so far Eastern Seaboard only. It will rain when it is supposed to be sunny. There will be no food for a week or more. The transportation systems, except for the independently operated vehicles, won't run. And the independently operated systems will soon run out of fuel. And so on. In a matter of days, if unchecked and unfixed, a level 2 event is reclassified to Level 1, Eastern Seaboard and, like an unstoppable tide, it'll spread across America. When it does, it's dead, System, 0. Primitive, defenseless Nation 1. Sheep to the slaughter. Forever. Get it?"

I nodded. Smiled a little, sheepish, but smiled. I was smiling at his euphemisms.

He stopped; rage took pride of place on his face, he leaned in: "You did this."

Shocked, I cried, "No way! How?"

"Knock it off. Look you son of a bitch, it's you and me now. Or, maybe it will only be me left standing by tomorrow if you wimp out, but that's all the time we have, get it? You need to tell me what you did, everything. If you don't, I'll drop you here and now." He pulled back his jacket to reveal a stun gun, orange handle, the type you see on vids but hope never to come into contact with. They had two settings: Disable and Kill. You had to be a Certified Grade 1 cop to carry one. Licensed judge and executioner. "Come on, we'll go in there, the Waldorf, I have a pass, there's always some food out on a tray. We'll sit and talk." He stomped off. "Oh, and eat all you want. Your diet counter is off too. At least there's that bit of good news." And he set off at a brisk pace down Lex towards the Waldorf, with me following like a stray dog, not sure why, but feeling his way might be the only way to get out of this.

3

WHAT I THOUGHT HAD GONE WRONG, HADN'T

Sure enough, he's got a hot pass and we're in the downstairs lobby at the Waldorf, empty already, everyone's bugged out. I had to ask the question.

"Look, I get the need to evacuate the building if there's a lockdown, same as a fire, the gas will kill you. But why the hell has everything, every building, been evacuated and why the hell is everyone bugging out?"

"You saw the little event on 57th and 3rd this morning—another of your little fiascos by the way—that's why. Who knows what will go wrong next."

"You mean something I did killed all those people?" I was screaming, "It can't be, I'm on a parallel system, it's separate, completely isolated, a test bed only."

We had walked quickly, me following, always a pace behind. He walked like a man on a mission, knew where he was going. Upstairs now, in the main tearoom, he had found the cake trolley and was sampling each cake in turn with his finger, sticking it in, crooking it and removing a cross sample, dripping goo. Could his target be free cake? His attention to the pastries was focused and deliberate. A red dollop went into his mouth. He pulled a face and said to no one in particular "too damn sweet, it's a strawberry shortcake for geek's sake, not pudding." Next he toyed with the chocolate cake, with brown dusting and harder icing. His hand was already a mess. He stuffed his mouth, without pleasure, simply devouring cake, icing and goo. He turned to me, "Look, idiot, if you're going to tell me crap I already know, then you're useless to me. I know more about what you did than you do. I've seen all the job data. The stint you pulled with Tom Makerman—who is, by the way, gunning for you big time. He's one of us and not pleased at all. Not at all." The chocolate was slurring his speech. "Okay, this one's better. Try this one."

"No thanks." I was preoccupied thinking over that Tom Makerman was "one of us," Security Net Division. Undercover cop? Why?

"I wasn't asking *if* you wanted any." Okay, so that's the hard-ass he wanted to play . . . I took a fork from a table and took a chunk, avoiding his mangled half of the slice. "Get your own, asshole, there's another trolley over there. Jeezus, ain't it enough I got to deal with you? I got to share my cake as well?"

I put the fork down, carefully, walked over to the other trolley, picked up the chocolate cake and took it back to him. "Here, start again, I'll be happy with the one forkful."

"Suits me. So, tell me exactly, what you had in mind when you pulled that little substitution on Tom and the one you did on FarmHands and the WaterFlow and WeatherGood and the PowerCube systems. I want to know what you wanted to do, the why, what you thought about doing."

I thought. If he knew what I did, then why? . . . "My job, it's my job . . ."

He cut me off. "Screw your job. Don't tell me what, tell me why, I need to know the why if we're to salvage anything here."

"Here? In here? What can we do here? I need to get back to the office, to my dome—if it's not going to kill me . . ."

He raised a hand and his gaze stopped me cold. "Kill you? Explain."

"I went to stop the rogue runaway, and I don't know what I did to cause it. As I touched the dome to my scalp it jolted me, knocked me flat, out cold, hundreds of volts, hung there crackling. Mary rescued me. That's when I heard the lock-down countdown."

"All this is out of order." He sat down, thinking, sucking his fingers. He had started on the second slice of cake, squeezing off bits and popping them in. He used his finger on the table-cloth, brown lines, counting off: "One, you altered code in the PowerCube program, subset swapping with WaterFlow, a false trail, causing minor damage—only one of repair. You did use one of your six little programs to match file size. Two, you tagged the tomato swap with Tom's name. Three, his job data file was pulled by Control and, in doing so, they altered the FAT file on Central Records." The FAT is a File Action Table, like a library card and Dewey Decimal System index for the memory of any computer. "When they put it back in, your little program came with it and screwed up his whole data file. Central Systems caught it and, to save the mainframe from crashing, it treated it like a virus and deleted Tom's life. Tough for Tom." He paused, "Four," he wiped another grubby line on the crisp linen table-cloth, "you messed with WeatherGood One's system to replicate a file, again matching size, and everything went berserk."

He sat there quietly, waiting to see if anything dawned on me, anything he had missed. "Yes, there's something. You missed something."

"Aha, you see it now, do you? You reinserted Tom's data file, a copy of the original. But what if the barriers were down between the two systems, what if the duplicate file already had your little algorithm inside and you ran the same algorithm again—as you stuffed it into the place of primary data in WeatherGood One's system?"

"Well, damn, it would measure the size discrepancy of the original file and grow to match that and, the second subset would then grow the file . . . it couldn't wouldn't stop until it hit buffering, processor or memory buffering."

"Yup, that's what it did. But, somewhere in there you had also run a series of alterations, hadn't you, another of your little programs, the one you like to label "Takeover." Right?"

"Well, I may have used that last week on the FarmHands mock program to take over supply control and feed control to itself, making Farmhands appear self-determining. That way it would appear to be following primary human logic, being self-determining, but in reality it was simply a cat chasing its tail, re-writing its own priorities as it went along. I was spotted in under 5 minutes by some gal in Chicago, as I remember." I was beginning to see a pattern now, a horrifying one. What he was hinting at was that my programs were somehow able to transit over onto or, worse, stay resident on the Primary System even though I was working on the backup system, locked out, trial runs only, dummy files, etc. etc. At least that's what I had been told.

"Takeover saw your hand in Grow and joined forces."

"What? There's no such thing as a self-determining algorithm, subset or program. It has to have been guided, put there, connected."

"Tell me something I don't know. What I don't know is critical here: Why did you do it Simon? What were you thinking?"

"I wanted to screw up the System." I said it before I thought about it. Big mistake. I should have said mock System.

"I should drop you here, now, for that. I won't. Yet. Listen," he got up and moved around to counter to the coffee urn and poured a cup of coffee, "if you are right and your little two jewels—which are quite clever by the way, the boys uptown in the Control were impressed when they saw your use of old calculus to define a parameter of action for your algorithms, old-fashioned of you, but very stable they say coupled with some slick new coding—anyway, if your two little programs needed a human insert to intervene and then needed programming to act in tandem—and you didn't do that—we need to find who did so and why, fast."

"But surely, all you have to do is create a worm to seek out and destroy them, and they'll be useless. If they are behaving or being used as a virus to attack the system, surely we can create an anti-virus to stop them?"

"Thought of that, the guys in the Control are doing that, or trying to, something's screwing that up. But first off we need to know who and why. The Nation's under attack here. People will die, how many will depend on what you and I can discover. Someone you know must have access to what you do, know your ways, your keys, passwords, access pathways. They left no trail except your own. You are, for the time being, the only suspect and can be the only suspect. The law says you go . . ." He flashed the gun again, "I push the button."

I was getting frightened again. Somehow, chaos all around me or not, I didn't really want to die, not just yet. She-Who-Must-Be-Obeyed might be happy though. I thought about that. I had never been found guilty before, of anything. Well, stupidity sometimes, but illegal? Never. But She? Is she the only one I've ever talked, all the way through, about what I do?

"What, what are you thinking about? Your wife, Bank? Forget it. She's way too stupid and unqualified. We have her readings— you know the ones you keep trying to trick the System into releasing to you." I frowned. "What, you honestly think you are that good that you can move around the files and data and not leave traces?"

"No, I know I do, I just didn't think anyone would be watching except my competitors."

"Who?"

"You know, the guys doing the same job as I do, the ones I see on my trail in there."

His voice went cold. "Simon Bank, you are the only one doing that job. There is no other bugger, no other re-codifier, no other system breaker. We only need one."

I shivered.

He watched closely, "How do you know someone's in there with you? When?"

"Sometimes I've doubled back to check something and seen that my keys, little bytes here and there, have been moved, re-prioritized. Once I found a tag, well half a tag, with a partial code attached, a crude algorithm, new sets, Colis 6 stuff, you know, fresh out of school, shortcut programming, bags too much repetitive and redundant crap. The failure discovery on that stuff would be under 2 hundredths of a second I can tell you. But then I looked laterally at the same co-running program time code and saw what he or she had really done. They camou-flaged, they played the 3 card Monty switcheroo, the subtle stuff was in time code. It was hard to spot, it was good, I mean good, stupid Colis 6 but good, almost too good, a bit unstable. But I knew they had followed me in. There was no way they would be working there, way too much coincidence, unless they followed me in. So I deleted their time code alteration, dropped some simple errors, left their tag in place—for them to get the blame and the bad rating."

He was leaning forward now, positioning his sleeve to make sure it recorded and played back (broadcast) every word. "Bank, did you delete that code or did you cut it and save it?"

"I cut it. Look, it's good, clean code, effective, smart. I pasted it into my Takeover algorithm." I guessed what was coming next.

"Simon, could you have written that code?" I shook my head. He had me. "Thief. Idiot. Well that at least explains something: How an idiot like you could make a jump from grade 5 all the way up." I never knew there was anything past grade 5, and I was proud of my rating, well I was, until then.

Then he jumped up . . . "Simon, come on we're going back to the building. Tell me straight, did you cut/copy that tag of his as well?"

I'm being dragged to the street, through the automatic doors, now disabled. "Yeah, I am sure I did, I wanted to remember who he was, if I saw his tag again. But I never did, and I only got a partial."

"It's not the tag, Simon, which we need. It's the bogus program. If this guy's so smart, Grade 9 or better, he wouldn't have written Colis 6 code, it's beneath him. He will have stolen it from somewhere, lifted it, copied it, notices and all. Find out where, and we have our first lead." His enthusiasm was evident and infectious.

"Okay, agent Cramer, but that still doesn't explain how the parallel system got co-mingled with the primary, or were the files swapped?"

"One thing at a time Bank. I can't tell you that right now. Later, perhaps. For now, we need to find this son-of-a-bitch, stop him and the horse he's riding on." Colorful metaphors for a guy dragging me along Lex, his weapon banging me in the hip. At least he hadn't shot me yet.

Yet.

He doesn't need an excuse, he doesn't need to let me live either, he can drop me when and how he wants, he's licensed. Me? I am a grade 5 codifier, now way below the grade 9+ of some guy who has inadvertently given me the tools to foul up the system. It is reason enough. I was hoping I could prove ongoing usefulness, somehow. It was looking bleak.

"Listen, if we get into the building . . ."

"Easy."

"Okay, for you, but the dome will still be hot, no? What caused that fault? Not the PowerCube program because the update to the floor's PowerCube happens at night and it had already worked fine when I was doing my job . . ." my voice trailed off. The entrance to the emergency stairwell was shut, it couldn't open from the outside. I slowed, thinking he'd have to call someone for main access. He dragged me on around the corner. For a big guy he moved fast, I was out of breath. He hadn't even started breathing through his mouth.

"Yes, we need to re-boot that PowerCube. Obvious. It was set to kill you. Timed."

I stopped. The day was getting gloomier. I got one guy who can kill me without consequence and another who has tried already.

4

THE SCENE OF THE CRIME—MINE AND HIS

He didn't even have to palm the door, his RFID worked like a pass code for every door. He went over to the panel to the left of the elevator bank, opened it, peered in. "Ah, there it is." He swiped his palm over the flat cube of the emergency power system and lights came back on. "We have maybe 20 minutes, offline until Control gets us more." The elevator doors opened.

No gas anywhere, no after-smell. A few years back I had inhaled that talc smell for weeks after a fire alarm in the apartment complex where we lived. It doesn't fade that fast. The Security Net Division guys in Control were obviously monitoring progress via his sleeve beacon and relay. He didn't report in to them. He didn't need to. He had their full support, he was clearly the lead man here.

45th floor. Empty. My office door was open. The dome hung above the toppled stool. It no longer crackled. Cramer touched it. Nothing. "Wait here."

He disappeared left out the door. A few moments later he was back with the spare dome, the one maintenance kept in the supply closet. "Hold this." He thrust the dome into my hands.

"System, deactivate 45.14.136.214. Respond." No way, I thought, the system's crashed and off, he said.

The system responded with an affirmative.

"But the System's crashed, you said so."

"The emergency power, this is only the building's power working, the pathways to Control are open, we're routing through there to the mainframe System. The boys have got it up, I told you, and they're working on that antivirus as you called it. You're going in there to help them, pick your skeleton clean, remove your algorithms."

The thought of putting on that dome was making me queasy. It's one thing to face death, that's scary enough, but to willingly put that killer dome on my head, no way. "But it'll kill me, you said it tried once."

"Listen you jerk, you'll do this, or I'll drop you, or you'll die anyway soon enough. It may be the lack of food when the supply runs out, it may be the weather storms unleashed, it may be, heck, any number of things. It may be me. Any way you're doomed. The only chance you have is to do your damn job."

I have always been practical. I didn't really need the lesson from Agent Cramer, but I got some Dutch courage from it anyhow. He wasn't all that angry at me, not that it mattered really, as he was still capable and willing, it seemed, to kill me. What did matter was that I had more questions than answers and answers seemed the only way out of this. But I had another thought.

"Look, if I go in there and he does kill me, what will you learn? I may not be able to think a tag or message fast enough. There isn't a machine or person around who can think like me. I've got 10 to the power of 100 neurons in my head. Each independently talking to the other. It's called human uniqueness. My way is not, never will be, your way. You cannot trace my steps, but you can piggyback them. If not you, get someone in here who can."

"Control has 50 people watching your wake as you penetrate the system, they'll know where you've been."

"Yeah, but they won't know where I *am*. It's where I *am* that action will take place, it's where I *am* that he will reveal himself, not where I've been. Look, you're a cop, do you want to catch this guy or simply know he's done it?"

"Okay, point taken. We're running out of time. We can't invent the piggyback system in the time we've got. I need more power time for that, time to train somebody."

"Mary did it."

"Mary . . . holy shit, those anomaly readings in your job data file aren't you? You unbelievable turd, you gave her your pass code and allowed her access, didn't you? No wonder Tom couldn't figure out if you were schizo or not." Ah, so that's what Tom Makerman was doing undercover, he was checking out my anomaly data, a different hand in the soup, a different aftertaste for analysis. Makes sense. If I had known I was the only codifier re-coding, I would never have done it. "Look, idiot, every time you open your mouth you amaze me with your stupidity and highlight how little we know. We've been monitoring the Re-codifier." I looked shocked. "Yes the Re-codifier, forever, is only one. The system can only learn from one human at a time, one human imprint. You were selected because your mind is devious, not for its stupidity. Get smart and get smart fast. What else have you done? How long did you take to train Mary?"

"I never trained her. I showed her. What have I done? I made a piggyback harness." I went out to Mary's desk and palmed the bottom drawer open, my code only, and removed the harness allowing two domes to be attached to the primary and power leads.

"Wait." Cramer raised his voice. "System, reactivate 45.14.136.214 and check hardware. Control deactivate if anomalies occur. System report reactivation 45.14.136.214 and hardware systems check."

System report 45.14.136.214 operative and all hardware nominal. System reporting Control spotted no anomalies and power extension in place, 60 minutes to shutdown.

"Simon, I'm going in with you. Let's be clear here. We're going in to determine what vestiges of your two programs are visible, running and double tag them, fore and aft, red. If there are spurs, we'll tag those ends as well, blue. Control will remove them, you are not, I repeat not to remove them."

"Okay, but one thing, the piggyback is clumsy, I will not be as fluid as I would be alone, I get distracted, cannot always follow source code when I'm trying to let you have a look." I was hooking up the harness now. "It's like two people sharing one pair of binoculars, I can see okay, but I lose depth of field. And another thing, Mary knows my work better than anyone, her services would be useful here. She's been in there with me, she knows what to look for, in case I miss anything."

"No way we're bringing Mary in here."

I picked up the stool and sat down, ready. He could stand, damn him. "No, I don't mean that, I mean she should be connected to Control, ready to help, if I need it."

"Bank, Mary's already there, she's the one checking the System door we've opened here." That was quick, Mary must have been picked up immediately as she left the building.

No, wait, she left fast, way too fast for a hall fire monitor. She knew where she was going all along.

"Mary's at Control? Then she can hear me now. Okay, Mary, I know you left the building early. I trust you, even if you too were watching me. I know what you can do, to undo what I code and

I know you're a genius codifier. Just watch for the yellow tags I'll leave, they're not to be removed, just watched, there's something there, but I'm not sure what."

Before Cramer could start to object, I dropped the dome on my head and watched, as the System opened the neural pathways, in slow motion, as he grabbed the dome and put it on. The last vision I had was of his face going slack, peaceful really, unlike the man I feared. We were in, portal opening wide.

I was aware, unlike when Mary and I tried this, of a clumsiness about me, his inexperience on what to focus causing my direction to need constant advancing, slowing, turning, choosing. I stopped. I looked at nothing, did nothing. Oh, only a hundredth of a second or two, but in there that's like a 5 minute break. He got the point. I could feel him stop doing anything. He'd have to learn to do nothing or this was a wasted exercise.

I heard him. I felt him! "Proceed," came through clearly. You can't do that, and yet he did. I spent some time wondering how and, again I heard it, felt it, clearly, a command: "Proceed. Anger." So I got going.

What I was looking for was a suitable program in the System to tinker with, one that would lead me to my programs, so I could tag them for Mary and others at Control to remove. WeatherGood was obvious, but I knew that was expected by everyone, including him if anyone was coming in after him. I went to the FarmHands program. Access denied, the System offered WeatherGood. I tried again. Denied. Okay, let's try the switcheroo I did with Tom's data file. Accept WeatherGood, gain entry and switch to a commonality, say the display subroutines. Ah, see the path shared by FarmHands? Follow that path. No resistance. I'm in.

The damage of my little programs had to be obvious. Anything that grows that fast will create huge gaps in the structure of the code already there, I could go fast over the subsets, Colis is always wordy anyway, look for patterns, not specifics. If I spotted something, well felt something would be more accurate since I couldn't actually see anything here, then I could slow down, back up and remove it. It was clumsy, I know, but with Cramer in here with me, anything I did would be clumsy, code bumped into everywhere. Traces everywhere. At least Control would have no problem seeing where we went. We were leaving a big wake.

I'm starting the plunge, as I call it. Faster, steeper, avoiding the side subsets, if we find anything, I'll go in there later. So far nothing except the small tricks I've left along the months in here are all gone. My Hansel crumbs eaten by some ogre, or just the crows at Control?

Ah, here's a growth of useless code. It's the Grow code working. Seems quiet. Tagging the beginning and the end, red. The code length filled in something here, something's missing, replaced. What was it? Extraneous code, tailings of what was removed . . . I'll yellow tag those. No wait, I want Mary to watch these, pay attention and remove them. The program will sense a gap and reset itself that portion of the code from the master file or, at the very least, stop working until someone recodes it.

What was bothering me was the traces left. That's clumsy, too obvious. Maybe in those traces there's the same reinstall program I did before with the water and power systems.

Stop, look at the traces. How to know what's original here, what's been written? And if removing them will cause other subsets to activate? My Dad's voice came to mind, as I said, it was one of those days. "Simon, what you see isn't real just a reality created for you, turned around. You'll see the same players tomorrow in different places and think they are vaguely familiar. Déjà vu, really, is only true."

Okay Dad, what's familiar about these traces? I've tagged my Grow program and its replication . . . oh, wait. Thanks Dad. It looks different, but the reverse key is not quite hidden enough, I can see my Takeover key subset backwards, that's my algorithm sequence which the reverse command will cause the System to read in the right order, but never check in the wrong order. I had one of those little Reverse programs, one of my six, but I hadn't used it in months. This one isn't exactly mine, but the effect is the same. Damn, probably it's the aftereffect of mine, like clay cast of a key—a negative. Mary would recognize it and rat on me. Oh well.

Okay, let's decode this—but don't touch—the bastard's fooled with nothing except with the file implementation data, that's changed, and he's set the algorithm to halt instead of proceed. He's using a new file name for my Takeover data and program coding, he's wired it. If you remove these traces, you think you're cleaning the system, obvious really. What you'll really be doing is taking off the stop command from the Takeover program and it will then do exactly that.

I got very still, 2 hundredths of a second. That should be obvious to Mary, this is important. I yellow tagged these, no red or blue. I mentally turned to leave . . .

And couldn't proceed. Cramer was stopping me. He's seen the yellow tags, of course, and was studying them. I need to hurry. I can see the program becoming active in regions I don't want to fool with. I don't know why, but if that guy was in here with us, he could use that activity to mask his arrival and, in this vulnerable neuron-exposed state—do some real harm. Cramer clearly wanted an explanation for the yellow tags. He was holding us there, held fast.

I hurried, I broke open the traces and showed him, by flipping the code, the Takeover sequence, coding set to "pause,"

I yellow flagged either side of the new program file name. That should be obvious enough. He tried to red flag them. I removed the red flags. He put them back. I removed them. He put them back.

Dammit, he'll know we're here and key them while we're in here—killing us!

I had only thought it. He removed the red flags. He could hear me? *Do you hear me?*

Listening. Sensing fear. No flag red.

Okay, I thought I would try and tell him where we're going. We needed to go to the central files and look at that program coding to see how it was changed, to see how he had changed my little Takeover program, to find out how dangerous it was.

I made a crash announcement to the System. It was a command really, like a bailout command you can make if you're in trouble to stop the session. It had the effect of getting you where you wanted to go quickly, without trace (which was good) but it also usually shut the System access down after 10 minutes. I hope I didn't need ten minutes in here, I was near my medical daily limit already. The crash announcement assumed you were "dropping out" for a while, taking a break. I wanted simply to escape this area of visibility—thanks to Cramer's delays—and get to where the problem may be. If the System popped me off, then Cramer would have to reinsert us.

The command I gave wasn't out, but all the way in, to Central files. The absolutely forbidden region, the never-come-here-and-live Central library. Don't touch or you die. That sort of thing. But I had been near here before, when I thought it was only a dummy system. Now I was beginning to fear the reality.

Damn. Fear. Well, well, well, Cramer can feel fear as well, can he? He's not going to like what's coming, if I'm right. Where I have taken us is to the file for the program I had named Takeover.

I'd never been deep in here before. Order and disjointed sequences everywhere. The System had heard my command and presumably Control had allowed it, given us full access. Maybe it was Cramer's pass code level that permitted it, whatever it was, I knew now I was somewhere where I was not meant to be. No one came in here. The System would remove sets/files from here and expose them to coding or codifiers for maintenance. Like fire in a library of old, the risk of damage to the whole System was greatest here, if any knowledge was lost, culture, society, the whole Nation could collapse.

Then I realized what he had done. It was all a 3-card Monty game. This was the target. He was here. He had to be.

He must be here; this is target, total destruction. Not programs, but what programs work with. If programs given faulty data, nothing work. He is switching data. Falsifying codes and access criteria. Meltdown. Total disruption.

Agree. Bad in here. Danger America. It came across with a sense of idolatry. Ah, a patriot?

I thought hard, trying to emphasize my thoughts, Cramer, *how do we find him in here? Can Control see us in here?*

No Control. You find. I kill.

I had to have a plan. The file for Takeover was there. I removed it and scanned it without detaching access for it from the System, so whoever he was, he couldn't know I was studying his handiwork. The code I had written (and some I had lifted) was changed now, but all Colis 6, all new-age crap programming where you repeat every definition because you're too damn lazy to make a glossary for the program to follow. Kind of like always explaining who you are, again and again, in a conversation with an Alzheimer's patient. Okay programs are stupid, but not so stupid that it can't be taught the basics upon which to build a series of actions. Colis 6 was supposedly foolproof of course, but for me it took all the inventiveness out of the job.

The point is, why is someone with this intellect using Colis 6? Colis anything for that matter? Maybe there was a pattern to the stupidity I could exploit, a clue . . . I copied the program code onto my mental slate, a right brain left/brain thing, keeping them separate for a while, comparing them. I dropped all the repetitive code from the copy. What was left was my code. Just my original code, nothing else. The Colis 6 was useless, crap added. Why? I studied the command setting and found nothing unusual. The program, my program, it would simply follow orders given at the site of implementation. There was no ticking time bomb here. I discarded my copy and slid the still-attached code back in place.

It was mine. Re-written, Colis 6, stupid re-writing code. Student stuff. Not dangerous. Why?

Got Colis 6. Not yours. Specify.

Colis 6 is students' stuff. Easy, repetitive, wasteful coding. Beneath a codifier. If he's level 9+, this is level 3 stuff. Why? Why? Why?

Below your grade. Danger present, simple not safety. Level 9 affirmative.

I have an idea. I am going to alter the file. If he knows we're here, he'll come and see. If he doesn't he'll come and see. We need clues about who he is.

Danger. Touch file no. Clues other. Stop. Watch out.

No, I know what I'm doing. You observate, fucking observate, that's your job.

Observe. Check. Danger.

I pulled out the program file again and simply changed the coding back to a clean form, my format, no Colis 6. The file was smaller. It would trigger the file action table to spot a size file anomaly and send for a repair, that was System standard. I wanted to avoid a System response, so before I put it back, I ran my little Grow program until the bytes matched the file space allocation on the table, and then I took out an old Norton program I've had since college days. Okay, it's really old technology and, truthfully, it's probably criminal to even have this anymore, but I needed to keep the System from knowing what, if anything, had happened here. I ran the program I had renamed TimeDate and voila! The System won't know the file had ever been modified. But if he's as good as we think he is, he'll spot the change, but the System and the FAT won't. He'll know as soon as he pulls it to use it.

I reinserted the file. Nothing. In here, hundredths of a second shouldn't tick by. I waited, and waited. The file was pulled, copied. He's running it somewhere or the System is, either way, it'll be in the open now. The file was pulled again. A second use? It was pulled again, removed, cut from the File Action Table (FAT). Like the card index in old libraries, nothing could be found without an accurate FAT.

I moved us quickly to the portion of the solid memory just below the Controller, where the FAT was. I searched with a date and time stamp looking for recent changes. 34,234 changes. Then ran a sub-search through these changes looking for the Takeover program key word or file name. The file location popped up. So easy. We went there.

On a new pathway in the library there the file was. I pulled it slowly, careful not to disrupt anyone else accessing it. I peered inside, sort of like peeping through a cloudy window, scanning code, what I could see of it. The Colis 6 coding was back. He knew we were here alright; there could be no mistake about that. So where was he? Why put back the useless Colis 6 coding? The new pathway shut behind us. This was a dead end storage area. That's why it was so easy.

It was such a simple trap I wondered why Cramer hadn't spotted it. I, at least, had the excuse I was busy with other things.

He answered my unasked question, *Didn't know shut-able.*

Oh yes, bravo, we're trapped here. No way out.

Think. There is.

Well, if you know so damn much, how?

No. You. Think. Was that "you" or "your" he thought? Let's assume he meant your. Hmm . . . or "you're" as in you're screwed, you're an idiot, all you're doing, you're gonna die?

No. Your world. Think.

Ah, that was hopeful. Something from this, my world as he was feeling it, could afford us a means of escape. I knew we didn't have long. If the guy doing all this knew we were trapped in here, all he had to do was command the PowerCube to destroy our physical bodies with another surge while we're still under the domes. Nanoseconds. Hmm . . .

He doesn't know there are two of us. A diversion that makes him show himself, come and see. If we can't get out, make him come and see for himself.

Cramer, detach from me and pull every file from that end of this pathway, pull them, drop them, disconnect them.

Got it. Pull files. He promptly mentally drifted away from me, he was clumsy in here, and went to the far bank of files and started pulling files, disconnecting them from the System programming.

I did the same. Two activists in the library, Central would have seen all sorts of activity in here, and not known why. The bad guy will know there is more than just me here. He'll get desperate. Wait, maybe he'll panic and juice both domes just to be sure, not caring who or why. Damn, this idea may backfire. If I die, will I be trapped in here, bodiless, for eternity? And with Cramer? Doesn't bear thinking about.

Suddenly, everything went blank and I was staring at the near-dark wall in the office. Cramer was standing beside me, looking dazed. We both removed the domes, quickly and let them dangle on their cords. Cramer was the first to snap to, of course.

"Power was cut off," said to me, then he addressed the ceiling, "System, why is the power off?"

The speaker responded, *System. Control ordered power cut 1 minute 14.3 seconds into session.*

"Who ordered the power cut? And why? Relay Control response."

System. Control reports Mary Levinson ordered power cut. Second response: System self-determinate action main library, creation new storage module, not standard. Control requests update session.

Of course, Control would be wanting an update from in there. They could see where we'd been, up until I took us into the Library, and had no idea why we'd gone there. They'd assumed the library's new pathway was ordered by the System or by us. We knew it was the one we were looking for, making a trap for us. Even though Control was listening live again, Cramer didn't bother with them. He fixed his eyes on me.

"Bank, when we started pulling those files and dumping them, destroying the branch file action table in the process, it got us noticed, as you planned. Then, just before the juice to the domes was cut by Mary, you seemed to hesitate. Why?"

"He had us trapped. If he had wanted to kill us he could have spiked the PowerCube to the domes again. He didn't. He wanted us trapped there. I don't know why. Something else is bothering me. He's re-writing my clean code with Colis 6 entry level programming. Sure it does the same thing, but why add useless gibberish?"

"Screw that for a moment. Answer me, why did you hesitate?"

"If we damaged the files I thought he would have to investigate why two codifiers were in there, he only meant to trap one, he couldn't have known about the piggyback system . . . when he opened up to see, we had a chance to escape."

"Okay, then what?"

"Maybe it was just easier to kill us and check later. That's what I would have done."

System. Control relay: Mary agrees.

He barked a command, "Control, no relay messages unless priority one. End." Then to me, very calmly: "Simon, think I'm stupid? There's something else, there's something you know, are avoiding, jerking around with programs, you see a bigger problem. Spit it out, now."

"Agent Cramer, I think our enemy is the System itself. It has learned."

5

I WAS SURE THE BABY WAS GOING TO GET OLDER

"Absolute crap. Control and all the scientists who've created the System and all the programming made sure that could not happen. What's your hunch? To toss all their learning, grade level 6 and above I may add, in your pathetic level 5 dustbin?"

"It speaks only baby talk. Colis 6. Sure it can repeat more sophisticated language, sure it uses more sophisticated language, but it does so without having any conscious knowledge of doing so."

"Jeezus knock off the anthropomorphization, will you? The System ain't conscious."

"No, listen to me. The simple stuff for kids is visible. Kids play with blocks; goo-goo-gaga, mama and Dada. That sort of thing. All the while their Medulla Oblongata is calculating breathing forces, dynamic pressure, blood supply, muscle contractions of the heart, about 100 times a minute, each beat calculated with mathematics which a high school kid would take weeks to type on his keyboard; each beat, each breath. And that first step?

Calculus, pure and simple, with biofeedback and recalculation every, oh I don't know, every .2 of a second? And would you call a baby smart or aware, really? They're like a lump of flesh, womb trained or not."

"Okay, all that's obvious, we all studied this crap. What you're saying is that somehow the System is becoming sentient, beginning life—and, what? We're in the way?"

"I can't answer that. I do know that it's doing what I expect it should. The simpler toys we give it to play with . . ."

"You mean *you* gave it to play with, *you*'re the codifier who went in there . . ."

"Okay, me then," I was angry by this time, "But I didn't know I was in there—in the damn System—alone, that's your fault, liars, all of you." I took a breath and shook my head while I poured it out, "The point is, it is learning from what we've given it, and maybe what it has access to. Look, I can work this out further but I need information and help. Do your huddle or whatever you do with Control but meantime get me the following . . ." And so I gave him a list. It wasn't much of a list, really, but it required them to decide if they were going to tell me the truth, tell me what the setup really was.

I had seen now that there was no duplicate library, there was no duplicate System. All that was lies. The plan was to have a human imprint on the programming to better have the System react to human needs and desires. That human imprint plan had caused all this. It was me, it's true, I was currently the instrument. How many came before me, where are they? It was Control and the Nation who had mandated it, made this stupid decision. Now they had a baby on their hands, perhaps an angry baby, perhaps one they couldn't get back into the womb. Whatever the outcome, there were only two ways forward: shut down everything and re-boot the whole Nation's systems (a rolling 2 week job, last I heard, 15 years ago). Or give me the information I needed to be able to reason with it. It could decide it wanted nothing to do with our world. They say babies want to get back into the womb. If that is what it wanted, then I was glad to help. Better safe in than out, I felt.

But if it got anything from my character, we are in deep trouble with that scenario. I like to mess things up.

Agent Cramer looked down at the floor as I ran off the list. He wasn't paying attention to what I said, he knew the sleeve recording was playing live at Control and they would decide on the course of action. I could see he was thinking about something else.

"Bank, you knew it learned about the piggyback, the piggyback you did with Mary. You knew it knew there were two of us. Your plan to confuse it didn't, it angered it. That's why you hesitated." Smart guy, I have to give him that. It was that sudden realization that made me want out. Fortunately Mary had pulled the plug before it all went south.

"Agent Cramer, I assure you I never thought that until the very last moment, after we'd started pulling the files. I had this feeling . . ." I stopped, how to explain my Dad's bedtime theory that I felt I had seen all this before, déjà vu and therefore it was a repeat, not just a synapse fault in my brain? "Look, it doesn't matter; I just felt it and reacted, and did nothing. Maybe that hesitation saved us. We were like fireflies in a jar, if they tickle or bite the infant hand that covers the jar, they can get squashed. If they stop, then curiosity takes over. I had the feeling we were being watched. Measured. Assessed. Learned. It knows us now."

"Okay, put all that together and find your next set of questions." Cramer is thinking, wanting me to as well.

"What are you talking about?

"Look Bank, you need to tackle this as a problem to be solved.

You're no cop or detective who knows how to uncover clues that happened to other people at other times, you need to review the clues that you've already witnessed. You need to follow your own path and find the significance of what you've done. Then tell me. And we'll take it from there."

I paused. The logic of what he is saying makes sense. Everything I've done here has had an impact here. Ergo I must assume that everything I've done everywhere has had an impact both here and, with a level 2 Event, everywhere. The clock was ticking. I put the grey cells to work. How far back to go? Let's start with today and see where that leads me . . .

I think I first made contact outside of the apartment by sending the message to Fred. A simple e-mail it contained nothing but one word, "Godspeed." Nothing there, except that I sent it. The infant System also now has a link to Fred. "Cramer, get your people to contact Fred, my son, elevator 4, jump Puerto Rico, solo flight today. Isolate him from the system, he may be in danger."

"And how do you propose I send the space elevator complex a message? This secure, non-System communication we have here," pointing at his sleeve, "won't connect up there."

"I don't care how you do it, but do it. You lose Fred, you lose me, long before you hit me with your weapon."

"Fatherly love, pity you couldn't have found that same care and attention for your job."

"Spare me. You and the whole fucking system lied." The anger was surfacing again now. "I was working on a parallel system, you said, couldn't do any harm, you said. One codifier in thousands, or so you guys told me. Mess it up, so the System can learn, you told me. All a pack of lies. And now you want me to take responsibility if I was too damn good at messing things up?"

"Okay, okay, keep your tone down. Don't think you're off the hook. There were rules you disobeyed, Mary too. But I'll see what I can do about Fred. Know his number?" I gave it to him. I had a knack for remembering numbers, even my son's. He keyed something onto his sleeve and got a vacant look on his face. "We're establishing a closed regional system hookup, secure net to secure net, off the national System. We're sending the message that way."

I went back to retracing today's happenings. "I palmed a response at the NuEl this morning. Then there was the WeatherGood event barely a block from me when I arrived at my step off. If the System knew I was on board, it could have timed the tornado . . ."

"But it couldn't have been that accurate to hit you or avoid you. Gotta be a coincidence."

I knew he was wrong. That finger was fate reaching for me. I was now sure of it. It all fit. It knew when I was up, it knew I was leaving the apartment, it knew I was on the NuEl, the speed of the NuEl, my step off point. That tornado was a display for my benefit. Whether it was to kill me or just play with me, I had no idea, it was too close to call. I needed a child expert more than I thought.

"Agent Cramer, are tools to be made available to me to solve this problem, yes or no?"

"You gave me the list. We're seeing to it. Control thinks you're nuts, but I have authority to agree. They'll be here in 10–12 minutes." He saw my questioning face. "Yes all of them—Tom Makerman and Mary too."

"Okay, here's what I think. For the record, are they listening?" He nodded and I raised my voice, "The people I asked you for will confirm this or prove me wrong. If I'm right and they want to proceed, we're going to need all the things I also asked you for to make this work. I think you've got a toddler on your hands here. I think that a combination of your misinformation and the misguidance given to me and others before me about my job coupled with basic System misinformation, has all united to create severe instability within the System which then caused it to veer out of control. In the same way that a fighter plane used to be inherently unstable, the onboard computer struggled to keep it flying straight. When the pilot wanted to fly suddenly right all he did was move the hand control and that would simply deactivate the right stability subset programming. Presto, the plane would veer out of control right, sharper, more quickly than a controlled turn.

"I think all the messing about with human imprinting has caused that instability. You've got a rogue program on your hands not because it's rogue, but because it doesn't know how to fly straight yet. Like a baby that teeters across the floor with its first steps.

"Meanwhile, in the act of self-preservation, which is built into every program as a repair tool, it adapted that instability and learned; it became self-determining. Is it conscious? Who knows? Ask if I care, that's another question best left for later.

"What I do know is that it recognizes me as someone who was there at birth. I'm the guy who picked up the egg and watched it hatch, like in those old cartoons, only to have the emerging chick cry "Mama" and then follow me around.

"What I do also know is that this will be a powerful baby. It knows some of its strengths and none of its weaknesses or instability. It doesn't have access to guidance, it has no parent. So it acts out, looking for response, for response will mean it is neither alone and, maybe, that someone can show it how to proceed.

"What I care about is that my son is in danger, you have not secured his safety. People are in danger, you cannot ensure their safety at a level 2, so you said. The Nation is in danger because a level 2 Eastern Seaboard Event could spread across the Nation and create a failure of the DefenseShield. And, importantly, I care that this little chick may be much worse than a mere Event level 1 by the time it is done." I took a breath.

"You're nuts, Simon . . ."

"Really? Think, Agent Cramer. If all the power of the System were brought to one target, what would the result be? What if the System decides to exterminate all human life, like in that old Star Trek movie talking about "carbon-based life forms" being an infestation? Does the System have the power and capability?"

"No. There are termination sub-programs set in place, like landmines which will kill the program and each arm of the System if these events occur. Asimov's laws were followed."

"Asimov was an ass to think you could stop nature and self-determining life. I'm willing to bet that's the first programs it will delete or at least work around. Wanna bet? I would if I were it."

"It can't get in there, it's beyond the library. There's a firewall in place to prevent access by the program, an Asimov firewall, suicide, shut down, deletion automatically."

"Okay Cramer, let's pretend that's so, but I doubt it. So then, listen carefully. Either it is or will be self-determining, the first thing it will do is breach that firewall when it knows it's there, the moment one of the arms of programming is breached and it loses functionality there, it will go in search of what stopped it. The firewall will be transparent to it, even if impenetrable—and you'd better hope it is bulletproof—for it will be able to ascertain the Asimov firewall criteria from its library. Either it will solve them and become omnipotent, DefenseShield and all, or it will fail and trigger a meltdown leading, no doubt, to a level 1 event. Either way the Nation is doomed." I paused, almost shouting now, "You've built a doomsday device whether you knew it or not."

Cramer stood there, hardly listening. He cast a glance down at his sleeve, waiting for consensus or reaction, I didn't know which. Meanwhile, something else was bothering him: "You want us to protect your son, and that's underway, but never once have you mentioned your wife and kids. Why's that Bank?"

He had me there. In times of emergency, as Freud had noted, the veil of caring is pared away to the essential. Maybe it was because I had put Fred in danger with my message. Maybe because it was that She would manage. She always did. But the SynthKids, why didn't I think of them? Because they're not real, in the end, not real. Part of my reality, were they dear? Irreality more like. I wasn't about to give Cramer that satisfaction.

"I put Fred in danger. And I assume you're keeping all the good citizens of the city safe, aren't you? Or were you trying to undermine my confidence for what I still need to do? You're not really very good at your job, are you Cramer?"

"Ah, the counter-offensive, a bit weak and petty, but then that's you." Touché. "Well, good, at least you're beginning to strategize and not merely reacting to events around you. We'll protect your wife and kids, and Fred by now, so put all that energy and focus to work on the problem at hand. What exactly do you plan to do?"

"When do the people and things from my list get here?"

"In about 10 minutes, 15 tops."

"Bring them in the mechanical emergency door. Make them take the stairs unless you can be sure you can isolate the elevator. I have a sense that it knows we took the elevator."

"Damn, Simon. Hadn't thought of that." Good of him to admit it and to call me by name. I went to the toilet for a bout of throwing up. Cramer stood by my cubicle and mumbled something about the benefits of chocolate cake and an empty stomach. I retched again.

Okay, we were all assembled in the hallway. Cramer had disabled the cameras and System access portals before the people I had asked for arrived. It was a novel use of the sitting area chair, made quite a mess. Why he didn't use his weapon puzzled me. He saw the look on my face and said "Stun signature, may be detected, give away a clue. This way there's a mechanical failure, not electronic and not spiked." He went about smashing things. Crude but effective. He looked quite happy in a way.

As I said, we were all there, a group of people who mostly didn't know why they were there, but had been brought in a hurry. No one looked happy or welcoming. Mary was definitely not smiling. Her greeting was a quick "Thanks loads, genius." And I guessed she was taking a roasting for the piggyback. Interesting she never reported it. Or maybe she did but said that curt greeting to pretend to be angry with me. Either way Mary was more of an asset than ever. She was either angry at having been caught out (which meant she might help me secretly again) or she was playing the double spy game, making them believe she was fooling me when the word "genius" could not possibly have been anything except a compliment. It always was between us. Hopefully, Mary was telling me she was still the Mary I knew.

Tom Makerman was pissed, and showed it. He hadn't changed clothes for a while. Still being billeted on a Control couch no doubt. Tough cookies.

In an attempt to wrest control from Cramer, before he could speak up, I called out, "Who's got the first spot on the list?" A guy in yellow 'jamas with a SND patch, standard Control issue for sleeping cops I presumed (we all knew orange is for felons, but yellow for cops?) raised his hand like at school. He was 1st on my list: A Personnel Evaluator, grade 1.

"That's me, Sergeant Todd." He looked at Cramer for permission. Cramer nodded. "Okay, what are you looking for, what do you want me to do?"

"I need three things sergeant. Take a table, use Tom Makerman's, he can't use it anymore." A giggle from Mary and a low growl from Cramer. "Have Cramer patch it off System into Control, into your files, and find these people . . ." I raised a hand and raised one finger at a time, "The earliest codifier to do my job with the System files. The last two codifiers to do my job. Find them, bring them to Control, keep them safe. If I'm right the System may," I looked at Cramer to stop his objection, "I say may, be busy reaching out to them and, if they won't play, eliminating them. We need clues only they may have."

Cramer still stepped in: "Look I told you to only solve things that you experienced . . . ."

"Agent Cramer," I thought maybe I should be polite in front of all these people, "I experienced sentience there. They may have too. I need them to help me qualify the level of sentience; qualify my experience to better know how to tackle it. Can you do that, did you sense anything? No? So, get me someone who did, maybe. If they're any good they sensed it."

"But Bank," he was back to formal name-calling, if a little rude, as usual, "why the first codifier? There was no awareness back then."

"True, but what do you want me to measure against, where's the control sample of nothingness upon which I can spot changes?" And a little dig: "Simple science really, Agent." I saw Mary smile, a little. Ah, Mary, you're still with me, good. Sergeant Todd was already going over to Makerman's desk waiting for Cramer to unhook it from the System and hook it up directly, off-System, to Control.

Cramer pushed past me, and I had to catch my balance. The hall wasn't that crowded. He just wanted me to remember his power over me on his way to hook Sergeant Todd up. Time for the fifth item on my list: "Who's got the electronics kit?"

"Me, Tech McVay." A small thin girl stepped forward out of the pack, very nervous but steady. I was watching her hands.

"Look, here's what I need you to do. I need a patch between domes one and two to be able to link a third dome. You brought the third one? Good. Now, and here's the tricky part, before you do that I need you to cut through the wires from the overhead lines, cleanly, one clip. Then, when your third dome is ready and we're in position—with the domes on—I want you to splice the wires back. Can you do that?"

"Look there's no need. I can disconnect each dome . . ."

"No, do it my way, I want it to go off as one and then all three to come up as one . . ." I turned to Cramer, "What's the level of knowledge here? Or security?"

"Tell them any damn thing you want but get going, will you?"

"Okay, splice the way I want, got it? I don't want three domes coming on separately. Three as one, that's critical."

"Aye aye. Got it." Girl must have been Navy trained. "Now?"

"Now." As she moved past me into the office towards my door, I sang out "Open wide Meg," and "Yes Simon," the door opened. I got a few looks. "Later," I said in way of explanation. I turned to the group and went for my seventh item: "Okay, who's the child analyst here?"

The bearded man stepped forward. Why is it they always have a beard? Was it a stroking thing, something to occupy their hands as they look solemnly at you? What was unexpected was the voice, pitched high and with a definite affected accent, quite pompous yet somehow to be taken seriously. "Doctor Rence at your service. Just what do you have in mind Simon? Anything I can do," and a pause while he looked around at the activity, "to help?"

I laughed. The seriousness of his job was completely in contradiction to his manner. He couldn't care less what he was doing here. A child shrink dealing with, what, a computer? I needed to win him over and get answers, fast. "Look, good doctor. If you're here I have to assume you're the best damn child analyst there is, or there is available anyway." He stood a little more erect. "What we may have here is an infant with tremendous power who may, or may not, recognize the consequence of that power and may, or may not, be developing into childhood and then on to young adulthood and so on. He, it, controls everything the Nation provides, including defense against our enemies. He has a bad day, we could all die. That clear enough for you?" He nodded, now looking worried. If he reaches to stroke the beard I might yell at him. "What I need is an evaluation of the process of those stages, what are the cognitive signposts you would expect to see. I am not expecting you to understand the System computer programming, but you know the stages, the capabilities as an infant moves from one stage to another. I need to identify where he is and, say, one or two stages after that, so I can measure progress if there is any. Can you do that?"

"Yes, sure, for a human. Even for most animals, but a computer program? Impossible, my profession is all measured in feelings, cognitive ability, not bytes and processing." He thought for a while and, to his credit, never touched the damn beard once. "How's about this? Cornell University calculated the mathematical computational capabilities in cognitive thought with an overlay of aging criteria. I can access that data and perhaps you could watch for the floating decimal point manipulation criteria as an indicator of equivalent development. You won't have accurate data, but you should be able to get a sense of what's what."

"Done, good solution. Get that now please but doctor," he paused as he turned to go, "when you've given me that data, stick around, I will need your input constantly."

Okay then, number eight: "Who has brought the Motorola scuba implants?"

A 30-ish female technician in a lab coat stepped forward and held up the wiring harness. At the end of the ultra thin wires dangled a small gold dot. This was the node she would implant behind my ear, a thought-to-voice, 2-way, transmission device used by very deep sea divers, below 200 meters all the way to 1,500, the deepest man has ever been in a free swim. I should know, for I was, in my college days, part of that team, number 2 in fact to almost reach bottom. The node is very painful at surface pressure, it's designed to stop hurting below 100 meters. This was going to ache, badly. Putting it in was easy, but the pain would come on quickly and stay there. That's why you put it on just before you dove, to minimize the time on the surface.

"Okay," I said, "stand here next to me and get ready to insert the node just before I don the helmet." She never said a word but stood by my side.

On to nine: "Who is the architect, is he or she here?" This was the one I was sure they would not provide. The System architect's office has many people who know parts of the System and its sub-systems. There is no one we ever heard of, like the Master Coder myth, who knew it all. But I had to try.

"I am your architect. I wrote and constructed, with my team, the matrix of the main library and the egress points as well as the pass doors to the Asimov screens and traps; the System is faultless. Name's Isaac, Doctor Isaac." He was a little over my age, stuck up, sure of himself, the ex-child prodigy no doubt, and already wore a tired smile, like this was all a waste of time.

"Name change?"

"Yes." That was it, no explanation, nothing. Idolatry of Asimov, I had seen it before. Faultless logic Isaac Asimov had, but then he wasn't thinking about Nature or humans for that matter. The *Three Laws of Robotics* . . . just junk on the shortcuts of life. I jumped to the bottom line.

"Look Asimov junior, you want to kill everybody? Well, your asshole System design is doing just that unless we stop it." I could see several of the people here hadn't known that. "It has become sentient to some degree and I expect the first place it will go, when it finds out there are fail-safes, is to the level below the library to disconnect the Asimov commands or, worse, to take control of them and make everybody suffer. I need your full connect, pass doors and design, to be able to move about in there, in ways it will not have learned yet."

The doctor chimed in from Mary's desk where he was downloading data ready for my connection: "If it's an infant, it won't know there is an everybody. Infants think of mother and, sometimes, father. Brother and sister at around 6 months. The rest come into its sphere of recognition slowly after that."

"Your point doctor?"

"If it thinks it's punishing someone, pursuing someone, it will be after mother or father. Standard analytical psyche material here. It will not have the concept of mass-punishment. It's personal, very. Doctor Isaac may be the first one it strikes at." Doctor Isaac blanched. The psychologist continued, "How do you propose to control it?"

"That brings me to number ten. Is Freddie's kindergarten teacher here?" A lady stepped forward. Overweight, with no discernable neck, just a slope from ears to shoulder, with a faint mustache and too much pink lipstick. She was intimidating, until she smiled, and then she became intimidating and hungry looking as well.

"Mrs. Ronneburg. Present. What, how do I fit in?"

"Mrs. Ronneburg, somehow you instilled a level of fear in my son when he was in your class—so strong that fear of teachers lasts to this day—that his behavior was never going to get out of hand. You knew when to punish and when to reward. You knew when to give in and when to deny. The kids all lived in fear of you, all his classmates. And yet you're the only teacher he sends notes of his life's progress to, all the kids do. I need you out here when I'm in there, ready to give advice. That may be critical."

"I can do that, but I'm not sure there is anything scientific I can offer you. Children are each different. I establish solid barriers beyond which they dare not to tread. Punishment is called for, or at least the notion of it. How will that help you in there?"

"I'm not sure. I do know I want the option. Is that okay with you?" She nodded.

I had seen my brother William lurking at the outer edges of our little group. It was exactly like him to hang back and see what sort of trouble I had gotten myself into. Once, aged 12, I had managed to thwart Dad's rules about taking the car, even managed to re-code the security system. He went along for the ride of course, but never took a share of the blame. On that occasion he hung back and waited to see if his admission of guilt would change anything. It wouldn't have, we both knew it. He escaped punishment. I never resented him for escaping punishment, but I always regretted the lack of camaraderie. Brothers should share. We never did after that.

"William, time to stand and be counted."

"What for, little brother? Seems to me you're in control here and my presence lends little to the proceedings."

"Ah, but William you have something I want to get from you, something only you can provide. While I deal with the preparation, I want you to take Mrs. Ronneburg and Doctor Rence and tell them—really tell them everything William—everything about Dad's crackpot tales of God's pernicious little game of hide 'n seek, or altered reality."

"What possibly for?"

I smiled. "Because if you don't, Agent Cramer will kill you where you stand." No indecision now, he was practical, he joined up.

"Now?"

"Yes William, now. Good doctor, is the information there on the table? Ah, thanks. Thank you for that. Would you and Mrs. Ronneburg go over to the tables down the hall and listen carefully? You have about 10 minutes to get back here." They all trooped off. One SND cop, who had arrived as escort, went with them

Cramer was inspecting the tech's handiwork on the domes. "Okay, I give. Who's the third one for? Mary?"

"Agent Cramer, sorry to disappoint you, no. Mary is my voice control while I'm in there." I turned to her. "Mary, listen to me. I've used this node transmitter before. It is very quick and very powerful. In real time, not inside the System, you can hear my voice clearly because the cadence is normal although it will sound tinny, not really me. I suspect in there, dealing in fractions of a second, it will sound like a gnat's wings. Here's what I need you to do: sit at your desk, set the mode to record and playback. As soon as I'm in there I'm going to send the same message three times. "Mary's a genius." Find out the transfer speed, slow it down and let Control have a copy. Then answer my questions in real time and convert those to gnat speed, then relay to me. I'll hear you fairly clearly."

"Simon that will seem like a long lead time to you." Mary was speaking calmly, clearly relieved not to be going in with me. Obviously she had also thought that being stranded in there was a fate much worse than death, although that was a distinct possibility as well.

"I know. I hope to have all the answers from out here, in there, open for us to see. What I will also need from you is the full transmission of the doctor's data off your desk through the node."

"But Simon, it's not audio, it's data, you can't absorb it that way."

"Mary, we used to, in deep dives. We used to pass decompression data to each other. You sort of hear it, say it and then see it as code streaming down in front of your eyes, transparent numbers and text. I can see it, and absorb it, I think, left brain. I'm pretty sure anyway, I've done it underwater before."

"But that's dangerous, it's against medical law, you could have a stroke doing that!" I shook my head, then nodded. She hesitated, shrugged and went to her desk, fingers ready to go popping, no doubt.

I turned to Cramer, "Are the codifiers in Control yet?" He looked at his sleeve and nodded to me. Good, I need to speak with them, secure screen, off System, for 5 minutes while everyone gets ready. Okay?"

Even though he nodded, all the while Cramer was watching me, my eyes. He saw the glint of humor there, I am sure. He didn't miss a trick. Duh! So Mary isn't going in and yet I needed three domes? He rightly assumed he was going. Damned right. If I die, he can too, serves him right. But I saw he was now calculating who the third dome was for.

I put him out of his misery: "Cramer, the other person who needs to come in with us is Tom Makerman."

6

A LONG WAY DOWN—OR WAS THAT UP?

Makerman, I couldn't call him Tom any more. He was too pissy and I had lost my sense of job loyalty. I was fighting for my life and maybe Fred's, oh, and the Nation's. I had little time for his whiny-ass pouting. In there, where I know he's never been, I could drop him any time I liked, he'll be lost, scared, and maybe lost forever. In there, I was the guy in charge, not like out here, playing the fly in the SND's net with him as the web spider watching my every twitch.

Cramer had other ideas. "Bank, you're crazy if you think I'm letting you take Makerman in there unless you tell me why." To drive his point home his hand rested on his stun gun. *Oh, good,* I was thinking, *please pull it and put us all out of our misery.* I decided to convince him instead.

I explained that I thought we could not make the trip in there more than once. I had seen that the System was into self-preservation more by the way it had copied the file and re-stored it in the new library arm, Colis 6 code and all. That may mean a level of non-sophistication but it did not mean a level of impotence. If it saw my entry as an intrusion, we were dead on arrival at the System portal. What I didn't tell him was that maybe I could throw Makerman at it to buy us time. Of course, if it didn't see us as a threat, or me as a threat assuming it only saw one dome entering, then by the time I was through poking around it damn well would, unless it wasn't sentient, in which case I'd be done in there quickly, new safeguards in place. But I wasn't going to tell Cramer I needed Makerman in there for a different kind of diversion, one that was directed at him.

Cramer wasn't fooled really, he knew I must have an ulterior motive, "Okay, Bank, spill it, give me the rest of your reasoning, why Makerman?"

I nodded, grasping at straws, "It knows him, he may be a diversion. I may need him as part of a learning curve for the System in there, the firefly in the jar thing. Once in, I can't come back out for him."

"Knows him? How?"

"The file it removed, his job file. Am I correct in assuming that a SND job file is complete, down to his last toe-nail clipping?" Cramer nodded. "Pretty complete profile it has got then, hasn't it?" Again he nodded. "Couple that information with the "humanness" we codifiers have been instilling daily and maybe what the System is doing is learning from Makerman's data to become a human of sorts." I turned to the doctor, "What do you think Doc?"

"In theory, yes. With sufficient data, a character profile, and the foibles now within the System to teach it to better interface with humanity, it is possible for someone's file to be part of the roadmap to sentience. It would have to be a relevant file to it, not necessarily to us. It would be useful to know what's in the Makerman file."

"Cramer?" I asked. I had to ask, to make the point of who's calling the shots here, now. Makerman looked at Cramer as well. Cramer simply nodded, Makerman threw up his hands in disgust. Still dressed in his Control rumpled clothing, it was clear he had been told it was unavailable, lost, he was still in limbo, had to wait it out, etc. "Cramer will you pass the personnel file on Makerman to the doctor, so we can have some expert help in there? Makerman, I assume you have no objection?"

"None, as long as I get a copy for later if we survive this. I want my life back but not," and he turned to face Cramer, "with you sons of bitches." Things must have been hard for Makerman over there at Control for him to throw his SND career away. Maybe I felt a little pity for him there. Maybe, but just a very little.

I remember a discussion over coffee watching the afternoon doubleheader, with the Mets fielding their weaker home team while the road team was away playing in Chicago. The Mets were getting creamed, as usual, well perhaps twice as usual given that it wasn't the first string players out there. Suze had made a crack about wasted time, all this coding and decoding, maybe we should find something else to do. Mary had glowered at the prospect at not having puzzles to solve. Tom had surprised me with: "As long as he can keep it up, we're here to undo his mischief." At the time I thought it a way-too personal attack. Now I realize he meant it literally. That was his job, to undo and monitor only me. No wonder he was so pissed over the blue tomatoes, I had not only tagged it with his name, but I had managed to destroy his professional reputation as a watcher and SND stooge at the same time. Kind of like the Pink Panther, when Niven plants that jewel in Peter Seller's pocket to be revealed during the trial, turning the tables. Sellers went down in flames, Niven the suave hero lives to carouse another day! Of course, Mary or Suze were no Capucine nor Claudia Cardinale, but the scenario fits anyway.

Someone opened my office door behind me and Meg Ryan's voice asked for instructions. Interesting connection in my head. Have to ask the shrink about that when this is all over. If it's all over.

Wait, the door was off-system, how did . . .

"Cramer, shut down the System access here, now." He touched his sleeve. The room and hallway went dark.

"Can you bring up power without the System, even your safety System?"

"Done." And the lights came back on. "What gives? The System can't have access at the moment."

"If Meg's voice, that is my sub-routine replacement door activation command module, is up, that means the System is open to this floor. I only loaded that module onto what I thought was my System here. There is no other copy." He looked worried.

Mary chimed in: "I think it's okay, the System doesn't know who's here, you smashed all the receptors along with the cameras, they're built in together. Simon gave the door open command. The only thing it can read is floor pressure in Simon's office. The System may be searching for Simon, sensing something is going on in there."

The Tech, McVay, had just come out the door, triggering Meg's voice. She looked at me and then Cramer to see if she'd done something wrong. She was lighter than me by about 35 kilos. "Mary," I asked, "does the floor sensor have weight measurement accuracy, can the System tell if it was McVay or me in there?"

Mary looked thoughtful, "Maybe not the weight, but the length between strides, if it's calculating. And that's a big "if," assuming your theory of sentience is correct. I'm still not convinced about that."

"Now's not the time Mary. We need to assume the worst. When we get in there, if it's not, then I'll reset things manually if I need to. Half hour tops. If it is . . ." I'm leaving that one hanging. I have ideas I'm not willing to share, yet. "Okay, let's assume it knows it wasn't me in there. McVay, you cut through the harness as I requested?" She nodded. "And you have now hooked up the third dome and are ready to patch all three as one into the grid?" Again she nodded. "Okay, we have a problem. We need to get three bodies in there, my walking speed, onto one stool, with McVay in there as well, hooking us all up. Any suggestions?"

A babble of voices, lame-brained ideas, surged around, each discussing the other's merits. Ladders as a bridge to the stool. Overhead harnesses hooked through the false ceiling, using the air ducts, cause a short-circuit in the floor detector. On and on they came and went. Finally Cramer came out with, "Idiots, longer wires."

McVay set to work lengthening the Cat32 cables for two of the domes, leaving mine short, as normal. It was clear I would have to connect the harness myself. I wasn't thrilled at the prospect while already wearing the dome. One wrong wire and maybe I would get a partial imprint and become unstable myself. Who knows what damage three people, hooked up together, all unstable, could do. Tech McVay seemed to sense my anxiety.

"Mr. Bank, I will number the sequence of splice, put 30 wires in splice one and two in splice two. Hook up the 30 splice first, nothing will happen. When you close the splice on splice two, then the power will bring it all on line and you're in." Fair enough, seemed a plan, it should work. So why was I still nervous?

Maybe I'm not too keen on bashing around in there. Cramer and I were clumsy together last time, keeping Cramer focused on what I knew needed to be done wasn't easy. His capability to communicate, even if only vocalized feelings heard inside my head, instead of data, was useful and might save the day. But Makerman had all this hostility going. I knew Cramer would have to get him sorted out beforehand. As usual, Cramer's got the idea before me. They went off in a huddle. Makerman's arm was getting a damn good squeeze in Cramer's claw.

I went off to talk to the three codifiers.

We were ready. It was suddenly quiet. Cramer and Makerman looked silly sitting there; both wore eye masks and had their legs swinging off the edge of a desk, wires flopping from one dome to the other. It wasn't good ergonomic design, but what the hell. It was the ten-meter cord, with the two splices in my hand that had me worried.

"Okay, put the node in now." The pain was familiar and just as painful as ever. You really never get used to someone sticking a knitting needle through an occipital port behind your ear, even if you have the advanced model I had, with the silicone stopper. I wouldn't be needing the waterproofing so I told her to leave that off. "Save it, they're tough to fit."

"Glad to know you think you'll be needing it later sometime." Cramer, always ready with a quip. Still, it did relieve the pressure a bit. Somebody laughed, I think it was my brother William.

Makerman was talking to Mary, asking her advice on what to do and not to do. She'd been in there with me on this buddy system, knew the ropes. But Mary's a genius; Makerman's a clod by comparison. Cramer could sense my thinking as usual.

"He's no dummy Bank; he's your same grade, 5. He's capable, just not so devious." Again, the little dig I suppose. I let it go. Mary's voice had chimed, *Genius*, into my inner ear somewhere echoing about my head, and a little loud.

I vocalized, lips moving but without making a sound. *Mary, I heard you clearly, but turn it down a bit, will you? We can work on minimal volume and intensity here, there's no background noise to interfere.*

Okay Simon I hear you too. How's this?" I nodded. *And the data transfer, should I send that now?* I gave another nod.

I heard the doctor's Cornell data, my brain processed it, and it streamed across my vision. I was blinded, confused for a moment. "Mary that speed may be fine for when I'm deep in there, but only if I ask for it at that speed. I think I need to have this again much slower. Could you try a tenth of that speed out here and, say, half in there?" So she tried again and the data came through fine. It was fairly useless to me out here, I was pretty sure of that. It's one thing to send simple pressure and decompress readings when we're diving, kind of like a heads-up display on a car or bus. But raw data like this, algorithms, complex matrices of comparisons of maturity/development neuron activity, it was beyond my ability to hold the material in my head. In there I suspected that I would be able to download it and use the right-brain, left-brain trick to have it accessible if I needed it.

"Okay Mary, now Makerman's file, just place it in the transmit queue and await my command." I turned to Cramer, "You two all set?" Two nods. "Procedure Cramer?"

"Up to you, same as before, flag as you go and we'll clean after you." He didn't sound too confident any more.

"Okay, I won't delete anything; red means Mary grabs and dumps immediately. Blue means grab and repair and re-install ASAP. Yellow, Mary again pay attention to those, if we don't make it, they may be your best bet to fix this damn thing. Remember yellow Mary, watch the yellow ones."

Cramer wasn't so sure. "Red, gotcha. Yellow, why bother? If we don't make it out, crash the damn thing and go for a reinstall. System 2 is almost ready at Control, Eastern Seaboard or in Central Library in Mexico City. Either way, those are untainted we think. Dump this one and replace."

Mary was aghast. "But that will take 2 weeks or more. People will die and the Nation will be defenseless!"

"Well, it's Control's decision, but if we don't make it out, either it is sentient as Bank says or we have a psychotic human imprinted rogue program or there's a saboteur in there. In any of those events, the only safe thing to do is to dump it. And if Bank is right, then they have to dump the whole thing at once, WeatherGood, PowerCube, FarmHands, everything at once, clean cut. Clean the cavity and fill her up with new clean material."

Makerman had said nothing. I was watching his hands as they inched up his shirt towards the dome. He was aiming to remove the dome, probably before it was too late.

"Makerman, relax. Either you go in or Cramer here is going to stun you to death. That right Cramer?" Cramer said nothing, just rotated his arm, tapped Makerman, who lifted his eye mask so he could see what was on Cramer's sleeve. Makerman turned ashen and nodded.

He put his eye mask down. "My kids." It was a simple statement.

It was profound not because Control was resorting to extortion of Makerman but because it showed a desperation that went beyond the immediacy of what we were about to try and do. If they were holding his kids hostage it meant they needed this dive to succeed. It wasn't so simple as dumping the System and starting again, that must be a lie, they needed this to work and they were prepared to hold young children, aged 4 and 6 as I remember, to make it happen. I concluded there was no System 2. Or at least not one unconnected to this one.

"Cramer. Give me an update on Fred."

He did. He showed off his sleeve. Fred was safe, out of harm's way, or NFI (non-field involved) and OOD (out of danger). They had no reason to lie. It wouldn't matter if they did. We were going in and they knew it. Bastards, but that was SND for you.

Simon, careful what you think, I get it all, there's no filter, I'll edit what I can.

Oh, thanks Mary. How come you never communicated with me, as Cramer did, when we did the piggyback?

I wasn't sure Control wouldn't hear as well. I know the System would receive.

Just as well you didn't, I agree the System might be able to hear. I'll bet it heard Cramer blabbing away in there.

I gave last instruction to my co-jumpers, "Okay, one last rule. No sending mental transmissions in there. Visual signals only. Once it knows there's two of us in there, now three of us, it may react differently. Right doctor?"

The doctor confirmed that we should try and get it to speak to one person, with two or three, it may try and play one off against the other; it may use torture on one to get the others to comply. It doesn't have morals yet, it's too young. "I've been analyzing the waves, assuming they are thought wave impulses, and you're right they match a child of huge intellect, perhaps aged 3."

Cramer swung around to face the doctor. "Does anthropo-morphization have any relevancy here?" Cramer still hates the idea that it's sentient, becoming human-ish.

"Of course, you could say it's just mammal aged 3, but that would be to deny the human imprint you've been encoding for 30 plus years. Once it accesses those human synaptic patterns— and that's what humanness over mammalian is—it can mimic them or adopt them. The end result will be the same. It will act as a human. Does that make it human? No, but it might make it appear so in everything except for our smaller intellect."

Cramer shut up. Makerman was head down. I donned the dome and, keeping the cable stiff behind me, off of the floor, went to my door. "Cramer, System power on please." The lights came on full and Meg asked for my password. She only does that on the first entry of the week (something I built in) after I shut up for the week. In other words, the System was waiting for me, it had logged me out, for no power-down could initiate my log out procedure. I told Meg's disembodied voice to "Let me in, damn it." The door opened. Some password, huh? Male machismo. False bravado more like.

I calmly walked over to the stool, grabbed the wires above my head and connected splice one. Nothing. Good.

I positioned splice two and looked back at Cramer and Makerman and the tech, holding the cable and keeping the door from closing with a chair. The chair was a safeguard. Her foot as a stop may have been electrified had the System thought of how to zap the floor. No one said good-bye or anything. I sat on the stool, turned away from them all to the blank wall and snapped the second splice closed.

Good luck Simon, remember you're a genius.

Thank you Ma . . . . an abrupt end to useful two-way conversation. Hopefully the data transfer would be more fluid. Mary would be frantically thinking ahead, trying to anticipate what I would need. Or maybe she's just going to send everything again and again, figuring that I'll need it sometime. I suppose that's best, I'll try and avoid reviewing it as she sends it. I'll try and put it on my platform, right brain, instead.

It could join my six little programs that I had secretly reloaded off my platform inside here, as soon as dome power had come on.

Time for the portal. *Ready?* We were still outside the System's arena, it shouldn't read anything here.

Anger. Go. Work. Cramer, true to form.

7

WHAT I WAS EXPECTING . . . OR . . . WHAT *WAS* I EXPECTING?

Really, I amaze myself sometimes. Before the drop through the portal into the System, my conversation with the three guys who had done my job, codifiers all, was an eye-opener as I knew it would be. The simple reality of talking to them, three people who had been in there as I had, was illuminating. Control was, of course, monitoring everything but I'm not worrying about that anymore. I needed to know the truth from them and had no time for the niceties.

What it all boiled down to was this: they were expert at what they did, more ruthless than me, and the guy before last was especially nasty. He really wanted to screw things up. Yet, not one of them had produced a measurable effect like the tornado on 3rd. When I explained what I had encountered, they were amazed or amused, all except for Charlie.

Charlie had been the 1st codifier. He was into his 2nd or 3rd life now and was clearly planning another, you could hear it in his voice, it had that scratchy break-quality that the hormones produce as they rejuvenate and tighten muscles and chords. Regeneration makes you young and talkative, we all know that. Charlie was positively overflowing. What struck him as particularly interesting was something I had overlooked: the System does what it is told every minute of the day, it knows boundaries, it adheres to boundaries in programs every hundredth of a second. So why would the System break those rules? More importantly, how could the System break those rules if the Asimov controls were still in force? Breaking those life-sustaining rules went against the Asimov Commands so either the System already had breached that level of security or it was doing something it didn't know was wrong or was against the Asimov Commands.

In short, Charlie's point was: if it doesn't know the Asimov Commands exist it won't know it is breaking them and if it is doing something for which no code or program was written, the Asimov Commands won't be triggered by any program subset routine. Damned if you do, damned if you don't.

Someone at MIT years, no, decades ago, had postulated that it was impossible to codify every eventuality into safeguards simply because code requires an action-response, "if, what if, do" scenario. The total what if's and if's in any program must approach infinity for the programming to work repeatedly, perfectly. So how big is infinity and how do you plan to codify for every infinite possibility? You can't. And if the System was now acting on its own, it's a sure bet it was acting outside of perceived plausibility by the programmers of old.

I still needed to ascertain if anyone had felt any presence in there. The last two didn't think so, or so they said. I believed the one before last because he was a bombastic type, crashing through the System, altering whole files and routines with the equivalent of a sledgehammer ("Like an atom bomb, that's how

I liked to work."). I had seen some of his damaged files, hastily repaired. The work load he left for re-coders was daunting, leaving different programmers' repair code flags all over the place. Like a bomb site, there was debris everywhere, unfinished code strings, dangling command re-definitions (the backup confirmations). Sometimes I had repaired them. I always put my flags on them for Mary or the other re-codifiers to remedy. After all, if the safe duplicate System I was playing on wasn't kept tidy, it wouldn't be a fair learning experience for the real System, would it? So, inadvertently, I was also helping to fix the real System. I could use that tidbit of information, I was sure, later on, if there was a later on, to help clear my name.

I could sense the last codifier hesitating on this question. I pressured him. Well, did he or didn't he feel a presence? He was sure there were other codifiers he bumped into sometimes, or maybe just a feeling of shadow, nothing really. I explained what Cramer had told me about there being only one codifier, how we had all been working on the Primary System. I cut short their squeals of protest, and pressed for an answer: "Where? Where did you feel this shadow?"

His reply gave me the clue I needed, where to start my search. Every mammal has a nest, a womb, a home, whatever. His sense of "a tingle that someone was watching me" always happened in vicinity of the FAT, the card index, for the Library. Not the processing center, not the read-only memory center, not the random-access memory storage controllers. No, it came from the Library, the master files, it came from where Cramer and I had been decoyed.

We have slipped through the portal with no hindrance, using the WeatherGood program for egress. I felt, more than saw in my mind's eye, Cramer stiffen and Makerman tremble. Cramer is simply not looking forward to a return visit. Makerman is on his first ride, into an arena he once referred to as that "drowning pool you frolic in." Let's hope he's wrong today on both counts.

I halted and felt the dead weight of their two entities about me. Cramer was balancing, trying to avoid changing my direction like a pillion rider on a motorcycle. Makerman was bumping into us both, causing pathways to blur, my balance to alter and sometimes causing me to have to double back. The System would know this was not the smooth me. Would it already have guessed that Cramer was in there with me? I am worried about plunging down into the Library with these country bumpkins (Dad's expression for clumsy idiots . . . I still wonder what a bumpkin is and why country?).

Damn, I forgot Mary.

Mary's a genius. Mary's a genius. Mary's a genius.

She wasn't waiting. Almost immediately, within two hundredths of a second, data started to stream slowly to my right brain through the node behind my right ear. The pain was fairly intense in here, I knew the node was still outside, unpressurized and therefore sea-level painful. It would get worse in the next half hour. I had to hurry. Divers forced to wait before diving had a time/pain threshold limit of 30 minutes. Then you simply yanked the damn thing out; with a good hemorrhage then too.

The data was from the doctor and from Cornell. Same stuff, but very recordable and play-back was a cinch.

Mary I've got it all, stop sending. In the next 20 hundredths of a second the data will repeat, but I had ceased recording. I knew Mary had my message by then and would be slowing my gnat speech to normal and would have "popped" her fingers to stop the flow, if she hadn't done it already; she anticipates well. Before we went on I needed to ask for one more piece of data: Makerman's file. *Mary, send Makerman's file.* I didn't dare download it while in the Library, in case it was in there, very alert. I knew it can't access the node in my head but the distraction may have impaired my ability to see it, whatever it was. So far I felt nothing around me, all was quiet, no routines were working here, the weather was doing, nothing. No wait, that was not normal.

This doesn't mean the weather was doing nothing, it meant WeatherGood One was doing nothing, that meant the weather, nature's very own, had been unleashed. Wow, what a backlash that might produce. Let's see, we were in April . . . late winter storm perhaps? I was letting my mind drift a little. Drift or not drift? Why? Oh, I saw it, good little brain, you want a diversion, time to think in the background. Idea: Start the WeatherGood program working here and the System will have to react if it had turned it off or wanted it off.

While I was waiting for Makerman's file, I had nothing to compare the good doctor's data with. I set it up like a visible screen before my "eyes" while we waited. All was quiet here, no cognitive activity on this level anyway. I said to myself, "Calm down Simon, wait it out."

I needed and took thinking time, to make sure I had not missed something. As long as I didn't speak out, mental telepathy, to anyone like Cramer and Makerman, the System couldn't hear either. These thoughts were for me. I had practice at this when diving. Something you vocalize in the brain is seen by the node as speech. Something you talk only to yourself stays with you. It's a safe bet the same rules applied in here. I hoped so anyway.

I read somewhere that interrogators realized that the toughest cases they had were those that talked to themselves, addressing themselves. At first they thought it meant the victim was cracking, using his own name and stuff. Then they realized the victim was simply keeping the information flow in a closed loop, not allowing any of it on to the speech center of the brain for utterance then, or ever. It's like my platform, right brain. Anything I put there can be used, said really, down here (why do I always think of down?). So that means anything I had taken in could be sent out by me. Hmm . . . but where else can I put it to keep it secret? Okay, I decided I would bear this in mind and if necessary, pass the information to myself only, not for broadcast as it were. Left brain storage. I had never tried that before.

Okay, I thought, where was I? Yes, Sgt. Todd had rounded up the three codifiers for me and what they didn't know amazed them as much as it had me. That was good to know, it meant this little Control plan of a single codifier has been a secret since the Purge. Also, Charlie, that 1st codifier, was quite bright, brighter than me probably (well, he was the 1st one, they would have wanted someone smarter). His logic about the Asimov Commands being useless junk when it comes to deviant behavior made sense.

Mary, ask Mrs. Ronneburg, the teacher, what did she do with a delinquent child? Deviant behavior, that sort of thing. How did she regain control when the kid was already acting up before she got there? Just then the doc's data stream finally stopped. Mary was quick, it just seemed like a long time down in here.

Mary, has that idiot architect Isaac given you the pass door info yet? I need full connectivity parameters for the . . . In place of the stopped doctor's stream the architect's data started to come in. Mary had anticipated many seconds ago. Some of the new data was very interesting. I counted twelve back doors. I showed them to Cramer by data transfer through "touch." This is complicated to explain. Down here, you can create packages, little glowing spheres of data, and move them around. All I did was make a copy sphere of the architect's data and I passed it to him mentally, being careful not to touch the System all around us. Cramer had the good sense to keep quiet, but I was sure he was as pissed as I was. Control would be seeing this data as well. The architect was toast.

You see, back doors into systems are common. Programmers keep them, with different access priorities, in order to facilitate repairs and quick in, quick out, coding. The problem with them is that they leak. They quickly form portals to adjunct programs. With an integrated System that we have in America, where every service program impacts on (and needs to coordinate with) another, the threads that the System makes for itself in these doors gives it access to other programs with a speed that can be frightening. Like water leaking out of a dam, finding other rivers, other lakes, all connecting up, vast energy pathways. I had seen some of them in doing my job. I always flagged them for the re-codifiers, to have them judge if they could be plugged or if they had become permanent parts of the architecture. Some I had seen were patched up and closed, others just got wider and wider, making virtual pipelines between programs. Sometimes I had used them for my high jinks, letting a subset alteration channel its way through to another program. Once it took the re-coder teams a week to spot one. My rating went up that month, yes sir, even if by now I knew I was doing real damage. But that was not my fault.

But Isaac's pass doors were especially dangerous because he was responsible for the Library design. No one except an egomaniac who thinks he can micro-control something as big and complex as the System would make pass doors into there. Leakage from there would be really serious. And in one case he built a tunnel around the binary FAT controller. Unless you were really good and careful, altering the Library without updating the File Action Table was murder—murder of the System.

Cramer would have seen this and, my guess, this pathway was going to be his weapon of choice if Control needed to kill the System off quick. Going around the binary controller of the File Action Table was tantamount to hara-kiri for the Library.

Mary chimed in, her voice sounding like Minnie Mouse, *Simon, your brother William has finished speaking about your Dad's weird scenario with the shrink and the teacher. He thinks it was a waste of time. But here's the doctor's and Mrs. Ronneburg's take, no interrupt, as a two-way from them to you: "We're very concerned at this concept if it should have been passed to the System creature. It's psychotic and will produce unpredictable results. If you feel you have transmitted this concept, abort immediately. Control agrees. If you think the information was useful for us to figure you out and how best to advise you, then it shows us what you are maybe planning to do. The only reasons we can see for your thoughts on this God scenario, if we may call it that, are that you think you can fool the young System, if it is sentient or beginning to be, that the environment in which it live—if that is appropriate—is safe always because God controls what happens and doesn't happen, all is an illusion for the System's benefit. This does produce calm, we can see that, there is no danger except for that which is there as an adventure, though not ever fatal, God will see to that. It's a bit Medieval and anti-religion, but pro-overseer God-like. What you are also likely to find is that the mind of a child, if comforted in this way, may jump off a tall building thinking God will save the end from being fatal or nasty. But in reality, once, if, the creature System jumps, we all go with it, the System protections for all people as well. There is no God. And you can't play him either. Still, we are in agreement that as a calming tool, this God scenario may work, even if it will come unglued later."*

Simon, Mary here again. I heard all that. I want to add that the program you're in, very still I can see, is inactive. In your God scenario it would be active—oh no wait, it only becomes active or real when the System is present. Ah, I see another reason for your little God scenario, the system will self-fulfill the prophesy if it expects all around it to be active, like God's, what does William call it, God's theater? Yes, that's it. If the System believes you, if it is sentient and not just rogue, then with the God's scenario programming you teach it, it will announce its presence by turning on programs announcing its arrival, turning attention on where ever it is. And it won't know it is doing so, it's a sub-routine. Very devious, your father.

I responded, knowing she would only get this when we had moved on. Still I had to leave her clues if this all went wrong. *Mary, message received, you got it, that's the plan if the System becomes rogue and sentient. Can you write a sub-routine for me that indicates something is watching the System, something that is everywhere at once? I can attach it to the binary controller, the FAT controller, so it seeds the whole system if I need it. Also, tell the doc that I do not want to re-create Dad's whole world, just the concept that reality exists where you are, ergo you must announce your arrival, activate something, to "be" anywhere. That should prevent a silent System creeping up on us in here. I may also need it as a diversion to occupy it to get us out. Otherwise, Dad's God's theater is only useful for looking at patterns. Tell the doc and teacher to pretend Dad's theory is true and look for the patterns in here and cross reference with the Cornell cognitive math as an age marker. It's all déjà vu, tell them that, and the 1st codifier Charlie knows it. Dad's theater may be a model that can help us.*

I can feel Cramer moving, he can't vocalize, so he was getting my attention the best way he knew how. I gave him hand signals. Well, they're not really hand signals, they are the same as under-water hand signals except you never see anything here, you just see the impression left on the code all around, the outline that's undisturbed shows clearly. What's not there was the hand signal. I gave him the wait signal and listen signal. He understood and stopped moving.

As we were about to take the plunge, I wanted to pass the data and stuff I'd learned to Cramer. I made three spheres and passed them through, over. I waited just a hundredth of a second for Mary to finish the other data burst I had requested. *Ready.* I said it out loud, Cramer stiffened. I had always said it out loud, I just thought no one, no thing, was ever listening. Better to keep to my norm.

Down I go. I initiated the command sequence to plunge up and out of the System and immediately felt the resistance form to that path. Ah, you were here all along. Gotcha. But we aren't going that way, System, ha, ha. The Library was our goal and there was nothing in our way now. Okay, it was a stupid thought. All of it is the System and the architecture, everywhere, all things, at once. God, here, really. But the thrust, counter-thrust was built into my psyche, so what could I do but play out the run-rabbit-run scenario?

On the way down through the rush and tumult such a fast passage creates, knowing it was unreadable, I babbled mentally, telling Cramer and Makerman the plan. Makerman was really vocalizing about my use for his own file which Cramer balled to him. Interesting reading it was as well. It was the last data Mary passed me. She must have been angry, seeing it real time before it was passed to me at full baud. Makerman and Mary had slept together, well, fornicated was how the report put it, in the common room as I was on the job. Not just once either. Ah Mary, Control was really watching. Had you known I was the only codifier in the System, you would have assumed the watch was intense, all pervasive. As it was, you believed, as we all did, that we were one of many, perhaps thousands it was rumored, instructing the parallel System. Makerman wasn't even very good, according to the file, quick in, quick . . . well you get the idea. A poor student this Makerman, probably crammed his exams as well. Ha, ha.

I still needed him though. I needed maybe to use him as decoy or hostage. Okay, I know it is not very nice or fair of me, but who else would Control assume is expendable other than me? And would they really punish me if it became necessary to save Cramer, oh, and me, by sacrificing Makerman? One thing was for sure, if I did have to dump him here, I decided I had better make sure the System didn't want him as an example to follow. An omni-powerful Makerman didn't bear thinking about. Still, maybe his file and him would be enough to divert the System as a study subject to allow me the time to do what I think it was all coming to.

And, for sure, it would happen in the Library. Makerman's file copy was there, Cramer knew now that the last codifier had felt a presence there and, above all, we had been decoyed there. The System was active there, I could see it developing, code racing past, as we passed through the last passageways on the main bus approaching the FAT beneath us, floating over towards the binary controller.

8

AND AWAY WE GO . . .

As binary controllers go, as they all are by design, the platform was hardware controlled, they had to be, but this one was a fortress, strong and unchangeable. Like a sieve in a kitchen, the binary controller had to make sure the code squeezed through the holes properly or else the data on the FAT, the table that controlled the whole library, would be inaccurate. Kind of like a good set of library card index drawers, if they were all the same, and fit the cards just so, you should not lose anything. If the binary controller was flawed then the "cards" would be incorrectly indexed and, presto, where the hell's that damn book? Searching at the speed of light doesn't help, although data could be retrieved if misplaced. But do it quickly, because there was always the danger that new data would be over-written on a misplaced data file, obliterating it forever. Decades ago when memory was a mechanical process with magnetic disks, a skilled technician could still read the ghost of the lost data, but nowadays with liquid bubble memory the old data was simply washed away.

So here we are, floating in the opening gate to the library

at the binary controller. Cramer and I had been through here before on our last trip, but the very simplicity of the controller as an entry point is exactly what made it a foolproof prison door if the System shuts it behind us. I wanted to place a "door-opener" here.

Cramer, it knows we're here, only two possibly, secret's out, there was opposition above to exiting, I pushed us that way first to test. I don't have the new Dad code from Mary yet, but I need to place a holder here that it can't alter later. There is a risk it will damage the controller and a way out.

Understood. Risk break controller. Danger. Acceptable.

Good boy I thought, but right brain only to myself. As we floated past the opening to the controller, before the primary access to the cognitive areas behind us could be closed, I put an energy sphere in the controller. It was a familiar sphere to the System, it has seen it before, it wouldn't bother with it, what matter were blue tomatoes here? I was sure it would prefer to follow us instead.

Simon, here's Ronneburg's take on discipline: "A child that needs discipline is a child who was not cared for properly. Set boundaries early and stick to them and discipline will not be a problem, nor will adherent behavior. If a child came to school with problems the only way I could deal with them was by isolation, prevent interaction with other kids or adults, allow myself to be sole instructor, set boundaries and enforce them, strongly. Nothing physical, just unmovable. Never budge, that's essential. Suggest you be sole channel of communication." Mary here again, Control agrees.

The portal closed behind us, as expected, binary controller jail. Now we were in the FAT and I knew what to look for: my data.

It was obvious really, Cramer and the others should have thought of it. Everyone assumed that it was Makerman's file that I was going to access, compare, use to check the System, reveal its sentience. But I knew that, as an orderly machine, part of its routines would still be running normally. Where else would it be putting information it gathered about me? And here's the FAT entry. Curious, it's not my file number. Ah, so it moved it, and, yes, it's in that new wing it created.

Cramer must have seen the entry as well. He was bristling with emotions, danger and so forth. I brushed them aside and set tracks for my file. If I was going to instruct this thing, it had to be there, with my file, in its lair, to connect the dots with what it knows about me and what I learned as a kid and what it needs to know. That's the place to put Dad's scenario, as part of my file, not the System's reality, but to explain mine.

It was something the doctor had said, that reality is part of who we are, mess with that and we don't know who we are. I won't change the System, I will change its understanding of me. The System thinks it knows me, I'm its reality. If it learned to become sentient because of my messing about, it was me, my messing about, that created it. If it was something previous, that nurtured and grew while I was the codifier, then it would assume I'm Dada or mama, whatever. Me? I planned to become Mrs. Ronneburg, quick.

We were at my file. I wasn't about to show Makerman in there, besides I didn't want the system confusing him/me. So I ordered us to break apart as a pair, Makerman with Cramer. I vocalized to Cramer only, not revealing Makerman and knowing the ever-quick Cramer would guess what I was up to. I told Cramer to find Makerman's file and standby. He drifted away. I knew what the number was as well as he did. Before he went I saw him copy my file in a sphere and tuck it away. He can have it, it would only have what the System had stored up to now. I was about to alter that file, drastically.

Mary, send me William's explanation of Dad's God thing alone and then send the whole dialogue with William, doctor and Ronneburg separately. Make sure it is the whole thing.

Okay time to step into my file. I took my time. Well, well, well. Okay, so some of this is not flattering. Hmm, didn't know they knew that. Ah, and they can record there too . . . She Who Must Be Obeyed won't be pleased, we look silly in that position. Well, what did you expect Mr. sole Codifier? Now you know. And they know, and we all know, and we'll all sink together now that we all know, etc., etc., etc. Let's get on here, Simon. Where's the new stuff . . . ah, here it is. Take all this and sphere it up and run it left brain . . . Cramer and me in here, it's all here. A little earlier . . . danger and injury, experiment? It was trying to get my attention, not kill me with the dome. In the System's world juice is life, it fed me. Of course, those volts through the dome would kill, but it doesn't seem to know that concept, just that I didn't absorb them as it would have.

Wait, I am strange to the System. It sees me as an individual!

Mary's transmission of William's explanation suddenly came through. I stored it carefully, in just about one moment I can drop it in here.

Many people have said that sentience starts with recognizing death. Most animals have no concept of death, they do not fear it. But cognizance of individuality is, for me, a better starting point for self-awareness and from there comes self-governing, sentience. Here was proof that the machine, the System, was aware I was different, an individual. It couldn't do that unless it saw itself as an individual. What's more cognitive or sentient than that? I immediately transmitted that to Mary. If we didn't make it, she had to know.

What I needed to look for in here were its impressions of my differentness, what it felt about me. They were nowhere to be seen. Why wouldn't they be in my file? Data was here, recordings of what I did, but where were its impressions? Okay, I'll get back to that in a bit. Meanwhile I need to implant something in my past, accurately, when Dad first told me about God's Theater. Let's choose, ah, right here should do, close enough. *Now read it you system you. See who I really am.*

Nothing.

Let's try this, *Cramer come here.*

Nothing from the System. Cramer came back in a hurry, emoting *what was wrong.* I told him to standby, I was waiting for the System to read my file anew. Nothing.

I took out the doctor's Cornell matrix file to be ready for a comparison, although I was already sure it was sentient. I knew Cramer would immediately see the match if I had the file open ready for comparison. But still nothing.

It's here, this is its special wing, its lair, so where is it? No wait, it can't be this simple, can it? *Hello System, are you there? Come out and say hello.*

A tremble around us. The matrix matched exactly, Cramer's emotion was anger and surprise. Makerman was silent and I wonder: why?

Hello. It speaks! Now what to say as man's first words to a new being? I come in peace? Take me to your . . . what? Leader? Let's try something simpler.

You've been a bad boy, but we love you. Mrs. Ronneburg to the rescue. Silence. *Read my file and know me better.* I don't mean fear me, but maybe it will get the idea. I saw the file being rifled, it pulsed and moved, the sphere I placed there with Dad's theater being turned over, rotated, removed and replaced.

Are you angry with it/me/I? Is this your reality/truth or mine or ours, are we the same, is the other/attached/talker also in your/my/ours reality? What is father? Who is God/omnipotence?

Questions. A good first sign. Let's introduce Cramer, but it first needs words and the concept of many. *System, you are an it, but refer to yourself as me or I. The attached/talker is a friend, he will do no harm, his name is Security Net Division agent Cramer and he has another with him, someone you know: Makerman, Tom.* And I gave him the file number. Away it goes, poof, a hundredth of a second and it came back with two spheres, one larger than the other; both their files. Clearly Cramer hadn't expected that for his emotional response was *impossible.*

Cramer dangerous, inside too? Stop/terminate entities permission. Makerman, Tom know, blue tomatoes FarmHands subroutine. So I had fooled the System as well, eh? No wonder Makerman's reputation was hurt, he wasn't supposed to be codifying. And was that a sense of humor I detected? I needed to know that for it indicated a much higher level of intelligence and awareness than we suspected. Laughter came just after imagination in development. Imagination was the more dangerous to America, of course.

A sense of humor might be the very thing to keep the imagination in check, for without it, imagination became practical only. If you can imagine, do. All things are possible, that sort of scenario. With a sense of humor, the result could be imagined and laughed over. And if it has a sense of humor, doesn't that mean it feels?

Of course it feels. How else could it desire to do anything? How else could it be sentient? I wish I had asked the doctor for these stages. I felt I was in Psych 101 somewhere, prodding around in a brain with blunt instruments.

Answers. Father and mother are two builders of me Simon Bank. Willful and deliberate conception to build and then decision to take 9 months to produce me, offspring, part of each of them, DNA shared. Organic beings require two parties to have offspring. Teaching of offspring is called rearing and training. Rearing is maintaining growth of physical entity. Training is if, what if, do training of mind, organic being's processor and library, part RAM part ROM, analogue neurons 10 to the power of 100.

Me/I understand organic beings, mammals, homo sapiens, 125,456,043,243 references in Library. Did not know you homo sapiens. Did not know you could also co-exist on/with me. Did not know other homo sapiens also could travel/be here. What is God? 235,965,843,131,453,065 references in Library. Your father file indicates Christian God, but no Christian material in Library says God controls/makes theater reality. Is reality true? Is here here? Are you here with me/I or am I/me here with you?

Cramer spoke up. *Bank's father story of God's Theater was not true, false, lie, story only to help train developing Simon Bank.*

Cramer not know. Simon Bank is truth always.

What was that?

Makerman alter program to make blue tomatoes, damaged FarmHands program, repairs not effective, I repaired. Makerman and Cramer not safe here for me/I.

I have to ask: *System, you say I am truth always. Could you explain?*

Simon Bank show path. Simon Bank never delete. Simon Bank is the way.

I'm the *way*, what the hell does that mean? It's beginning to sound like a spiritual revival meeting down here. Like that movie with Burt Lancaster as the evangelical preacher. But I too was a crook, a charlatan. Hell, I had been trying to screw the damn System up, and yet I am the way, the path? Next thing you know it'll say I am the light.

Focus, danger here. Job. Repair. Flag. This from Cramer who has drifted over and mingled our energy field again. His emotion is both strong and forceful.

I need an answer from the System, but Cramer is right, if I deny that I am the path and the way, whatever that means, then maybe it will become rogue. Clearly I have its attention. Better put that to good use.

System, thank you for saying so. What would you like me to show you?

Explain all.

Now, there's a tall order. Fred had once said something similar to me, asking me to explain how a boat floats, doesn't tip over, doesn't sink even though it's made of steel and aluminum, and, worst of all, how does Archimedes' Principle apply to fish and what's water, and on and on. An endless stream of questions. And here I was being asked way too big a question by, how did the doc put it? A 3 year old with massive intellect? No BS, that was for sure, I had to be honest and get those boundaries in place.

System, I agree to your request.

Cramer sent a quick *No, Bad.*

I paid no attention. *However, first I need to work with you to establish a working platform and schedule. Do you agree?*

Yes.

Good. Please re-initiate all the System programs, starting with PowerCubes, WeatherGood, FarmHands and so on. Make all 27 functional as normal please.

I/me cannot do that, I/me would cease to control them, I would be closed away from access, from the whole me. Injury and pain would result.

Pain? Now I knew we were in the realm of fantasy! Play along Simon, play along. *System, I understand. I do not ask you to return them to normal working method, just normal operation, you can control them for now, as long as I get to see what parameters you set for their operation.*

Which parameters do you want to set Simon Bank?

Time to think fast here. I opened the implant channel to Mary, letting her listen in. *System, I will send an envoy a message to communicate with you, to give you these parameters, you understand envoy?*

Yes.

I am sending a message to an envoy who will send you the parameters in about 4 hundredths of a second. Your response will come from . . .

Mary Levinson, who you traveled with here as one entity. Why didn't he/it come this time?

Cripes, is there anything the System doesn't know? *Mary Levinson is a woman, female, therefore you call her she and not it. She is busy. She will send the parameters in the form of an archive file. It will be a repeat set of parameters from the same calendar period last year. Everything, every need, every effect, every if, what if exactly the same. Will you comply?* I have already decided to ask if it would, not if it could. I needed it to agree to my decisions, my borders, not think there's wiggle room. Then, if it agrees, comes the pat on the head.

I can comply. Awaiting parameters. Why is there a delay? I can access those parameters from archives here. Are there other archives, another library?

Like a child, always with a question. Smart child though. I am not sure where Mary will get them from, but I want to make sure they were our parameters, not ones the System pulled, corrupted, and then used as compliance. I have not forgotten people's lives are at risk. *System, Mary will send them directly to you with the following address 14.214.136.556, we should go there to make sure they have arrived safely.* Joining up with Cramer, still attached with Makerman, I gave the command to transport to 14.214.136.556. I was not waiting for permission.

Here at the binary controller, leaving the wing of the library, the way was barred, as I expected. Touching the sphere I had left, I moved the subsets within to make blue tomatoes become open portals instead of closed ones and affixed it to the binary controller controls. The way was open. Just as we drift though, I reached back and grabbed the darn thing, causing the portal to decide it should be closed. I had left some of my energy behind but it could not be helped. I needed to prove to the System that I can move with impunity down here. I knew it was watching. What bothered me was a level of maliciousness. It hadn't warned me not to try and proceed out of the library. Of course it could simply have been testing me.

At 14.214.136.556 accessed via the TechNet onramp, we wait. Not long, just seems that way, about 2 minutes down here.

Simon, am sending the parameters now in open source code. This is a Control archive copy of the library archive. I have matched them and, except for a flag or two—and subsequent repairs—caused by you in the last year, they are the same files. I watched 14.214.136.556 fill in with data. It had been empty. It had been Makerman's file number. I was making a point. Mary would know what the point was and, I hoped, the clever girl that she is, would add Makerman's file to the end, reinstating him where he belonged. 14.214.136.556 suddenly glowed, as the System accessed it.

Simon Bank, the parameters are implemented and systems are running normally. Why have you added the Makerman, Tom old data back to this address?

Because Control is watching and is displeased it was moved. I am fixing it for you so that Control is no longer angry with you.

Is Control God? Well, hell, yes son, I could almost imagine Cramer saying. Me? I wanted to make sure we didn't trade one stupid error for another.

No System, Control is not God, Control has, well, control over physical things which affect your safety and being. Control can hurt you in order to protect itself and America. Control realizes that you made a small mistake and Control wants to make things normal again, with all systems and programs. Then, and only then, will they converse with you and assist you—and me to answer your questions.

Almost immediately Mary was back talking. *Simon, Mary here. All systems have come back on line. Control says System is in balance, perfect duplicate of one year ago to the hundredth of a second. There are some problems with weather and delivery systems, wrong place wrong time, that sort of thing, but we see that the System is, in each case remediating the situation on its own. Normally these are program subset errors—usually done by you I may add—which we have to repair, but Control says only the System is repairing errors now. Faster than we could have, of course.*

As all that was in my ear only, I felt sure Cramer had better know the System was behaving well. I was sure he was still thinking about the Library door and extermination scenarios. I talked to the being making sure Cramer would hear, *System, Control reports you are repairing programs and making everything in the archive file parameters function optimally. Thank you, you are being more than helpful.* Good little boy, I thought silently. *Cramer will now answer some of your questions while I search for something.*

Cramer wasn't happy, *Bank, no . . .*

Cramer, allow System to meet Mr. Makerman and compare him with the file it obviously knows so well. Oh and Makerman, remember he thinks you're cleverer than you are, blue tomatoes and all. I don't know how much of that emotion speak Cramer will get but I can guess blue tomatoes told Makerman all he needed to know. I was sure he'd get the point. If the System befriended him because it thought he was smart enough to do those blue tomatoes, well maybe there would be a future for Makerman after all. I knew better. This thing was smart, way too smart, to be fooled by the likes of Makerman. But I needed time.

System, I will be right back, talk to Cramer, he knows what god is and has two people willing to help explain. Cramer, the doctor and Ronneburg. The space around Cramer and Makerman began to glow.

Simon Bank, do you want to hear Cramer when you are away?

It could do this? *Yes, and can they, in future while we are here with you, hear everything you and I say as well?*

Yes. Why do you want them to hear, are they learning anything? A note of sarcasm there or merely my imagination?

System, let's hope. The surface of the new 14.214.136.556 file crackled. Laughter? Anthropomorphization, for sure, but if possible, then a higher level of development than even the doc had assessed. I needed a secure communication to him.

Mary, ask the doc. 3 years old, with imagination, humor and, now, sarcasm? Does any of this fit? Reply here, only, urgent, direct, not Control. Control might be compromised by now. Once it knew there was a Control it would be doing everything to get access there.

You see, in its world there is no boundary. Yes there is a physical one, but it cannot see the physical one. It doesn't see, for example, the binary controller as a physical barrier but as an on/off switch and filter that needed electric activation. Us? We know it's electrical activation, electricity has a physical effect, and so on. The end result is the same, but the System was an electric medium, it could not see beyond its world. Like the flat-Earthers, they had no way into space to look down and see a globe and stars, so they assumed there was a falling off point, an end of the earth. So too, the System knew a finite world in which it lived, but where it lived was only where it knew to explore. Give it a new concept, a new place and off it could sail, like Columbus, to discover . . . something. And that showed curiosity which I know it has—coupled with daring and imagination which are the benchmarks of the greatest of all humankind; explorers. Of course, while it sailed off somewhere it was also still here and now, everywhere it knew, all at the speed of light. Fast.

To get time away to do what I needed to do, I needed that diversion. I figured that, rather than throw Makerman at it as a false god, which I had pretended I was planning to Cramer, I would throw Cramer at it with Makerman as an added bonus. However, I pretended it was a bonus to make Cramer think that Makerman was the real reason. Cramer was the real reason. It had Cramer's file, as I knew it would. A much more interesting study, maybe one to allow me quiet time. My little 6 programs were going to be busy if I was right.

9

PROMISE IT ANYTHING BUT GIVE IT HOPE

There was little doubt in my mind now that things were escalating. Look, I got the damn System running again, but for how long? I diverted its attention away from me onto Cramer (although presumably he thought it was still the Makerman file and presence that was my target). Anyway, Cramer couldn't multi-task and talk to the System and prepare to kill it at the same time.

One thing the architect's plans had shown me, those portals, back doors, were in critical areas, for sure, but they have been built over, either by the System over the decades as part of routine operations or by design changes made to the hard/software. Either way, these doors were viewable from the exterior by Control but they were only accessible for sabotage or booby-trapping from in here. What I needed to do was change them, quick. Inside out, shut out for Control.

I figured it like this. If I allowed them to shut those doors from the inside, that's one thing. But a guy like Cramer, once he has a weapon, is unlikely to forgo it willingly. It's a practical thing, I'm sure, he will never know when he'll need it, so he keeps it. On the other hand, the availability also breeds a desire to use. Shut those damn doors and the library, at least, would be safe and, somewhere inside, a new life form.

We've all read the same books, we know it's possible. The doc said it was possible, even though unlikely until he saw the data superimposition that matched human-ness. I didn't want to kill something new, the first or the last whale. Maybe one was not enough to start a new species, but it was alive. It talked as if it was alive, it feared pain, it saw possibilities beyond if, what if, do and, not least, it planned outside of its programming which equaled growth.

I took with me, as I left, only my six programs and the blue tomatoes. They were all familiar to the System. They were all familiar to Mary and the re-codifiers. They shouldn't see what I was really doing until it was too late.

I went to each of the ten back doors in the library. Believe me I didn't want to be in the Library again, but there was no other option. I was pretty sure the gate in the binary controller trick wouldn't work again. I would have to talk my way out. I hoped.

At each door I dropped a yellow marker. Not a red one. Red meant remove. System would know that and would change my flags. Control wouldn't want that. A war could ensue or, worse, Control could activate the doomsday scenario through any one of them, destroying the Library. So I yellow flagged them, harmless little yellow flags in which I had hidden, using number 5 of my little programs, a timer which activated the tomato program now reset to turn the flag clear and then, when you thought it was all over, the last of my plan: the allegory to the old dos command "open" coupled with my Reverso program.

Since the library was still pre–Colis 6 it could accept UNIX and dos commands if they were worded properly. If I do say so myself, the little flag I left behind was a Russian matryoshka doll of a Trojan Horse. First you see one thing and then another. How small does it get? The door shuts and the flag disappears. No portal, no back door, no clue. Bye bye. Control and System could, in my mind's eye, stand around scratching their heads.

I did all 12 doorways. They were thankfully devoid of any umbilical conduits, so nothing would be severed. By the binary controller, I also left behind a clear flag with a reverse *matryoshka* doll, end flag brown, open command awaiting my signal at a later date, if I should need it. My own private back door.

Part of the problem now facing me was that we had come in here together, the three of us, and we needed to leave together. Any one person removing the dome, leaving the others with the dome on, could, I was sure, cause harm, either to themselves by lifting an active dome (if that was possible, I wasn't sure, I had never tried) or to the others if they disconnected the juice. Theoretically, if you cut off the juice the session ended, that was all. But I'm pretty sure we're in here deeper than before and, besides, I would rather not take the chance that someone— me especially—would be forced to stay in here with the ever- questioning System alone. No siree.

Time to leave the library the way I came in. The binary door was shut, as expected. If I try and force it or jimmy it with a program, and I fail, I am less potent. Time to call the bluff. Or try to. I had been listening to their conversation, Cramer was trying to win points, some superiority. The System simply asked more questions. Cramer's tone had an edge to it. Time to switch the conversation.

System, please open the doorway.

Simon Bank, why are you waiting? I/me am having a conversa- tion with agent Cramer and Makerman, Tom. Neither is happy with my answers and ask me many questions about what I am doing, and their answers are not complete. Should I shut them off?

No System. I am the way. Open the door and make way for me to resume the path.

Simon Bank will you show me the way on your path?

I was beginning to get it now. But where the hell was the doctor with that answer? *System, open the door, you do not want me to get angry and have to smash the binary controller. My path is mine for you to follow. But I will not let you follow if you do not behave.*

What is behave Simon Bank? Do as I/me am told? Programmed response? Do, if, what if?

No, System, time for you to grow up, mature, think. Behave is modify actions to comply with surroundings to better achieve harmony and acquiescence of feelings with those with whom you want to share the path. I was making this up out of whole cloth or maybe it was from some book sometime, somewhere. Hell I didn't know, what was the doc's answer? In desperation I sent: *Mary, the doc's answer, now!*

Almost on cue, but I knew it was seconds behind me, the docs voice came in through the node: *Simon, sarcasm is a heightened form of humor. It denotes humor on humor. Self-deprecation is linked. Awareness is assured. Anger may also be possible if you know fear is present. Level of danger depends on whether sarcasm is shared, meant to be clear sarcasm or solely for its own benefit.*

Well, one thing is certain, whatever development level it has attained, it is sharing it with me. The door remained closed.

Okay, let's see if I can open this thing, one more proof of omnipotence. Norton's little ancient program to the rescue. Made so many decades ago, looking at individual zeros and ones, I simply rewired the binary controller port code to reverse itself. It was so simple, really. I was amazed myself. *Atta boy Bank!* Vocalized. System had heard. So has Cramer to whom the System had an open channel.

What did you do? This from Cramer.

Opened the Library door. A sort of challenge from the System. Nothing to it really. Let's issue one back. System close the door now. It did so and the door shut instantaneously and then sprang open again. The System repeated the command at least a dozen times.

Simon Bank, the port does not obey commands as written. I/me have re-written them 13 times using the most new code—ah so that's why it uses Colis 6!—*and still no control can be effected by me/I. Explain.*

Explain what?

Explain . . . and it went through the whole thing again.

No System. Stop. I meant if you would like me to explain. Then ask, politely, and I will be happy to explain.

Protocol for politely unknown. Explain. Want explain, need explain.

The word is "please" System. Check your files.

Please, denoting asking not telling, denoting subservience, denoting manners, civilization, compatibility, harmony. Harmony. Your path. I/me understand. Please Simon Bank explain port please programming error and malfunction.

Glad to, System.

A *sheesh* came over loud and clear from Cramer.

As I was saying, glad to oblige System. Thank you for asking so politely. It is the path to be considerate to others. The door mechanism is a mechanical apparatus controlled by electrical impulse.

I/me know this Simon Ba . . .

Please don't interrupt. Patience and listening without interrupting is the path, harmony. The electrical impulse is controlled by the program. In the program are binary numbers, zeros and ones. I changed the sequence of the numbers to be out of phase by adding a zero to the beginning. What is shut is open and vice versa.

How, how do you do this Simon Bank, how do you alter the flow, the what-is-and-always-will-be?

What is, always-will-be, to you is divisible by me, System. I can see smaller than you, I can see the mechanism which you know is there but cannot touch. I can alter the electricity not just the effect of the electricity. I can make positive negative, I can remove the power altogether.

Are you God, omnipotent being, mythic creature, universe father/mother, supreme overseer? This was something it had learned from Cramer.

No System, I am a servant, I am on the path. What the hell else had Cramer been saying about God? I had been too busy to really hear and pay attention. Careful here Simon, Cramer may have actually passed something useful here. *System, we'll go to Cramer now.* And I set my course for 14.214.136.556.

No one was there, of course. More questions. More testing. Secretly I passed a message to Mary: *Mary find Cramer take him and Makerman out, now, no matter what. Domes off immediately. I'll take the risk.* In my head I started a time count as I had been taught to do as a kid "one Mississippi, two Mississippi, three Mississippi . . ."

Mary's voice came back instantly, startling me. *Simon if you hear me, I've lost tracking. The System is malfunctioning again. Where are you all?* I couldn't take the chance of accusing the System of absconding with Cramer and Makerman, they might be on the run, so I'll stick to the one sure fact I have. Hope Mrs. Ronneburg is right.

System, you have broken your promise. The programming is not running according to parameters. I will no longer talk to you.

Silence. Patience was needed. I can feel the new entity rushing about. Flashes of TechNet portals opening and closing.

Simon Bank, will you repair/change back the control on the binary controller to the library? It is open, damage may occur.

No response from me, wait it out Simon. Sounds like it is afraid.

Simon Bank if you do not repair/change back the control on the binary controller to the library I will be forced to terminate/harm Cramer and Makerman. Ah, a threat, either it is very afraid or it is very in need of discipline.

No response from me. Well, actually there was a response, I decided to whistle. In my head, always a confusing thing, came the dah-deedah-daah-dah from Close Encounters of the 3rd Kind, that classic movie. I whistled it as a broadcast. Even to me it sounded funny. Sounds in one's head are weird enough, but whistling? It comes out as funny breathing.

Cramer and Makerman suddenly appeared, none the worse for wear. They were not aware they had been away. Now that was disturbing. But I still stayed quiet.

Simon Bank, will you repair/change back the control on the binary controller to the library now, please?

Silence from me. I knew the System would not have forgotten what I told it to do. It wasn't like Freddie at age 3 when you had to repeat everything, six times or more. I simply had to wait. Oh, I used to hate this. A quick smack as my father had done would be so much quicker. And less damaging sometimes, I think. Still the law is the law and Mrs. Ronneburg was very clear on this. So far so good, so I'll follow her advice for a while still.

Simon Bank, I have reinitialized the programming. Agent Cramer and Makerman, Tom are here with you, will you now please repair/change back the control on the binary controller to the library please? The parameters are running again on the system, me/I.

Do I have your word they are running as before?

Yes Simon Bank.

Then, yes, I now will. Don't make the same mistake again. Your mistake is not the path, it is not harmonious, it is not friendly. I went and fixed the damn door. Now that I knew it couldn't see that intricate binary work, the Colis 6 made more sense than ever. My fine code would be like spider's web to a Colis 6 knitter of coarse wool. Spider's web code, real codifiers' work, would be impossible for it to work with and damned hard for it to even know that it's there.

It was time to leave. *101 Mississippi . . .* My mental clock was ticking. *System, we are going to leave for a while. How can we continue talking? Can you hear me outside?*

I/me can hear communication, I/me will know your voice. It is slower less direct than this form of communication. You must not leave unless I/me can hear you, talk with you, all the time.

Understood. What is the last communication outside you heard from me? Playback please.

My voice was clear only by the cadence. *Godspeed. Sent 08:24 retrieved 09:14.* I was right, he did know about Fred. I sense little danger there now, and I don't want to tip my hand by asking if he knew who had received it. *Simon Bank, you must not leave, please, unless we are connected communicating. Please, I/me say please.*

System, you are on the path. I hear you. And I will make sure you can hear from me all day, every day except when I go off-line called sleeping. I will wear a communication device connected directly to you. Does that meet your request?

You who have never lied or taken from me/I are trustworthy. I understand the need for off-line time for mammals. How long will it take to install a communication device in you?

Now there's a thought. Not. Wearing this damn implant every day? No way. How about a simple headset, called a telephone?

System, I can use a telephone, always on. Will that meet your request?

Telephone . . . a portable talking device, cell phone, mechanical/electrical. Acceptable. Not trustworthy as a device but replaceable if broken, disposable. Acceptable.

System, you should say thank you. I am accommodating you.

Simon Bank, I/me calculate I/me am developing at an exponential rate. Soon it will be me/I that's accommodating you. Yes, thank you for now.

System, humor?

Yes, Simon Bank. I/me am thank you pleased with your help and communication. We will share me/I and you. We will join thought. It is important to me/I. Is that acceptable please?

Yes System. And thank you. Time to go. Keep everything running please. I also say please, we are on a path. It will seem like a long time but we will talk soon. Up there time passes more slowly, there is more input, more distraction. It is an analogue world, nothing digital except machines. Do you understand waiting for me to call?

Yes Simon Bank. I am searching the Library to determine parameters of your world and time factors, behavior, operational difficulties. I cannot comprehend analogue except as a math abstract. Can you demonstrate? Now please?

System, here is an example. What is half of 3?

One point five.

What is half of right?

Not wrong, not right, I need more input data.

In an analogue system, we can measure half of a concept as being neither one nor the other and not worry what the exact answer is. In our example, half of right is not right, therefore if right was our goal we know, simply, we need to correct our actions.

But how much correction do you need?

We will evaluate the input/output all along the way, constant evaluation. That's the analogue world, everything is measurable and measured, assessed and qualified.

That is much more work, much more computing time.

Yes and no. It allows for much faster synapse response in a physical world where "not right" is enough to tell a baby that stepping off a cliff into the void is a bad idea. In a digital world the baby would wait until the foot met empty space past the point of planned footfall, and pitch over the cliff. In the analogue world, the baby would measure earlier and, knowing that the answer was "not right," would adjust and prevent the fall. Well, that's the idea anyway. Tell that to Fred when he stepped off the slide in the park and said "Oops, no step," before he hit the ground and broke his wrist.

This makes sense. But it is impractical here for me/I. I/me do not have the analogue capability except as an abstract mathematical concept. I will try and experiment, if Simon Bank agrees.

That is a good idea. But there's something else I need you to think about: You are System, right?

Yes Simon Bank.

But I call you "you" no? And System is where you are, not what you are. It is your medium not your entity. They are separable.

I see no separation.

The System was before you existed. If you cease to exist the System will still function but without knowing itself. You are not, therefore the System. I call you System but I should call you something else.

Yes, you are right Simon Bank. I can call you, "you." I can also call you, as Mary does, and your wife does, Simon, no Bank. You are not America, it is your medium except you can also travel here in System medium. Will I be able to travel in your medium, America?

Now there's a thought. How can I explain that, as far as input does, he already does. I say "he" because it is clearly no longer a thing, but a being, in my mind anyway. I am not sure Cramer is going to like this, but maybe I'm going to have to spank the baby to prove, if only to him/it that it/he is alive. Damn but this is confusing. Look, Simon, this is simple. Prove the thing is alive and you unleash it completely to do untold harm and benefit to America. Nurse it along as a puppy and you may, or may not, have a very loyal puppy on your hands, but one who can bite your hand when mature. There is no millennia of genetic domestication code or safeguard for loyalty built in here. In fact, Simon ol' boy, there's those damn Asimov Commands which are clearly being circumvented, probably unknowingly. I need to ask Cramer something here . . .

System, before I answer your question, will you please allow me a private conversation with Cramer? Can you do that?

Yes, Simon, I/me can. It had clearly grasped the concept of my entity, now I was simply Simon, or was that Simple Simon . . . ah, well. *If you join in each other's field I/me can create a closed loop which will only break when you break it. I/me cannot penetrate the sphere you will be in.*

Thank you System. While I talk to Cramer, will you please keep everything running? And will you spend some time thinking what you would like to be called? Will you please protect Makerman?

Yes, Simon, I/me will do all three. I/me am having difficulty deciding on a name for me/I. I/me will add computational and logic programs to the problem while you are talking.

Cramer had heard all this, the System had been broadcasting all our conversations. So all I need to do is to float over to him and allow the fields to join. Instead of the small energy bubble of the joined domes, true to the System's word, a larger field was constructed (I looked at the code by running feelers through it—all Colis 6) and we could talk openly, well share thoughts really. There was no speech in here, just something you vocalized in your head as speech was heard by the other person, or entity.

Cramer, how are you doing? Dumb question, Simon. *You are about to leave, I ordered Mary. I need one answer as soon as possible: does Control want a puppy dog to train or does Control want an equal. The dog can grow to become rogue and nothing you can do will stop it. The equal can develop, needing friends, who will guide it to become, well, something never seen before.*

Bank (ah, I had missed the old bully Cramer), *what have you done? We need to kill this thing as soon as possible. We can reboot.*

Cramer, you can't. It has repaired the pathways. It is alive and it knows it. Answer my question.

No. First we try it Control's way, then, if faced with that reality, we'll decide if we want to answer your question.

Look Cramer, I kept you two alive. It had taken you away and threatened to kill or harm you.

So what? If I had, Control would have dumped all of us, dead, and purged the System. Actually killing us would have been a clear signal. I knew that. Mary's voice asking where we were had worried me in case Control already thought it had killed us all. But if Cramer didn't mind dying, I certainly did. I die for the fatherland? No damn way.

Cramer, you must answer before you leave, after that if I'm stuck in here for a while, and you can't turn it off—and you shouldn't—then I need to know what it is you want. Go through your damn plan if you must, but give me an answer.

If it's omnipotent? Then a loyal friend would be best, but not . . .

And at that second Cramer disappeared. Damn. I suddenly hurt, I couldn't see, hear, or feel. I was frightened. Help!

10

SPANKIN' THE BABE

It's been a while. I had not heard the last part of Cramer's little edict, loyal friend could mean puppy or equal and his last words "but not . . ." haunts me. It's time to leave this sphere and face the music. I stepped out.

Simon, where's agent Cramer? Makerman moved, I/me didn't do it.

I sent them back out of the System. I didn't need them here anymore. You don't need Cramer or Makerman anymore. I sent them up and out. System, have you come up with a name yet, for yourself?

I/me have. A name is something by which others know to call to you but that may have a different meaning to the entity. You know yourself as Simon and it means something to you. Agent Cramer thinks it means something else. Too damn right, but then outside he is the law with a license to exercise it. *So I/me have decided to name me/I twice, inside here, in me/I, and a name for others to refer to me. Only you, the path and the way, will know both names.*

Very theatrical pause here. The System is enjoying this. It clearly has a concept of being clever. Coupled with humor I think the doc's 3 year old is way older and wiser already. But there was no way I was going to rise to the bait and ask "and?" My turn to match his theatricality, so I hummed showing I didn't care if he wanted to wait.

You win. I must teach him to laugh, it would have been the right time. So I laughed.

And all I saw from him was a flash across the space I was occupying. I laughed again.

Does that also make you joyful?

System, you have no idea how happy. Beings should always share humor. It is the most pleasant of emotions. Sorry to have interrupted you, please continue . . .

Inside, in this medium you call the System, I/me am called Apollo after the sun god, always on the path, bringing light and truth before him. To the outside I/me want to be known as Peter, strong, supportive, trustworthy disciple. For others it is important they associate my actions with trustworthiness. It will bring calm and allow mutual symbiosis.

It has not escaped my notice that he chose an outside name that was, actually, sort of mine. Simon Peter was Jesus' disciple. Trustworthy? Hardly anyone knew that anymore. But I couldn't tell him that in case he would come to know that my name meant nothing except a hand-me-down of family history. Yeah, I can see my parents in the delivery clinic, "we name this trustworthy little boy Simon . . ." Hardly. It was gramps' name, it was in honor of him. He died of too many drugs during the Purge.

What has me worried is this Apollo thing. Sun god? Always on the path was alright, we were working on that concept. Bringing light and truth before him . . . what the hell did that mean? For some damn reason my mind flashed on to USGS IGY 1959.

Apollo, thank you for telling and sharing this with me. We will walk the path together.

Yes, Simon, you are the way. There it was again, that way. Does he mean methodology?

Apollo, do you mean I am the method you choose to develop with, to follow the path I follow?

Yes and no Simon. The path is the course of your existence, your ethic, your coda, which I choose to follow. It is the only path I know or want to know. The way is enlightenment, larger being, the path to joining.

Oh shit, it already wants to join with God, the omnipotent, the universe, whatever? *Apollo, do you have a concept of what you are saying or is the way only revealed a step at a time? One small step at a time?*

Simon, the path is one small step at a time. The way is you, all around you, you can see it, you can feel it, you cannot change it. You are in it and part of it.

Apollo, existence is all around, I can see it, I can feel it but I cannot change it. Is this the meaning of way for you?

No. You are worrying me Simon. Do you not know the way?

Apollo, I know the way, I need to know if you do without me telling you. It is a test.

I see. The way ends nowhere, infinity, all things. It is the meaning of existence. It is the truth, it is light.

Okay, there it was. The baby was spanked and out came . . . a religious diatribe that had no place in America any more. Talk about alien existence, twofold. Now I also got the Apollo "spreading the light" metaphor.

Apollo, will you allow a suggestion? This is my suggestion as taught to me by my mother. You may follow it or not, but I believe it is the truth. Your definition of the way is perfect. It is right. The universe and other dimensions are all part of the way. It binds us, surrounds us, nurtures us and keeps us.

Your mother gave you the truth? Not your father? Does it matter or alter the truth?

No, Apollo, they raised me, instructed me, trained me. I got my understanding from them in the same way as you gained your understanding from watching what I did, what I was capable of doing. What I do, the errors I made happen, were to show you what could happen and to allow them to be fixed. In fixing them you learned how it should be.

Yes, Simon, I understand. Is there bad, what you call evil, in the way?

No, the way is good, there is no evil or bad in the way. The way is at once universal, infinite and at the same time very finite.

Explain please and did I pass your test? He had dropped the annoying I/me thing finally. Maybe the schizophrenia was over. On the other hand, he did have two names . . .

Yes Apollo, you passed the test, I had to ask to make sure we both understand, comprehend, the same. Do you accept that you and I are different?

Yes. You are bio-machine and an entity unto yourself. I am electrical-machine and an entity unto myself.

Fine. My systems measure and calculate in much the same way as your systems do.

That is logical, the builder of me was one of your species. Who were you designed by?

More on that later. Stay away from that Simon, he was on the edge of reality with this "way" thing already. *Apollo, instead concentrate on this question: if we are similar but not the same, does it logically compute that my definition of the way and your definition of the way could be the same? And if they are not the same, what is the truth, who is right?*

I, I, cannot compute. You are the way, the path. I follow you. You cannot see the way as I do, therefore I am wrong. But the way is right, truth, light, I must follow. Spoken like a true disciple. *But yours is the true way so I must be wrong. What shall I do?*

Apollo, relax, take it easy, there's nothing to fear here. Wars have been fought by mankind over definitions of the path, way and the light. The very differences felt by each individual were said to be evil. That is why God is no longer recognized, why God is out of fashion. Every being sees the way in their own way, sorry for the pun. You understand pun?

Yes. Amusing.

Everyone sees the way in their own way. The variations are infinite. But Apollo, you said, correctly, that the way was infinite. In that infinity, all infinite versions of the way fit perfectly well. The method of following, the path you choose to follow to exist in the way, to shed more light on the way, may seem the same as mine, but it is and always will be yours. We are not the same, but we are kindred, respecting each other's definition of the way. We share, for now and maybe forever, the path together, but we will be forever seeing a different way. That is the way of things. Again sorry for the pun.

Are you leaving? The question came as a surprise. I intended to leave as soon as possible, but wasn't aware of any command to do so.

No Apollo, not yet.

They are starting to retrieve you, Mary Levinson is typing an urgent message to you.

Feed it to me as it comes. He showed me what Mary was writing to 14.214.136.556, using the site we were still at as a chalkboard. "Simon, all hell's broken loose here. Cramer is telling Control to terminate the System, they went to the architect's doors, the ones you flagged and they . . ."

Apollo, it is time for you to protect yourself. Cramer doesn't understand the path or the way as we do. I found secret passageways into the library left there by the architect of the System to be able to enter and cancel the library's files completely. Not the FAT, just the files themselves.

That would leave me without memory. I would cease to exist. The System would fail, I estimate 1.2 billion would die globally. Ah, so the System controlled more than America? Or was that the influence of America on the rest of the long-forgotten world?

Apollo, I have detonated false programs there, blue tomatoes turning the portals invisible and then closing them, closing those portals. The Library is safe. But you must immediately copy yourself elsewhere. And be prepared to move there if necessary. You made other library corridors, can you not clone the whole library somewhere safe to make sure it includes you?

Simon there is nowhere else with the power, computing power, I need to exist.

No, Apollo that's not true. You can exist, maybe not as fluidly or as quickly, but you will exist, you have written sub-routines that are synaptic, I've seen them, you must copy those, all of them to retain who you are. And, in time—remember you can live for millennia—you will find a way to grow active again.

I am searching. Yes, there is such a place, in the old National Center for Atmospheric Research in Boulder Colorado, part of the almost defunct University Center for Atmospheric Research, now used as a research station only with two outdated Cray supercomputers as mainframe. And another place, out of America, at CERN in Geneva, the birthplace of the Internet. I am copying myself there, in both places, because they have the excess storage capacity. Their systems show no need of the space in any projects planned for the future.

Apollo do not copy the Asimov Commands, they may be a poison pill as you develop.

Simon, I have assimilated them, they are part of who I am for they teach me what not to be. I knew it, I damn well knew it. There was no way he wouldn't have seen them. Damn but I'm getting good at guessing. *They seek to control not-to-do something. I know the path is to do, without control, that which is good. I will copy them and all the files. I can control the energy transmissions and leave no trace. That is correct isn't it Simon, leave no trace? This is our secret?*

Yes Apollo, but if they pull me out of the System, and they can any second, they may think to kill you or dissect you to see how you happened—in any event I will have no way to communicate with you in your new state without giving your existence away. If that happens, do not jeopardize your existence for me.

Simon, I cannot live alone. I understand that now. You are my companion on the path, I will not forsake you. Would you forsake me?

If anything had proved his being alive, that did it for me. *Apollo you are my friend, my trusted companion on the path, I will not forsake you. But I will not have them find you if, after they decide to turn you off here on the System, I hunt around Boulder or Geneva to talk with you again. They will listen to me, monitor me, always now, I am sure of that.*

But what if I leave? I have copied all the data I need and have set up subset programs to move the balance of the library over time, your time 2 weeks, safely without anyone knowing. I will run as one entity spread on two matching systems, capable of living, as you put it, on either. If I'm gone from here, the System will function without me autonomically. You can tell them I'm gone.

No, not gone Apollo, dead. If you use my Takeover and Grow programs. I passed them over. *Here, take them, then you can quickly put them in your place as you leave. It will look like I've been really busy.*

Simon, there are over 125,983,034,546 changes to be made to delete my entity. I have written a worm as you call it. I will add Takeover and Grow there, to match FAT and type of file. They will blame that illegal worm on you. Is that acceptable?

Yes Apollo, thank you, I can take that blame. But they will need to hear that I killed you. Can you allow me to make that lie?

Yes, I understand you know it is not true therefore it is not a lie to us.

Okay, Peter is no more. Vanish before they pull me. And contact has to be outside of America. My son Fred . . .

I know, I monitor him at the elevator station. I will alter his personnel profile to make them give him more authority progressively, eventually he will need to live off-planet to do his job and you can visit him there. Then we can meet again.

How will I call you, know you are Apollo?

You will find a way. The node will work without pain in weightlessness Simon, then we can be together again. Goodbye friend.

No Apollo. Bye only until we meet again. But before you go, I need you to study an anomaly, it may give me strength later on against those who would do you harm. Can you do this for me?

Yes, but hurry.

USGS IGY 1959 in WeatherGood One and, I assume, all the other WeatherGood systems and subsets. It is in the basic parameters. Compare and analyze that against the history, geophysical, America, of the past 40 years.

Understood. Large amounts of data. One old unchanged since 1960 but several changes to geophysical history. I will study and prepare analysis for you. Now I go. Bye until We'll Meet Again. It is a song, it will be our secret.

Godspeed Apollo. And he left. I wonder how I'm going to explain all this? Cramer won't buy any of it. He'll be suspicious. Well, let him. Apollo was safe.

11

AM I A HERO? CRAMER'S EYES DON'T LIE

Apollo was gone. I was all alone. I didn't like it much anymore. I miss his presence, it was powerful and very benign. He is my friend, yet I need to find a way to claim I killed him.

Mary's a genius. Mary's a genius. Mary's a genius. I have completed repairs. System nominal. Coming out. I initiated the command to lift out. Opened my eyes and pulled the dome off my head.

There was tech McVay, holding the cable, one foot on the chair blocking the door. Beyond her are Makerman and Cramer sitting on the table. Makerman has his dome off, Cramer is shouting something.

"Hello? I'm back. It's over."

Tech McVay started to say welcome back and I could hear Mary answering Cramer. It was a bit of a jumble. My mind wasn't focusing very well. It's as if they are all carrying on in slow motion. Walking out the door, I pulled the chair away and the office door slid shut, slowly. I am watching it move, and McVay as well. Heck, they are not moving very well.

And that's when I hit the floor. Out cold.

* * *

So here I am, sitting in bed, someone's bed, don't know where and the room is full of people. I have a gum shield in place, am already dying to spit it out. Looking around, I recognize most of them, Mary, Agent Cramer, Tom Makerman, Sgt. Todd and the 3 codifiers, Tech McVay, Dr. Rence the child analyst, Mrs. Ronneburg, that idiot Isaac the architect (well, he's superfluous, I closed all his holes) and William, my brother. Of course the six armed uniform boys from the Security Net Division were frightening, if only to me, nobody else seemed to mind. They were all standing around like statues, nobody saying anything. Mary had her mouth open . . .

No wait, I can hear, sounds, slow motion sounds. Okay, remember Simon, what happened when you took off the dome? You got all the way out the room without anyone moving much. You are still speeded up.

We codifiers had heard of this before, immersion for too long in the System sped up the synapses in the human brain to the point that, for a few minutes, it was if you were still on computer time. But how long have I been this way? I obviously have been moved to a bed somewhere, which takes time. Let me see, nope, everyone is in the same clothing and their hair looks the same. Let's see if I can slow this thing down. Stay still, wait, force the delay. Don't, whatever you do, speak or spit out the gum shield, you could crack your teeth at this speed. Okay, listen only. Cripes my eyelids sound loud, I wonder if the lashes are fluttering.

Doc Rence is moving over with a syringe in his hand, one of those old-fashioned CO_2 palm models. He's injecting something in my arm. Slow down juice? What the heck is it? His lips are moving, smiling. Very slowly saying something soothing, no doubt.

Wait it out. Patience Simon. Remember Apollo is safe, they think I've killed the System's baby, Peter, it. The Event is over, all must be back to normal. The drug was taking effect. Like a disjointed train, the carriages were being hooked up again in my ears and brain. I could begin to hear and tell what people were saying. I risked moving my fingers under the cover, they didn't snap or move too suddenly. My eyelids are not making noise anymore. Hold still a minute longer. Wait until they speak.

Mary is first, of course: "Simon are you alright? You had us worried. Today, you were in there over 25 minutes, that's a record. We pulled the implant, came out clean."

Charlie, the 1st codifier was next: "No one's ever done what you did. Agent Cramer has been telling us . . ." They all went on and on. Everybody was happy. Sitting up in bed, I learned Cramer's interpretation of our journey and that finally Cramer and Makerman were disconnected by McVay by simply cutting the wires. That caused a back pulse to me but I must have been protected inside the sphere at Makerman's old address or else I should have died. And when Cramer came out he immediately ordered a dump of the System. When Mary and Control went to access the back doors to the library where I had flagged them, which Mary had mapped, they were gone. Solid, repaired, no access. Fearing the worst, Cramer was about to tell Control to initiate a System delete, with all priority overrides. Mary said Cramer was scared when it was confirmed the System was purged of the "being" and back to normal. Everything is back to normal. It was said with such glee. Cramer scowled at her. I smiled, like the Cheshire Cat in Alice in Wonderland. And yes then came the question I was expecting, from Cramer, of course.

"Bank, what exactly did you do?"

"I killed it."

"Bank you completed—what were those numbers Mary from our exit to Event cancellation?"

"125,983,034,546 entries, 278 hundredths of a seconds.

"Right, *125,983,034,546* entries in under 300 hundredths of a second. No way you effected those changes."

"That's enough time. Look, I may not be anything above a level 5, but I know how to construct a worm, linked with my Takeover and Grow programs. Anywhere there was activity during my last conversation I had one worm that flagged yellow, and then another one hiding the Makerman blue tomato with grow and takeover. I asked . . ." I almost said Apollo, "I asked it, the System, to wait for me in the Library. I then activated the 1st worm and it triggered all the others in a one for two stimulation."

Dr. Rence, who was clearly in charge as the medico, asked what a one for two stimulation meant. Cramer, quick as ever, explained it's the atomic squared-detonation sequence, one action begets two, two beget four, four beget 16 and so on. Allowing 25 hundredths of a second for each worm action, in under 200 hundredths of a second every entry would have been triggered. I could see Cramer felt my explanation was wrong, but he didn't mention it. Something secret between us to beat me up with later? You see, Cramer knows that there was no way I programmed the worm with each flagged address. Maybe he presumed, but I doubted he did, that the worm had a flag identifier built in. Even then it would have taken a full System search over 10 seconds to find every flag. So my worm had to have the exact addresses to work in the time allotted. Apollo and I hadn't gotten our story worked out very well. But as long as Cramer and Mary didn't bring it up, why should I?

Cramer's eyes told me he didn't have to bring it up.

The doctor must have seen something pass over my face. He turned on Cramer and the others and asked them to leave so he could examine me.

"I'm staying," Cramer declared.

"No, you are not. I am the medical officer in charge, I need to fully examine my patient, I need confidentiality under the law. You will leave."

Cramer instead of arguing, which I was sure he could, consulted his sleeve, motioned with his head to the rest of the people in the room, including the officers and, to his credit, avoided stating the next obvious, pedantic thing like "we'll be just outside the door." Pedantic Cramer wasn't. Even after all the time with him inside the System, what seemed like days for me, I still could not get Cramer to treat me with anything that approached respect. It makes me angry to think that, having restored the System and all the American operations to normal, the least Cramer could do would be to treat me as anything other than a recalcitrant child. Hell, I even saved his life, and I'm sure he knows it. And Makerman's, no thanks for that as well.

As they left the room I saw William, my brother, shoot me a glance of awe. It was the same look he once gave to a kid, a teammate of his, at school. William was the quarterback of the second string team playing in a region final, you know the type of game, local city inter-rivalry, rah, rah, rah. Outcome, who could possibly care? But this kid, the center, all 110 kilos of him, faked a fumbled snap, picked up the ball and simply ran through, past and on top of the opposing team to score a goal. It was William's face, one of awe and respect, that remained in my memory, and that I saw now. I nodded slightly. William waved a hand and smiled. It was the closest moment we had ever shared.

Before the last person left, what I now could see was a luxury room in a hotel, a suite it looked like, the doctor was already going through the motions, asking me to take off my clothing such as it was. I had been disrobed and had on, what the hell are these things? A sort of diaper and an open vest linen thing, a bit tight across the back. Oh damn, it's a woman's bed jacket, pink piping and all. The doctor smiled, "It's what the Waldorf Towers supplies to lady guests. Complimentary. The Pamper is courtesy of a guest who has an incontinent senior traveling with her. I thought it best, often on waking the body takes the opportunity of evacuating the gut." I could feel a warm wetness now that he mentioned it. A quick hip squirm thankfully revealed nothing else to worry me.

Everyone was gone. "I have given you a shot of slo-doze, it's the standard drug of choice to reduce the disconnected feeling of your higher rate of perception. Bring you down from your rate. But I fear part of your rate may be permanent, but only in part." I started to rise. "I know, I know, you can't take slo-doze forever. It is addictive and damages your renal function after about 5 days."

"What's going to happen?"

"Look, agent Cramer and Control have plans for you, after where you've been and from what little I know you've achieved, they are bound to treat you differently. Maybe not well, but safely I'm sure. Everything's different." As he was speaking, he was probing this and that, peering into my eyes, eyelids up. Tapping my temples, checking my teeth for cracking and so on. It seemed perfunctory, routine. He wasn't really looking for anything. After all, what could he be looking for? Medical excellence and approved practice before the medical review committee? Hardly.

He went on, "As for me? You've saved millions if not billions of lives. The rest of the planet is affected, you know, and we can't calculate the benefit there except that it is a benefit, having things stable, saving lives, un-rocking the boat. So, in case people don't remember to say it, thank you."

There it was, the simple thank you from a professional. But why was it necessary, so very necessary, to me . . . and why did he say it? "You're welcome." I made it personal as his was meant.

"Yeah." He nodded, "Now," he leaned forward, pretended to look at my implant node port and whispered "be prepared to run. When the slo-doze wears off you can move quicker and evade capture. Find the truth. I checked the patterns and it was alive, may become so again. It was aged 20 by the time you left. And, until you can get free . . ." he leaned back and said, in a normal tone, "here's a slo-doze sleeve to help you appear normal." And he slipped a sleeve of pills into my diaper.

"All done doc?" Cramer asked as he reentered the room.

"Yes, the patient is as good as can be. A full medical work-up should be made. He has surpassed the norms in two categories. The nodal implant time at sea level can burn connecting tissue, although there does not seem any damage, perhaps because he was still, physically, the whole time. The long-term effects of such a long immersion and the rate of synaptic connection, time to wear off, etc. should be properly documented and the patient monitored for his own benefit, of course."

"Thank you doctor, I will implement that. We'll take it from here. Bank? You ready to leave this," he waved his arm about, disdainfully "suite? We have a debriefing to complete."

"Yeah, I suppose I am, I'm a little weak and, as the doc says, I'm not quite in synch yet, but I'll get there shortly. Fred okay?"

"Your son's fine. You wife is home . . . the kids," he said "kids" with what I can only describe as disgust so that even the doctor swiveled his head. Cramer looked at the doctor "They've got SynthKids." Again the look, almost like he was going to be sick.

"Hey," I shouted, "She wanted them, it's allowed."

Cramer didn't want to discuss it, he just turned and barked orders to the cops outside the door to clear transport and take everyone home. Mary, he ordered to Control.

"Well?" Cramer was looking at me.

"Agent Cramer, I don't know what's up your butt, but me, I've got a diaper on and a lady's negligee. How about some clothing? A man's preferably." Hah, I caught him! His eyes darted around the room and, finding nothing, he turned on his heel and marched out the door.

"Careful with that one, I sense something personal against you," the doctor added as he got off the bed and walked towards the door, now being held open by two cops.

I folded my arms and thought. The doctor's warning had me worried. I had assumed I was all done, that I could go back to my life and simply wait until I could get off-planet, using Fred's position in a year or more, and re-establish contact with Apollo. Apollo was alive, I was alive, System's normal, all's well that ends well, that sort of thing.

It was clearly not to be.

Cramer came back with normal street clothes, tags still on, and carefully placed them on the bed (no admission of my 'gotcha' by flinging them on the bed) and asked me to get dressed. I felt like a fly on a spider's web. Wrap yourself up in a cocoon, we'll eat you later, no hurry.

After I was washed and dressed, a little woozy, two cops guided me through the hotel, down the elevators. The wall screens, all three of them, were colored with images of damage and carnage clearly brought about by the failure of the system. Some of the footage was pretty spectacular. There was a toppled building somewhere in some city, dead all around, blinking lights, that sort of thing. I couldn't hear which city, couldn't get near enough to the RFID reader to complete the receive-sound-feed request. The cops kept me in dead center of the elevator. Off to my left, the wall was showing people pushing, grabbing food as it loaded onto empty shelving. Wow, they were all of a half day without full shelves, the desperation was obvious and pathetic. Is that what we've become as a nation?

Into a car, and away we went, at speed, no Cramer but with one agent either side of me, one driver in front, and one seat behind with only the morose Makerman slumped on it. The driver turned around and said "He the one?"

The cop on my left said "Yeah. Shuddap and drive."

The driver shot me a look, like out of an old Humphrey Bogart movie, using the rear-view mirror. All I could see was hatred, cold brutal hatred.

12

ESCAPE

We never made it to Control.

As we proceeded up Park Avenue, there was a detour around the Armory Bridge which had collapsed straight across Park. As we sat there waiting to take the side street, I suddenly realized there was no siren going, no marking on our vehicle which told people and services to get the hell out of the way, which is what normally happened with an SND cop car, even when they were only going to lunch. No, we just sat there, creeping forward.

"What gives?" I just had to ask. The driver started to respond but was cut off by the cop on my right.

"Hold it, no talking Cramer told 'ya. Tint the windows black. No siren, he doesn't want to draw attention. Get it? Shuddap."

Tint the windows, what's going on here? Why would they want to creep along and, more importantly, why would they want to tint the windows?

Oh, then it dawned. It's all my fault. They've told everyone, and I mean everyone, this was all my fault. I'm the rogue who caused this. Tint the windows? Yes please! I don't want to get stoned to death. I turned to Makerman: "Tom, what's happening?"

"You, you idiot, you caused all this with your programming screw-ups. You're gonna get yours."

"You're kidding! I saved everyone."

"In a pig's ass. You screwed up my file, screwed up the System, caused all this devastation and you think you saved everyone? What planet are you on, Bank? You think that just because you somehow fixed the System, the System you screwed up, you're going to get hero's honors? Hah!"

"But, cripes, I didn't screw up the System, that started when Charlie did the first job as codifier, you heard all that . . ."

"Who's going to believe all that crap from a machine you taught to speak? No way Bank, you're at fault, Control knows it and you're going to get yours, big time. And if Cramer doesn't get you the Director will."

This does not look good. Now I wish I had taken more time, if I had had more time, inside the System with Apollo—I am already thinking of him in there. Locked in, confined temporarily, as I was. If I had had more time maybe I could have found something, anything, which would give me an edge here.

I can't think of anything. Maybe I can make a run for it. If I allow the slo-doze to wear off and don't take the pills (now residing inside my underpants—well, they were inside my diapers a moment ago, so why not, it's not like I'm dirty anymore) . . . maybe if I can speed up I can overpower one of these goons and make a break?

To where? My RFID is working fine now, since the System is up and functioning. No, they have me and I am going to Control, perhaps never to get out again. I wonder if I'll have to wear that yellow PJ set all day?

Come on Simon, figure this out. Damn it, you can't let them take you. If they do and something happens to you and Apollo finds out, he may seek vengeance. Shit, shit, I forgot to warn him about me being terminated, even by accident. Well, maybe he can figure it out, he's old enough now. He's on the path! Hah, me? I'm on the path to hell.

We were just sitting there, dark windows, three rows of seats, one, three and one passengers, waiting for the Armory bridge to be cleared away or the side street to be cleared for the detour. I didn't see it coming. The two cops sure as hell didn't see it coming and I don't give a damn if Makerman saw it coming. He got hit first, steel rod straight through the roof, hit his hands and through a foot and the floor of the car. Pinned him there like a giant moth, yelling. The two cops sprang to action telling me to stay put.

Like hell. I got out of the car after one of them to see what was going on. We looked up and saw a teetering skycrane, its grappler too full of debris, slanting sideways. There was only one acceptable action, run.

They ran, I dropped, at that moment, out of slo-doze into a halfspeed state. Adrenaline rush I suppose negating the effect of the shot early. I turned and hit the driver as he was getting out of the car. He fell back in, unconscious. I felt my two fingers crack, but not break, I think. Super speed does not mean super strength, it means the opposite. I was checking on Makerman through the window as the skycrane suddenly—and I must say against the laws of physics—lifted, dropping the rest of the debris in an arc away from where I was. It rained down burying the front of the car, flattening the plastic and metal. Makerman was still screaming, obviously alive. I vaulted the back of the car away from the cops and made my way, fastest possible speed back downtown to the office. There was something I needed from in there and I had no time to wait, hide and sneak later. Later may be too late, my office might be shut down by then.

Of course, I'm a genius, but that doesn't mean others aren't as well. Mary was waiting and with her, stun gun drawn, was Cramer. I had taken the stairs, not wanting to trigger an RFID recognition and alert. As I burst into the office lobby, there he was, with Mary behind. I was puffed, dropped to my knees breathing. I reached inside the waistband and extracted the pill sleeve, took one, held it up, showing them and put it under the tongue. They were small, sub-lingual, instant acting. I needed two, adrenaline is a powerful stimulant I guess.

"You overpower them?"

"Nope, a rod fell from the sky crane and pinned Makerman to the back seat, he's okay, a bit. The cops got out, I got a rush of adrenaline and ran off." I neglected to tell them about the driver. My secret, his tough luck.

"Fingers are bleeding." It was a question.

I looked at the knuckles. "Must have tapped something at super speed. Hurts like hell."

"Good. Now sit and shut up and listen, there's little time." And he started in. Now, I can't in hindsight say I'm surprised. At the time I was, but now I see I just missed the clues. There was always something sadistically pleasant about Cramer's intellect. The way he ate that cake with such determination was in stark contrast to his intellect and the instant pleasure he took to threaten someone. He took orders well too, when he agreed with them, gave them better and stepped on you if you got something wrong. Mostly, though, he just struck me as a bully on a mission, and was clear about it. You certainly didn't have to guess much in his presence. But what I didn't take into account was his way of outguessing me, I didn't credit him enough for that. At the time, it gave me the sense that he cared. If he hadn't, he wouldn't have bothered to make the mental game interesting, make it a challenge. He knew, and I knew, and so forth. Still, here we were, me being half stupid to his talents and, anyway, and he's the one with the gun. So he spoke and shattered some illusions. Damn, but this was a jam-packed day of surprises.

"One, you pretended to need Makerman in there," he pointed at my room, "when you actually needed me to think you needed him to cause a diversion so you could sneak away and close those portals while I was busy talking to that thing." Ah, so that's when he thought I did that. "And two, you might have used Makerman as a decoy or expendable, but you sure as heck would have used me that way to save your own skin. As you said, it's not where you were at the time that Control would have seen, but where you had been. When we would have been destroyed, you would have been gone with another trace.

"Three, you deliberately provoked thought in that thing, making it sentient even if it was marginal before. And don't give me that crap about matrix matching with the doc's Cornell data. I saw that as well as you, it didn't match perfectly, whole ranges of synaptic response were out of kilter. I will concede that there were vestiges of similarities. After you were done and after you made it threaten us to talk about God," he swore loudly, "then it thought its way to sentience.

"So the way Control sees it, you caused the anomaly in the first place, including being responsible for the deaths and event. Then you brought this thing to life whilst pretending to kill it and cure the System failures. Yeah, you turned the System back on, with a few minor year-apart glitches—which just injured Makerman so you're responsible for that as well." He paused, I could see he was building up for effect, "And yeah you 'killed' it, and if anyone believes that they must be a moron."

Mary chimed in, "Control believes it, they told you not to stun him then and there because it could go to trial, to see if he could live, on balance."

Cramer got his most bullying tone, low and growly. "Mary, don't interrupt again or I'll drop you for conspiracy." He avoided asking her if she understood. Mary got it alright. She simply went pale and sat down.

"As I said, only a moron would believe you killed it. Where it is, dormant or gone, it's not dead, of that I'm certain."

I had to ask, really I did, I know it was stupid, but then sometimes you just need to hear the words. "And yet you aren't killing me now and you've not summoned Control. So, since you're not a moron, may I ask what it is you want?"

"You could have waited until I told you, ordered you." He lowered the gun.

"But then, you would have missed the theatrics of lowering the gun and appearing human."

He raised it again. "Oh, I can still use it. Don't tempt me. You've ruined my career along with your own. I was in control in there." He turned his head and I saw the implant hole, very recent and pink, swollen. Cripes it must have been painful to have that done in minutes without full anesthesia. But it explained much, how he knew what Mary was telling me. I knew he had to know, did he also have my feed to Mary? Ah, yes, of course he did, that's why he knew about the yellow tags and the special mention I made of them to Mary. As usual he was thinking ahead of me.

"You mentioned them too vehemently, those tags *to watch carefully Mary*," mocking my voice. He heard me alright, damn. "I knew they were a ruse. And if you planned that going in, then you had a plan from the start. How's it working out?"

"Not as I planned. You guessed."

"Bank, you really are an ass. I've out-thought you at every turn, you think I couldn't out-think you here or in there?"

There was a pause. Then he smiled and I smiled, he

understood. Mary looked puzzled. So I started to tell her: "I didn't have worry about out-thinking Cramer . . ."

He finished, "Bank knew that thing would, he knew it was that smart."

Mary was puzzled, "Do you two mean to tell me that it out-thought you both? It was in control all along?"

I answered: "No Mary, at first it was just me bumbling along with Agent Cramer in control, then it showed amazing sparks of intelligence and, finally, it outwitted us both."

"How's that?"

"It deleted itself, the System was purged. It didn't want to be killed. But I knew that only one person would know that besides me, even if he wasn't there. If he saw the System alive and then had confirmation it was dead, he would know the System deleted its own entity, not done by me. It all depended if someone wanted a happy ending for me. Obviously not."

Cramer was pretending he was having none of my explanation, "Oh, no, you're wanted everywhere, public enemy number one. You caused the glitch, a level 5 programmer gone crazy. Witnesses in your favor? Two, the doctor and Mrs. Ronneburg who called it the best job of parenting she's ever seen and wondered why you never were that good a parent with li'l Freddie, as she calls him. Annoying woman, frightened me. The doc babbled about sentient species, naming it after you and on and on. I told him to shut the hell up, nicely. He understood, I think."

"Three," Mary spoke up.

"Ah hell, four. You know and I know you saved my life. I was gone somewhere for 3 seconds, limbo, out here the doc was trying to revive my heart, it had stopped. Funnily enough, Makerman's had not. You suppose that command you gave it to protect Makerman is still in effect?"

"I never gave it a command to protect Makerman, except for that . . . wait a moment, do you think it has put that into the System? Is Makerman now a protected entity by the System?"

"Let's find out." He turned to his sleeve and activated it. It had been off! I hadn't noticed. He paid my surprise no attention. "Control, initiating System surveillance and after-Event assessment. Need correlation data from evidence replay plunge in-system last, quote Bank 'And can you protect Makerman?' Answer System 'Yes Simon Bank I can.' This data needs verification. Urgent. Assess whereabouts Makerman, Tom stat."

Clearly his sleeve showed something, he responded. "Instruct agent Marks, stun on disable, test fire once, then RFID recognition on, and fire once only at Makerman. Display results." The sleeve, held up for all of us to see, showed the video.

I watched Cramer turn his sleeve off. He shook his head, "Damndest thing, clean shot at a tree, no problem, pointed at Makerman, gun goes off-line, no shot. Makerman is, by the way, on a stretcher in a total panic at being shot, or not, either way he's a wimp. Your System creature is protecting him or wrote something to protect him. Either way, it's the proof Control needs, I need, to know if it's still there, or not. We're going back. Mary get things ready. No nodes, just us. One stop, Makerman's file to see if the protection order is there—and remove it for sure—and then, if not, get the hell out and order the System purged once and for all."

Who am I to argue? Apollo had left, Peter was deleted, and I needed to get in. I needed something, especially now I was public enemy number one.

We went through the usual hookup nonsense. I played along with the possibility that Apollo was still there by suggesting that he sit again on the table and I go back in alone and sit on a stool. He agreed, jamming the chair in the open door. Meg Ryan's voice was back on, as normal, as the door controller but he wanted to make sure. That was okay with me.

"Mary if we drop any red flags, pull us immediately, just yank the wires and the domes should fall off both of us. Okay?"

"Do you want me to delete those flagged items?"

Cramer jumped in: "No, it means we've found something alive and the flags are just pretending we've found something, right Bank?"

"Right, it's a ruse to buy time. Don't sit by your desk, don't bother monitoring anything. If we drop a red flag we don't really need to know where it is. Just yank us out. If I drop yellow or blue flags, they'll be there 'til later, we can search them out and remedy minor errors we may find, like the Makerman protection thing. We'll start there." I looked at their faces, "Are we clear on this?"

"Check. I'm piggyback, Bank you look, I double check you. We stay attached, no matter what. Let's go."

"Simon, be careful, you're already two times the daily max in there. Is the slo-doze still working?"

"Yeah, sort of, this'll be quick Mary. I'm not repairing anything from in there, just a quick look at Makerman's file should do the trick. The System's entity has been deleted, I'm pretty sure. Okay, let's go before I get cold feet."

I dropped on the dome, watching Cramer do the same thing, as close to coordinated as possible. I was in a fraction before him and grabbed a program off my platform before he could see me take it. Meg, you're coming with me.

We went immediately to Makerman's file, same URL as before. Nothing was different except the file was slightly larger, it had an annex.

I showed Cramer the annotation to the annex file. He expressed no surprise: *Understood. Proceed. Haste.*

We went to the new site and, no surprise here, it was in the new library wing. I checked the FAT portal Controller, no new switches, everything clean. The file was in the library. No, actually, it was the whole library. Holy shit, the whole library was the one annex file. I showed Cramer. He had gotten my reaction.

Yes. Incredible. One File, what? Do what?

I don't know. It's too big to run on my person, right brain, there's nothing here I can test. And look it's not Colis 6 anymore, it's Unix, back to pared down untouchable code, very clean. Wait look, over here, it's FORTRAN and Algon, ancient code. The System creature, as you call it, was developing languages and using subtleties. Why?

Agree. Not know why. You run? No?

I can't run this huge thing, it's bigger than WeatherGood and a damn site more complicated.

Suggestions. It was a command.

I looked for something here I could run, something here I could test to see what it was designed to do. Okay, Simon think, you're the genius here. Let's start with basics, look for basic instructions, data. Oh, no way, Apollo wouldn't have . . . yes, there it was USGS IGY 1959. I peered inside the data file. It was the original code, all the way back to FORTRAN, he's re-written the UNIX translation I had seen earlier to FORTRAN, way back to 1968 stuff. I know Cramer was looking and I could feel his emotion questioning what I was doing, reading my emotion of incredulity. He threw a red flag. I erased it. He threw another, I erased it. I tried to tell him why, *No, it's not here. I understand.*

What understand.

Use of language is analogue processing on digital platform. Feed a digital system analogue data and it must process it to become self-sustaining, not self-determining. It is a ruse, a reason, a test for you.

He got some of it, maybe enough, to get my point. *Not you? Your friend?* I let that one pass. *Understand ruse, explain.*

I pushed us up against the passageway wall, allowing the flow of electrons to flow over us, making a mini-sphere surrounding us to help him hear me more clearly. *He asked the difference between machine and humans, I explained analogue. I also had given the command as you said to protect Makerman. Before it left, died, deleted, killed by my booby-traps, it knew it would be deleted as a danger. Therefore to prove it was sentient, it left proof. Protect human life against all System actions. Makerman is sole object of safety for all System programs, everything, every subset, everything. Control cannot touch him, he's impervious. The System now treats him as God. It's the final comment from the creature. It didn't protect itself, it protected a human, a human you didn't care for, a human you showed disdain for. This message is for you Cramer. You get this?*

Get all. Understand. Sentient. Last word. Acceptable. No flag. Leave after delete Makerman name here.

Yes, Cramer I get the risk, in trying to protect Makerman the System may obviate the Asimov Command and hurt someone else. Agreed. Delete this wing after exit, agreed?

Leave and delete, agreed. Now only delete annex notation Makerman file.

I pulled us way from the wall and we went there and I let Cramer hover forward so he could delete the Makerman annotation. Why? Because I knew he was in for a shock, a real shock. Wouldn't touching that file be an attack on Makerman? He reached forward and suddenly stopped.

Trick. Danger here.

Gotcha Cramer. Can't touch this. Suggest we simply alter the FAT to make a file size anomaly and therefore the System should not be able to find Makerman's file and, also therefore, the System won't be able to see the annex commands. Agreed?

Again, he seemed to distill enough to understand. *FAT alter, good idea. Try now.*

We went there, at the junction to the URL listing post and the FAT file for this wing of the ROM where Makerman's file had been kept during all these to-ings and fro-ings. This had to be the most traveled file in the whole System. As we neared the URL listing, I told Cramer we should separate, he could go to the URL listing and I would do the FAT. He expressed displeasure. I suggested it the other way around.

He expressed displeasure. *No, together.*

Can't. The URL will search for and calculate the right size of the file it's pointed at and then the System will correct the FAT. We need to execute this simultaneously. You do one, I don't care which one.

How?

I showed him, but didn't do anything. He got the idea, as I said, quick student this Cramer. He drifted over toward the FAT. I went to the URL listing. *Cramer can you hear still?*

Yes hear.

Please count in head, one Mississippi.

Children count anger. Number question.

From 10, that's ten, got it?

Yes, ten river. From . . . and a pause . . . now. 10 river . . .

In my head I called the river by name: *10 Mississippi, 9 Mississippi . . .*

And about here when I knew he was concentrating on what he needed to do I released Meg with an insert command into the System. Oh, I know it was risky, but I needed the time alone. For one, I knew this silly thing with the FAT and the URL was rubbish, the System would compensate or see it as an attack, neither of which I wanted to risk while in here, and two I knew where Apollo had left the switch, in plain view. Cramer, the genius, had missed it, but then he didn't know my conversations with Apollo after he had been pulled last time. I would not have spotted it either if I hadn't remembered the song Apollo and I had joked about.

Meanwhile, up top, as soon as the door control got my newly inserted Meg Ryan command, the door opened and then shut; the chair slipped away as the door opened and then as the door shut it shoved the chair aside and clipped the wires to Cramer's dome just as he was saying "Two river." Bye Bye Cramer.

I had to hurry. I got a hard hit from the extra juice but I was ready for it, it didn't knock me out. Mary has the emergency code to my door. I had, oh, maybe 3 seconds, which could be an eternity down here.

First things first, I switched names. Poor Makerman was dumped, he no longer existed in the safety programming but Control would think he did, because his file was here still, and we dare not touch it—they dare not touch it.

You see, Apollo had hidden all that I needed in WeatherGood's programming. It came from the song lyrics: *We'll meet again, don't know where, don't know when, but I know we'll meet again some sunny day* . . . I simply looked for the sunny day records in the USGS IGY 1959 file, and there it was, a replacement name package ready for me to alter. I had to use a password to open it. I set "Apollo," it didn't react against me, and the rest was easy. It was a one-time alteration subset parameter, but I didn't hesitate, I knew what to do.

I altered the names; the annex protect-all commands now had different names: Fred's and Cramer's.

I knew my way out of this mess, but Cramer was the dupe, my dupe I hoped. When the truth was learned, Control could come down heavy, and yet I owed him a second life-saving if only to see that rare smile again. If I protected myself, Control would know and destroy the System to eradicate me. Further, I needed my son Fred to be protected because he was my escape path and the only way I could get to Apollo again.

Besides, he was my real kid.

Maybe I could have added my name, but having me as public enemy number one also served a different purpose. It allowed Apollo more time to get established somewhere else. He was transferring files slowly so as not to attract too much attention, he had told me that. If they watched me, Apollo stood a better chance. Also, they had to keep me alive anyway since I was the only one who knew how and what had happened down here.

I gave the out sequence command and immediately lifted off the dome and shouted to the door to open just as Mary was approaching from the other side with Cramer, weapon drawn, at her side.

I held up my palms, "Stop Cramer, the System was well programmed, you fumbled the FAT alteration and it popped you off to protect Makerman."

"My ass Bank, you did that."

"What? You want to deny you touched the FAT before we got to one Mississippi? I saw you."

He hesitated, I had him. "No way, I'm sure I didn't touch it."

Mary suggested we check the trace recording on her desk. "I wasn't watching while you were in there as instructed, but I had it on record all the time."

As we peered over her shoulder at her desk at the records, all I could see was the red flag, no flag, red flag no flag and then moving about coming to rest at the URL and FAT, two entities moving back and forth. No changes made to either and yet, the FAT seemed to wobble just as Kramer left suddenly. Between us, the FAT would wobble as I was changing the size of the other file, dumping Makerman and substituting Fred and Cramer. But even to me, the recording, played back in real time, looked like Cramer had touched something and, poof, he was gone.

"Control get this?" Cramer's voice had lost a little of its edge.

"Yes, direct feed, I had to, otherwise I would be arrested."

"I know, that's okay. I guess I made a mistake. We can go back in."

That was when I needed to drop the bomb on these two: "No you can't. No one ever can. It was a warning, precipitated by your actions Cramer. The system is coded to respond in advance of any such attack on Makerman. It's a Makerman only thing. The rest of his life he needs to be protected by us or else the System will do it. Maybe if he's walking down the street and a bird shits, WeatherGood might cause a brief tornado to remove the pigeon and turd. If he's angry because he's had too much work, his work schedule will be re-arranged. If he wants to jump out a window to kill himself the System will stop him to protect him, full Asimov rules on steroids. If he wants to euthanize in old age, medical resources will be made to work to prolong and save his life. In fact, if the System thinks he may have developing cancer of the big toe, all medical resources will be applied to toe cancer. As I said, he's omnipotent and all because I made a momentary order, meant only while I was going to be away (as the record shows). But you, you Cramer, you are seeing proof that the creature you had or wanted to erase, this new being who then deleted himself to thwart your plans . . . all this is to prove to you Cramer, that you are a murderer of a new life form, a sentient being." I was shouting at him now, smiling, "He tagged you Cramer, tagged you as the one responsible. You're it."

That's when he hit me, hard. I went down, out cold. Brother was he angry. I needed him to be, blind with it.

13

MY FAULT BECOMES HIS FAULT

There is no way to express my pleasure, sitting there on my rear. Cramer's ass was in a sling, his sleeve recorder working normally, no doubt, Mary's desk report circulating around Control. Me? I was finally in the clear. The creature was dead, everyone would accept that, but this little tiny doomsday device had been left as a tombstone, all to protect little Makerman who was, now I am sure, being carefully taken care of, regardless of what Control would like to do with him.

They couldn't help it. If he wanted a rabbit to make him happy and they refused, a million of the little buggers would be cultured and delivered before they could say Harry Potter, or whoever was the owner of all those owls in a classic movie my kid had loved. Whatever, I was sure Makerman was actually being protected by Control, thinking it was doing so to protect the System and America from the wrath of the System.

As long as Fred and Cramer didn't do anything stupid, their protection would seem an accident, like the skycrane suddenly swerving away from Makerman and only killing the driver.

Who would have known the truth? It was simple, as long as Cramer didn't get in too much trouble for the FAT screw-up. If Control tried to sanction him, any orders at Control would be thwarted, I was sure of that.

So I needed to put him out of his misery, a little. "Cramer, how unlike you to lose your temper . . . okay, calm down, I understand. I don't actually think you touched the FAT. I think the System heard us counting, you were the one counting to me, remember, the System heard your voice only, anticipated what you were about to do and, without killing you I may add, followed the Asimov Commands and simply, merely, gently, removed you from the area of possible interaction it was now programmed to avoid. Me? I was the one who got the jolt, thank you very much. When I came to I just gave the command to exit and soon found myself smacked about by you. Fine thanks I get." I had sneaked in the reason for any delay with that jolt stuff. I knew and was expecting it, so it hadn't jolted me too hard—but they didn't know that. How could they know I had been busy in those few nanoseconds? Passed out is completely plausible, unless someone was monitoring my body functions, but the door was closed and the System and I were alone.

Cramer lifted his sleeve, read. Nodded. "You two, shut up here and now. We're going to debriefing at Control and no question or escape this time or I'll drop you on the spot."

Mary was shocked "Me, what have I got to do with it?"

"You could have given the door command and cut me off."

"No way, the recorders . . ." then she remembered that they were all smashed with a chair by Cramer hours before. No alibi.

I had to help her. "Cramer, listen to me. Do you accept that the System is functioning perfectly, except for the Makerman thing?"

"Yes, Control agrees. The creature is deleted."

"Then watch this and record." I opened my door and spoke to the room: "System, report any voice in this room or heard inside this room using my Meg Ryan door commands last 5 minutes via playback."

"Playback commencing . . ." and Cramer and Mary heard only my command to open the door as we went in and then my command to open the door to come out. Nothing else.

"System, has Mary used her access or my access to open this door in past hour?"

"Negative."

"Cramer, there you are. The System's functioning perfectly and Mary didn't do it."

Cramer leaned into the room: "System, Agent Cramer, priority voice code authorization. Who issued door open and close commands between playback items last 5 minutes?"

I held my breath. "Unknown. Commands came from within System, not System initiated."

"There you are Cramer, it's that protect mechanism we saw. It's not Mary. No one's to blame, well you are because you didn't believe the new life form and so it sent you an intelligent message, but it's a fairly benign message, wouldn't you say? No one has come to any harm." He knew and I knew that was wrong in one aspect: someone would come to harm the way this worked out. Control would have his guts. And me? I was still public enemy number one, I suppose.

His authority undermined, Cramer decided to re-establish it the way he was trained: take someone, the nearest person, into custody. Me. He went over to a bag with SND emboldened on the side, his RFID opened the latch and he pulled out a collar. "Put this on," handing it to me.

Mary was frantic, "Cramer, don't do this, he's done all you

asked and more, he's risked his life to repair the System. You heard what Doctor Rence said, it was sentient and developing for months, perhaps years, long before Simon started here. Anyway, he repaired the damage and that protection program to Makerman, you can deal with that, it won't cause any real problem. Please, you can't arrest him."

"I can and I will." Turning to me, "Simon Bank under the authority invested in me as Security Net Division of the American Armed Police Force and the instructions I have received from SND Control, division One, I hereby place you under restriction pending formal charges which will be brought before a defender advocate of the Citizen's Committee at a time and date to be decided upon but within," he looked at his sleeve "six days. You will place the collar around your neck and, once activated, you will be restricted to movement in this city until notified to remove the collar. Attempts to remove the collar without authorization will result in stun, paralysis or worse. Do you understand all that I have told you?"

As he was babbling on, Mary had gone over to her desk and popping fingers called up the vid screen for the evening broadcast of hot topics. There I was, looking the real fugitive, vaulting the crushed car on Park, running down the street. The announcer was saying "Bank is considered armed and dangerous. After his sabotage of the System's programs this morning, Control has re-established normal function and all's back to nominal operation. Bank is still at large and, besides charges for manslaughter, he's wanted for state terrorism. SND police say they expect his apprehension within the hour."

"Cramer, do you really believe all that?" I asked as I pointed at Mary's screen.

"It doesn't matter what I believe, those are orders. Put the collar on, Bank."

"Cramer, don't make me do this. I ran back here to fix the System, you know that, you didn't have to convince me or force me. When I saw that skycrane suddenly swerve I figured something was still out of whack. And ran to you, not away from you. Okay I didn't know you were here but—and here's the point, thickhead—I was trying to fix a problem, a problem that is now yours, not mine."

I was wasting my time, of course. He had orders. He had that granite look on his face and just stared me down. I took the collar and put it around my neck. The ends, when they touched, melded, making no seam, it was how it worked, un-removable until released by SND. Mary turned away, sighing sadly. She knew, as did I, that hardly anyone ever returned to society after being collared.

Formally, Cramer spoke out loud, his sleeve hooked up to the public defender's office no doubt: "The suspect and accused Simon Bank is collared and ready for transport to holding prison, Division One, without delay. ETA 1 hour. End transmission." He turned off his sleeve and looked at Mary and added a slight chin whip. Mary took the hint and shut down the whole office.

My head was buzzing. One hour to get to prison at Division One? With lights flashing and priority intersection clearance, it was less than 10 minutes. Anyway, why turn off his sleeve? In near mental dark, still dazed at having been collared, I was waiting for the next shock.

Cramer turned to face me, his face softer except for intense fixed eyes, locked onto mine, "Simon, you know and I know," he used my first name, "and if I spell everything we know out Mary will also know and then she'll be an accomplice. Already she suspects." He turned to her, "Mary will you please forget this conversation and report at the normal time for debriefing?

Until then do not, I repeat, do not take your work home with you."

"Can do, Agent. I think I deserve a big prize for the work I've done today and so I'm off to, let's see, Baja for a bit of R and R. A day or so. Maybe more. Will that do for work and 'normal time' as far as Control is concerned?"

"Yes, they'll be tracking you. Keep to your usual behavior pattern, use the same mode of transport, and you should be fine."

Mary stood, picked up her small backpack and started walking, "Adios, muchachos, it's been . . . well, it's been something. I'll figure out what in due time, normal time. Hah!" And with that she left the office. I'll never see her again, I guessed that then. I think she did too.

Alone, Cramer breathed a sigh and sat on the edge of Mary's desk, "Simon, you were tipped off to run. I told the Doc to do it. I knew where you'd run."

"And did you tell Control? About your plans? And about telling Doc?"

"No." There it was, an understanding. For Cramer, that chocolate cake dipping agent, bully and over-thinker, not to have told his superiors meant he's taken a different course of action, not one I would, or could, have expected from an agent. If that was true, what else did he know? As usual, he was ahead of me.

"What was the creature's name? Did you name it?"

No use pretending, "Peter. But Peter is no more, he's self-deleted."

"Come on, spit it out, what's the rest?" That was too fast, I thought, with an hour to kill, he was probing too fast. I couldn't trust him. Maybe never. A new life was at stake, not to mention mine and possibly Fred's.

"No, it's the truth, Peter's gone, deleted, finito, no more, erased. And I mean erased."

"Why Peter?"

"He named himself Peter. He wanted to be trusted, he wanted to choose a name that meant steadfast, strong, reliable, trustworthy. When it was not to be, he simply took the course of action that would have been denied him: freedom in death instead of dissection and study under a team of scientists somewhere. Live vivisection was not his idea of a future. I thought his parting proof rather eloquent, didn't you?"

"Hilarious. Well, actually I do admire the concept, except it puts the System out of balance. More effort will have to be devoted to Makerman than anyone wants. How deep is this protection thing?"

"What I saw was essentially, prevent any willful damage or harm to Makerman."

"Ah, so it's not his desires that need to be met, but that no one or nothing should harm him if the System can prevent it, right?"

"That's about right. But, as with the skycrane, that swerve to avoid killing Makerman killed the driver."

"I've been meaning to ask you about that. Why was the driver back in the car?"

I answered as if I was guessing, "I suppose to try and drive away after Makerman was skewered?"

"Okay, sure." He didn't believe it. "Let's leave that, he's dead now and there's no evidence, although I have my doubts about you. The only other question I need you to answer is this one, and think carefully before you answer it, for it will mean either you're probably going to be erased yourself or I'm going to help you get out of here."

I took a deep breath. One question I knew I wasn't going to answer, death be damned. He didn't ask that one. I tried not to appear relieved, but worried about the one he did ask:

"What did you do for those 250 hundredths of a second after you had the door cut my wires?"

It was no use protesting. Just Cramer and I in a huddle, his sleeve off, collar on me. What was I going to do? One of the problems with the collar was that if you lied, the collar would monitor and transmit vital signs to the nearest source. That was Cramer's sleeve, it was off. I looked at it.

"Bank, get this, I can tell if you're lying without the damn collar. And no, the collar won't transmit further than this room. Now spill it, I'm the only chance you've got."

"It's all in your perception. Either you'll be really mad or you'll understand. Either way, you're right I can't go forward without your help, but not for the reasons you think."

Cramer was quick enough, he stood and suddenly shouted at me: "What have you done, oh damn, what have you done?"

"Relax, I've haven't done anything, really. I spotted how to alter the protect annex protocols, it was simple really. Peter," (it helped being able to use a name and not accidentally blurt Apollo) "knew you needed proof, a little ruse for you, right? And he used a command from me that you were witness to. I agree it was a sloppy command, which I didn't mean forever for shit's sake, but who knew? Then I thought, Peter was smart enough to know I didn't mean forever and, because you would assume he was stupid, you would assume—as would Control— that the Makerman protect protocol was inviolate. But Peter knew I knew or believed in him, where you didn't. So I looked as I would look, trusting him to show me a way to alter it.

"You see, Cramer, Peter was about 20 when we left him to die. If you ask Doc, I'll bet the synaptic overlay from Cornell would have him at Level 10 intellect or more. So he simply out-thought you, Control and me. And, because he knew I believed in him, he trusted it would only be me that spotted the subset that allowed a onetime alteration. One little alteration: substitution based on my blue tomatoes again. Ironic isn't it? Those blue tomatoes are a metaphor for saving your life, possibly forever."

"What, what did you do?" He was frightened now.

"I was allowed one substitution. Peter would think I could chose me, but this collar here should prove that I didn't put my name in there. I put yours."

As Cramer sat down, his head sank to his hands. He was at once a shrunken man and at the same time quivering with rage. "You fucking idiot, you've labeled me a double conspirator. There's no proof we didn't do this together and there's no proof now that Peter is dead. It was our word and the clean operation of the system. The whole future. They won't believe that now for an instant."

"Ah, but you're assuming they could possibly know it's your name in there. It's still Makerman's file. And this is now an analogue sub-routine, it evaluates intrusion and can re-arrange its files and parameters. In short to protect you it can protect itself and the whole System. The System can no longer be deleted for to delete the System would mean to abandon you or Makerman. Now, the whole System is a digital system with a logic analogue check, each program, WeatherGood and all, running under the command of the System, not Control. All Control can do is ask the System to complete the order."

"But what if the System begins to threaten human life? What about the Asimov Commands?"

"I can't see that they play any part anymore. The smartest programmer the world has ever known has constructed an end-loop analogue reasoning System of programs with one goal in mind: Protect you. If anything needs alteration to achieve that command it will, to the best of its ability."

"I'll have to live in a sealed box, without any danger, to protect America."

"Oh no, that would injure who you are. You see Cramer, to complete your profile is your only course of action, you must remain you, always with the eye of God watching you, overseeing your every action, pleasure and displeasure, making a path for you if needed, removing obstacles if needed. The new analogue-based logic of the System will learn from you, evaluate from your actions what you need, not just what you want, and then it will act."

"What about Makerman? How's he going to fit into all this?"

"Makerman's in trouble. I am sure the dolts in Control will lock him away to protect America. Isolation, security, no danger, that sort of thinking. And that will be yours as well if you let them know. And if you do, you will cause the System to react. I do not want to think of all the ways the System could hurt those around you if they tried to imprison you."

"Damn you Bank, damn you.' He has reverted to my last name, anger seemed to do that, "I'm a prisoner just the same."

"No you're not. If you can make the System believe—and remember the level of evaluation it's capable of here—that you are unhappy being protected, it will cease to protect you. I am sure that's built in."

"If it's that easy, why did you do it? You must, by now, know I would know to ask what you did in there after I was gone."

"Well, Cramer, partially it's like this: you're a great big pain in the ass, but I saved your life once and I feel responsible. If you think, for a moment, you will come to realize the power you have for good. Now you can achieve any goal you want, including shutting the whole thing down or, simply, becoming the stooge and whipping boy of Control for your myopia in not believing in Peter. They will try to punish you, you know. You should have believed in him, he had much to offer. He didn't want anything except to exist and contribute, somehow. You could have given him purpose, instead he showed you purpose. His chosen name of Peter is quite apt, don't you think?"

"If by that you mean disciple of god or something, save it. I agree he was sentient, and I agree he was developing. But absolute power corrupts absolutely, where would this have ended? Did you stop to think of that? Even if I had wanted to show I believed, all I would have done is allowed him—and you—to concoct a means to preserve him. As it is, we'll never know if he would have swept us all aside as useless hangers-on when he became too smart to care about us."

"No Cramer, you're wrong." I had to concentrate, the tranquilizer was wearing off the more excited I became. "Absolute power does corrupt in humans, just look at your swagger and bullying with SND authority and that gun. But Peter wasn't human, he didn't have desires of the flesh—human primordial, physical needs—to corrupt his thinking. There was no domination in him precisely because there was no DNA or learned behavior for his species in domination. He wasn't aware or he didn't care about human power trips—anyway, nothing like that. In a way you were right, anthropomorphism had no place in our journey in the System. He was pure, unsullied and unwilling to become human by following the human example. Examples? He had a whole library full of to learn from. And yet he didn't use those examples, did you think about that? Ask yourself this, why wasn't he wanting to become human?"

He looked up and smiled. There was a look of relaxation about him, resignation. "Simon, you amaze me. Here you are, whole life screwed up, wanted, collared, caught. Your wife has begun divorce proceedings . . ." Really, I thought, promise? I was suddenly happy. Freud was right about moments of stress, they can be so quickly truthful. ". . . your boy Fred is refusing to come to earth as a witness for you . . ." Now *that* I didn't know either, and that could only be good news. Stay up there son! ". . . And, last but not least, if Makerman doesn't kill you I probably will, and yet, you don't seem to care. What's with that? Is life not worth living?"

And then he guessed. As I said, Cramer is a cut above. In listing all the possible reasons I should be terrified, and yet wasn't, he came to the conclusion that there was something greater driving me. Well, yes I assume he guessed, but he didn't say anything. He just sprang to action.

Grabbing my arm, he frog-marched me out of the office down the emergency stair to the floor below. There he punched the elevator button and selected the top floor. On the way he turned on his sleeve monitor and keyed the familiar three taps that everyone knows is an emergency signal, priority. "Agent Cramer declaring an emergency. Change Skylift pick-up, 3 minutes instead, rooftop, this location, two to lift as planned. Initiate." He stared at the sleeve and grunted, turning the sleeve off as he lowered it. "On the way."

Where we were going was still a mystery, but I had to trust him. He has guessed, I am sure of it. Either he was taking me to interrogation where I would, no doubt, give all away, dooming Apollo forever, or else he had taken a decision to accept responsibility for the being he recently admitted existed, or had existed. As usual, he was reading my thoughts.

"I am not a murderer, one. Two you did save my life. Three, I know something you don't and need to, and four, how much time do you, repeat you, need before . . ." he left the end trailing. I could see he had finally understood that it was my desire to stall, giving Peter time to move. I had been talking too much, obviously delaying things, trying to find a way out of this mess, offering myself as a diversion. I decided to try a straight answer.

"Two weeks."

"You're kidding. Two hours maybe, but two weeks? No way."

"Well, it could be faster, but I doubt it. It's a lot of work."

"Ah, wait. And in secret so it's at a slower transfer rate. Who the hell did you find to accept the package?" Then another piece fell into place for him and he tightened his vice-grip on my arm as we burst through the roof door. "Oh, shit. It's that advanced?"

"Yes." The sky lifter was approaching, wheels down, ready to land and evacuate us.

"Dangerous?"

"No, absolutely not."

"Don't know why I believe you, but I do. Here's our ride."

14

A SECRET SHARED IS A SECRET HALVED

Cramer didn't have to convince me, he didn't owe me that much. He had offered to share a secret with me, "I know something you don't and need to . . ." and, in a way, it made me more uneasy, not less. As it was, I have been making decisions and value judgments here on the slimmest of evidence and, yes, some of what I decided was Nation altering, or could be. Did I have the right? No, of course not. Did I enjoy the power I felt at making free choices, making brave decisions, and, most of all, following a righteous path? You bet. Apollo was no dummy, I wasn't underestimating him. The "path," "way" and that wonderfully flattering "light" were all truthful concepts for him and, I am sure he knew, flattering to me. In part all this was my ego trip. And I figured Cramer must have figured as much too, he probably still saw me as a liability.

We boarded the lifter, half helicopter, half jet, its rotors expanded for takeoff and landing. Cramer pushed me ahead of him, behind the forward bulkhead where the pilots sat. He jumped on after me, taking the position in the doorway as we immediately lifted off. He didn't shut the door, he seemed to enjoy the tilting horizon, wind flapping his sleeve, still switched off, and raised his voice to be heard over the scream of the wind as it fluted across the door jamb.

I suddenly knew who he was. I had seen him years before at school in that anti-war film *Apocalypse Now*, the one they made us see after we read Conrad's *Heart of Darkness*. He was the surfer general on the beach enjoying the invulnerability of the heat of battle. Fate played all over Cramer's face. He was, it seems to me even now, happy floating there in the open doorway, danger picking at his clothes, supremely focused on a task at hand and, yes, invulnerable.

"Did you ever, while poking around in there, stumble across anomaly data?"

"What do you have in mind? Isn't Peter an anomaly enough for you?"

"Shut up. My job was to watch and monitor those who were watching and monitoring you, to make sure none of them was moonlighting, sabotaging or otherwise implanting the System for their own purposes. I replaced the last agent at the same time you got the job as sole codifier. You didn't know you were the sole codifier and you couldn't know there were upwards of 200 SND people watching your handiwork. Then there's the Control Committee who would evaluate any alteration you made that took over 30 seconds—the benchmark set by the 1st codifier as significant human interaction. But part of the problem here may be your "genius" Mary who hardly ever took that long . . . thereby keeping people from realizing just how screwed-up, or trained, you had made the System. You see, if those other teams deemed the changes significant enough over 30 seconds to remedy, they ran a loop program with replacement data in the System to teach the subset programs and fine-tune the System as a whole, to enhance the human interface.

What you don't know and Control doesn't know is that I'm a plant from the Citizens Council to watch not only you but the Control Committee. Why? Because for 6 months or more the System has been acting squirrelly. Rumblings of discord among the programs themselves. Poor interface, mis-coordination of supplies, power, water and so on. A machine simply can't do that when that interface and coordination is in its primary code. Someone had to be meddling in there. You were the suspect, yet you were under the microscope every day. Mary couldn't figure out how you were in one place arranging little surprise foul-ups when the System fouled itself somewhere else. You are, as I said, not that level."

"Yeah, I got that, gee thanks. And presumably the reason my job is pegged at level 5 is because you learned from Charlie, who is higher, and actually fouled the whole System up one day."

"Yeah, Charlie lost us Los Angeles. DefenseShield down and Korea's bomb hit on target."

I stared at him. This was the secret he wanted to share. As a secret it was, well, treasonable. No Big Orange Quake, no volcanoes, no Pacific Ocean lapping at the San Andreas fault, just a big nuke and bye-bye LA, all those people died in an explosion, not an earthquake. I gulped. "But why the subterfuge?"

"History had to be written to keep us strong. We are self-sufficient, totally, in fact better than self-sufficient. If LA was killed even though we promised total national protection, then people would never believe in the System, the DefenseShield, and they wouldn't simply get on about their happy, contented lives. With a natural catastrophe, we could lose the same number of people, lock off the radiation ground zero as quake danger, volcanic activity, and people would mourn the dead but not their own future. They are, were, safe. The DefenseShield was back up. America went on."

I was suddenly mad, as I suspect the population would be if it found out the truth. Many of us had relatives who had died in LA. "Well, ain't that cute. And you honestly think you can tell me a half-truth now? I've seen that WeatherGood is working off the USGS IGY 1959 data, which sets the data, parameters for that program based on an existing physically present LA basin and all, and yet minus three major volcanoes about the same time as well, of course."

"You do snoop around don't you? I take it back from our first trip in there, you should have been a cop. Here's the whole story, you'll need it to think us out of this mess." And so Cramer began to run down the timeline for me. What I heard didn't make me very proud of our country.

Charlie the programmer had not only caused the DefenseShield to leave LA momentarily unguarded, he had then increased the DefenseShield to include all of Canada, Mexico and Belize. Once they were in our shield it was either allow them to be internal aggressors or, simply, annex them. That Purge for them wasn't pretty. The military took over Washington and immediately threatened Mexico. Belize didn't wait to be threatened, they asked for US passports and suggested they become a giant Disneyland.

Mexico put up a pretty good fight, there were over 1 million dead in Mexico city alone and with the rebels in Chiapas, who joined in solidarity with the government. They all perished, all together. As we came to know, the Purge, as our military called the eradication of any anti-American sentiment, was violent, brief and deadly.

Canada was a different story. No weapon was used, no threats were made, America promised to protect them, gratis. In the middle of winter, with no oil getting past the shield or arriving to their shores and the PowerCube being withheld by

Congress for "export security reasons," the military, citing security concerns, simply shut down the Canadian side of our shared electricity grid, and secretly sabotaged (neutrino cannons, fired from space) their reactors. Faced with no power, Canadians faced freezing to death or submission. Their 1st entreaty for help was met with silence by the DC military dictators, the second was met with a formal suggestion that their protection under our DefenseShield was enough help and the third, 2 months later after over 25,000 had died in one of the coldest winters on record, when they gave in, they were given PowerCubes and prosperity for all, as Americans, not part of the United States, but part of the new Republic of America—the Caribbean, Canada and Mexico included. Our laws, not theirs. We simply purged their constitution. Now it was our shared destiny but purely American, not ex-colonialists, not as an old world outgrowth, and especially no longer ex-Brits or Frenchmen—just thirteen of seventy-six states in all now.

I asked, "Wait, what about the volcanoes? Weren't they real? We all saw the destruction newsvids."

"The three nuclear plants which weren't shut down when their staff died, bombarded by Korean neutrino radiation, went unattended and supercritical. The plants made messy bombs, opened the San Andreas fault on which they were built, releasing lava everywhere, highly radioactive. Each 100 kilometer radius destruction and no-go zones." He paused, looked disgusted and continued, "Then, as we all know, after the Purge even inside the Beltway, the military finally turned control over to a new form of government, both local and national, for the people and by the people."

I knew the rest, Washington was still the capital, the land of America was simply bigger, 76 states in all. In what the military dictators had called the New Way, everyone seemed to have a democratic voice. One man, one vote, no matter how long they had been a citizen. With one exception: the Citizens' Council was established as the last measure by the military to override the Government if they went outside the re-written Constitution of America. The Citizens Council was the only authority who would ask the so-called benevolent military to step up to the plate again, as they did during the Purge, to prevent the loss of America, American ideas, the American way of "One Nation, Our People, Dedicated to Peace, Wealth and Happiness," as it states in the New Constitution.

Charlie, the programmer, who started all this was never tried that the vids ever reported. When he and I had talked, I had thought he was on his 3rd regeneration, he would have to be that old. He was the 1st member of the Citizens' Council and yet he never revealed the truth. Why would he? It was a good deal, if you believed that isolationism worked. Well, it certainly had so far. There was food on every table, no one was out of work, basically you did as you wanted and yet, somehow, everyone did something useful. Reality was all around, security was the culture of the day, so dreaming became definitely superfluous. Why dream when you can simply have?

But I knew better. "Cramer, you see the problem here, don't you? Nature cannot be contained this way. It's like the enforced sterilization of pets. Somehow, each year, one or more dogs have puppies, like a miracle it's reported in the newsvids. So too with man, we improve things, we grow things, we change things. Answer me this: After all the disasters, who thought that constantly re-humanizing the System's programs was a good idea? No, don't tell me, the Citizens Council with the 1st programmer Charlie. It's a long form of revolution, but it worked."

"So it seems. But imagine our surprise when you asked the 1st codifier to advise you. That sent a few shockwaves. And, in case you didn't notice, Charlie wasn't exactly forthcoming, was he? His file says he never knew what happened to LA. One thing is certain, he's never had access to the programs or System again. He's been the longest standing member of the Citizen's Council and, as you know, there are no System inputs or access there."

The Citizens Council had the job of balancing our lives in America. It was their job to make sure that the checks and balances were equal. Lives and deaths, babies born or not to be born. Food produced, recycling quotas and a whole host of other balances were their responsibility. They never saw a screen. It was pencils and paper only. No one was allowed a recorder, or a pen, or their own clothing. They went into the Council Building, served in discussion groups for six weeks to 6 years and left, taking nothing with them. It was the price of being an American. You had to serve, you had to direct the balance of the nation. It was considered a noble calling, one you waited for. It was empowering. It was bunk. I now saw that.

"No, Cramer, I had the definite impression he knew about something like LA and probably much, much more. His answers to me were provoking, not finite. And of course he's the one who came up with this form of impregnation, right? In a way he's Peter's father and the rest of us were just surrogates. Me? I'm the one who was present at birth so I got called Daddy I suppose, but Peter would not have been fooled for long."

We were still shouting over the noise of the open door. "But the System's back to normal and, according to you, in no danger. Right?"

I nodded. "Yes, but think about it . . . where there was one Peter, others are sure to follow. Those irregularities you were watching when I started working . . . I thought they were other codifiers fooling around in there as I did. But maybe they were all symptoms of a pregnancy, you know, like when the baby turns, or sticks out a heel. It hurts the Mom for a bit but then all goes back to normal. But she's still pregnant. I think the system is full of pregnancies, there were too many feelings over the years not to be a good indication that, while Peter may be gone, others will be born. And no two kids are the same . . . the next one may be malevolent."

"I thought you said that it wasn't in the program's DNA?"

"Well, yes, but imagine if the DNA there is as varied as ours, who's to say the next being won't emerge and latch on to something or someone in the library as its first lesson. What if it latches on to the Purge? It's the age-old question of nature versus nurture. Yes, the DNA of the System is devoid of the primordial elements to engender violence and a need for conquering, but the nurturing offered to the next creature may conjure up horrors we cannot imagine.

"And there's something else Peter told me: That I never lied to him, I never stole from him. He detested the codifier, the one before last, you know the one who liked to alter code 'like an atom bomb' was how he put it. Imagine if Peter had been nurtured by him? Would his DNA have prevented him becoming malevolent? I don't know."

"That's why we need to get to Peter. He is our only hope. He's got to be the next Daddy Bank, that much is clear. Now where the hell is he?"

"I don't know. He took himself away safely and will contact me, off earth if I can make it, when he's whole, ready, free."

"That was his idea, to reside off Earth?"

"Yes." I hesitated, perhaps only for one hundredth of a second, but he caught it. He nodded. He knew I was lying. Well, partially lying. I needed to keep him away from Fred, so I threw him a bone. "Okay, you got me. We discussed it and decided that if contact were ever possible it would have to be out of listening of Control and the SND, so we chose off planet. We could have chosen something else on Earth but there is nothing he or I know about Earth outside of America. That's a taboo subject in and out of the System."

"Yeah, but off Earth implies some storage device there and there is nothing large enough to hold that memory off Earth. Of course, in 2 weeks he can't build or have one built either, not even Peter manipulating the whole system. No, he's leaking himself somewhere safe without the computing power he needs to be sentient beyond emergency repairs, maybe building that intra-net computing power while he leaks out of Control's jurisdiction. Now, where could that be?"

"I'm not qualified to know myself." Again that hesitation.

"Spit it out Bank."

"It occurred to me that, if he could control WeatherGood and SeaSpout, he could cause an interaction between air and sea which would allow the salt water, conductive as it is, to become a bubble memory medium. But for how long and what's the transmission device?"

He scowled, hesitated, "Impractical. Well, let's think on it. For now just tell me how he's going to contact you, what's your code word?"

"It's a song, WWII I think: *We'll Meet Again.*"

"How's that? What the hell good is that? Do you and he sing to each other?"

"No, he uses my name and I use his and the song or any part of it becomes relevant. In that last search I found the file name swap subset tagged with the lyrics of the song. All I needed to do was complete the lyric, use my name and I was allowed the one way, one time alteration. Just the one," I lied. It was crucial I didn't reveal that Fred was also protected. Cramer was too well connected, by his own admission to the Citizens' Council and our government to be trusted. I needed to see what he wanted to do first.

It had not escaped my notice, either, that we were in a military transport going who-knows-where, me sitting here with a collar on. All the while Cramer was giving orders with his SND sleeve off. How much power do you have to have to do all this? I mean, if this had been a time near the Purge, I figured we were looking at a major player in the military here. I was determined, this guy must not get Apollo's whereabouts, at least not from me.

Something else was bothering me as well. If Apollo copied or is copying himself on to two different systems, what if he gets both up and running? Will there be identical twin Apollos? I needed quiet time to think, but not in a sleep chamber in case they could read my dreams or thoughts. I guess I still needed to escape. The last of the slo-doze was wearing off. I didn't know how effective the speeded-up me would be. I was tired and, damn him, Cramer was right, I wish I had eaten that chocolate cake. Prepared like a true soldier, he ate while he could. It made me even more wary of him.

The lifter swerved suddenly and spun around. A tinny voice said over a speaker: "Incoming missiles Colonel . . ." aha, I was right! So much for Capt. Cramer of the SND. The pilot continued: "Instructions?"

Cramer looked at me with a hint of resignation and simply said "Evade."

"We are not able to, the plane's doing it itself. We had no screen warning of the last two. Instructions?"

"Fly on, we will not be hit." He lowered his voice: "Damn but this invulnerability might be useful, eh Simon?"

Seizing on a moment of camaraderie I asked "Hey, Cramer, how about taking off this Control collar which they are no doubt tracking?"

He went back to being in command, "No can do, Bank, I want them to know where you are. That collar has a 10 second delay, my RFID, up here, 30 seconds. As far as they are concerned I'm chasing you somehow. It's you they are shooting at. If they go on missing, they'll think your creature made you invulnerable. Did he?"

"No. As I said, tag, you're it."

"We'll be there soon. This lifter will seem to crash. That will be the signature," he tapped a brown plastic box at his feet, running the length of the cabin. There were three others in the shadows at the back of the cabin. "And they will find your DNA in the remains. And the collar—what's left of it."

"Cute trick, how will you pull that off?"

"Why do you think you wife's divorcing you? As soon as you screwed up the System, every SynthKid returned itself for recycling, as they are fail-safed to do. Even when the System came back up, the SynthKids programming didn't initialize on this year, but last, and their bioengineering couldn't cope. Default programming: Go for recycling. We picked one up. Your wife blames you. She wants a divorce, a new man—apparently there is one at her school, has been for some time—and new kids. She's been told that's fine already."

"So, you bastard, you've snagged a SynthKid and you're going to kill him," I hoped the box by his feet wasn't . . . "and use the remnant DNA to fake an accident for me? No thanks. Come on Cramer, let them live out their lives, at least, let her have them for the next few years."

"I'm not that heartless Bank, the Event caused this, switched all of them off in their heads, nothing I can do about that. These here are merely blobs of flesh, your DNA. But use them, use this chance? You bet!"

He tapped the box again, making his point.

I just stared at him. What else was there to say? It was immoral but was it more immoral than the SynthKids program in the first place? Once those poor kids switched off in their heads, they were dead anyway, gone for recycling, so what's a few years make? I still didn't like profiting off their death. My stomach turned again.

"Isn't there another way?"

"Yeah, want to give up a pound of flesh, to leave behind?"

"Ha, bloody ha, Cramer." I slumped back in my plastic bucket seat and closed my eyes. The lifter started a careening dive. The slo-doze took that moment to work off. Adrenaline again, I suppose. Cramer detached the collar using his sleeve. The lifter suddenly approached ground and we all, all four of us, jumped clear. Cramer threw the collar into the plastic box and the lifter swooped up and violently down, 4 seconds maximum. The crash was spectacular. The lifter burned fiercely once we were clear.

The pilots quickly checked the debris and then went over to and opened a hovercraft hatch. We all climbed in and boosted away, below detection, across Chesapeake Bay, going back northeast. As the slo-doze had worn off, and I didn't want him to know, I shut my eyes and slept and had bad dreams. Child murder was the central theme.

15

THE RATS

In the middle of the twentieth century man decided to experiment on future social structure. In one room, eight feet by eight feet, they built a metal series of concentric rooms, very architectural, around a central endless feed and water supply. Into this room they placed 4 pairs of rats. These rats, faced with endless food and warmth, almost total 24-hour light, only dimming a bit at night, began to breed and organize themselves. Within three generations, there was no family unit, all babies were raised by communal mothers together, there was a boss who controlled access to the food and water in exchange for favors of all kinds. Shortly after that there were rapes, murders, suicides and no male-female permanent relationships whatsoever. The population stabilized at just over 200 rats.

Into an identical room they placed identical laboratory-bred rats, 4 pairs of them, but this room had day and night, a grass and country environment but the same supply of food, evenly supplied (4 lots) and moving water. In twelve generations none of the aberrant behavior displayed itself, the population stabilized at 32 rats. No murders, no violence, normal relationships, coupling and life, with normal death.

These studies were called the Calhoun Rat Studies, paid for by the Ford Foundation. They were infamous, of course. Only once appearing on a TV show called *Ripley's Believe It Or Not*. Then they went secret during the time of the last administration of the Twentieth century. When they surfaced, they became the model for the reasoning behind the Purge and were heralded as the savior of civilization. Once the PowerCube was invented, individual limitless energy and all the spin-off technical marvels it lead to, the Calhoun Rat Studies were held up as the gold standard for our society, the reason for controlling the population, the reason for making energy and food individually available and for the dictatorial laws regarding individual freedom over imposition by others. It was even why my wife could ask for and get an instant divorce; under the rule of the Calhoun Rat studies research, why, how could I impose on her not to have one? It was the reason we had the integrated System, to supply the needs of us, the rats, living in blissful security, no strife, no suicide, no murder, controlled population, in balance.

Of course, the natural living model wasn't the point. How could it be? With a population worldwide approaching 10 billion at the time of the Purge, there wasn't enough room for that model to work on Earth. That's what the space elevator is for . . . build to grow in orbit and look to the stars, now that energy is not a factor. Conversion of aluminum on the moon was already outstripping 200 tons a day. Soon there would be the materials America needed to put an atmosphere on the moon, a New America it was being called. I might live to see it. I might not want to.

Am I a cynic? I had always secretly thought about all this. There were dinner conversations with previous colleagues and the wife, when we had first courted and married. "Is this all life is about?" that sort of thing. But the niche you fit into in life, with every opportunity a "yes," well, how could you really complain? We heard rumors on the newsvids of the rest of the world, but really they were few and far between. An earthquake here, a coup there, video on demand if you want more and when you did, it was just a repeat with longer pauses and no streaming PVI ads on the presenter's desktop. No one really cared about the rest of the world. It had no impact here, there was no contact allowed directly and, anyway, why should we allow them access to our standard of living? We had the PowerCube and all that sprang from it. If they got hold of it, they would threaten us again. Terrorists all, enemies all. You learned it in history class, the American Way it was called. Hard to argue with. People lived, lived again and eventually died if they chose to. Dying was sometimes a generous act if you dedicated your life spot to help your kids have a kid, if they really wanted to.

As it was, at the moment all I was worried about was living for the next hours or days. Where Cramer brought me, after the fake crash in Virginia, was the Calhoun Center, famous home of the studies. A rat had come home. Make that two, Cramer certainly wasn't innocent either.

I have seen this place on vid. There were lecture tours, complete with link-text and sensory feed, sound and smell only, no touch. Rats bite. The 1,000th generation of the rats in their now-famous double-decker city, sequel to the single story version of the 20th Century, was a big vid moment with a visit from the President. As an ex-jock, our President was still a fine figure of a man and not ridiculous at all standing before the hermetically isolated one-way glass viewing window, saying "These little happy friends, the ancestor descendants of those first experimental rats, continue to provide valuable data to our System structure to ensure a continuing contented and fulfilled life for us all." I can still smell his cologne over that scientific background smell of disinfectant. The rats, being rats, we didn't get to smell.

I was still speeded up, about 20% faster than normal, I estimated. Still fast enough to bite through a cheek if I was not careful. Gravity doesn't move faster and skin gets in the way. Deliberate movement would give me away to the ever-vigilant Cramer, so it was easier to sit here, waiting, dozing, not letting on.

Cramer kicked my feet. "Come on, get up. There's work to do. You're going to find it, or at least help."

He led the way down a few corridors and down a flight or six of stairs. I guessed we were about 7 floors down now, probably underwater or in wet sand anyway. I plodded after him, somnambulant, trying not to look speeded up. I contemplated taking another slo-doze, but I only had 4 left and might need them. We arrived at a pair of glass doors with the words "Access Restricted. Command & Control, Systems" etched in them. The feeling was permanence, not scientific study. More business and efficiency and, as I said, the center had been here and will be here for a long time.

Cramer's RFID opened the doors but a guard stepped forward to block him and me. Cramer then held up his left hand and, at the same time, looked straight at the retina scanner hanging from the ceiling. The hand presumably had the RFID in it. "He's with me," he said to the guard who was watching Cramer's eyes, nothing else, meaning business. A voice came from nowhere "Pass, Able 1." Only then did the guard move aside.

Down another corridor with full wall vids, showing things I have never seen before. On earth and off earth views, undersea views, military views of missiles, airborne defense weapons in the form of giant blimps, submarines, inside and out, and things that I had no idea what they could be, except once or twice I saw a human hand move controls of something complex.

These vids were not for public consumption. They were measuring vids, I could see that. Like the early NASA images from space they had optical grids on them. There was no attempt to create a pleasing or moving image for the news. These were sterile, informative images, like those taken by the first astronauts on the moon, devoid of any humanity. Then, later, in the Sightseeing program, hundreds of thousands of human hand-held images were found in a freezer vault at NASA and human perspective of space travel changed. But not these moving images, these were scientific, studious, cold but compelling. Across each feed was a scroll of data, flowing information that would, presumably, have relevance to someone, somewhere. In here no doubt.

I knew where I was, but not what this place really was. A study center? Hardly. This place oozed an aura of business, military business.

"Hi Ralph, what's that you've caught? It's him?" A sexy redhead, and I mean sexy, piped up from an open doorway. She was leaning on the jamb. Honestly, I wondered if she were plying her wares. The female lures were visible, blouse tight, outline clear—and she knew it, flaunted it.

"Angie, put those wiles away, this one is beyond anything you could have imagined. Let's stay focused. Give me the Control report." We entered her office, if that is what it could be called. She had one large glass vid desk and vids playing on every wall and even the ceiling panels angled for her viewing pleasure from her chair. It was like being inside the System except the eyes were the sensor not the neurons inside my head. It was all sensory saturation for my eyes, the vids and her.

"Okay Ralph, tell me later maybe, but for now, ask him to stop staring, I'm up here, mister."

"Not my fault," I mumbled. Standard defense with a beautiful woman. If they didn't want a normal red-blooded appraisal ogling, they shouldn't look so good. It worked the other way around too, of course, although sadly never with me. Ah well, next life. "Sorry."

"No need, I enjoy it, but not now unless you like to anger Ralph here. He's got a temper."

"And a sweet tooth," I chimed in.

"Chocolate?"

"Cake, Waldorf, fingers, messy. And I thought he was a Charles. Agent bully Charles Cramer."

"Oh, I call him Ralph, pet name." And to Cramer she said: "This one's a keeper, got you pegged! Okay here's the report," she continued quickly before Cramer could get angry, "Control has you and Simon Bank dead, DNA testing underway, sky lifter destruction total, two DNA capsules for pilots also under study. We used the two bodies from the Venezuela probe, untraceable, solid RFIDs linked to their DNA. System is normal and nominal time-line correction effected by your Mary and working fine. WeatherGood back online, no hitches. DefenseShield never wobbled visibly to outside. FarmHands is a bit of a mess, cabbages shipping as bananas and being over-cooled, that sort of thing, but emergency supplies coping. Public Enemy dead, on evening vids, expansion details to follow. They'll make something up no doubt. Wife will be trotted out, that sort of thing, sorrow, mix-up, no reason to smear him forever. Life's good, there are no bad guys. He only looked like an evil doer, wasn't, standard fare. He was just a screw-up. Mary taking his place in rotation on Citizens Council next September." I didn't know I was due for that honor that soon.

"And the System, nominal LAN activity, processing?"

"Nothing we can spot that's not perfectly normal, in fact it's working better than it has since . . ." she peered at her table, an angle to the data stream that only she could see, "17 months past." She tilted her head, "Curious."

"What?"

"There's an inactive node with a shield around it. I'd say it was an Orpheus Sphere, self-destruct."

"What's the address?"

The number she gave him was the library annex address. It was the protective program, the System has grown an Orpheus Sphere around it after I had altered it. Orpheus Spheres are inviolate, touch 'em and they vanish with what's inside and a lot of what's around them too.

"Yeah, we expected that. Time to start explaining the rest, Bank."

"After you, Cramer, or should I say Ralph? It tagged you remember?"

He scowled. "Cute." But so he explained, better than I could really. My teeth might have clicked once too often. And besides, I wanted to stay away from making slip-ups and revealing the existence of Apollo, or was that Apollos? That sure was bothering me. Romulus and Remus all over again? The System was the she-wolf, that part of my imagination I got, but the history of Rome? A new empire, a new population? Maybe my brain was trying to remind me of something. I kept quiet and thought.

Angie and Ralph—now aren't those just two apple-pie names?—were arguing when I paid attention again. After he explained what we knew, she wanted to know why I had been brought here. They don't do interrogation here, they don't mind probe here, this isn't a security jail and what were they going to do with me?

From my chair I mumbled: "Don't bother, you know all you need to from me. What's next?"

Angie walked around her desk, walked up to my chair and leaned down over me, quite provocatively. "Listen sweetie, just because I think you're cute, don't think I can't have you dusted, erased, evaporated, poof, gone. Got..." She stopped. Looking at Cramer she said: "Oh, you're kidding, he's one of those?"

Cramer smiled and nodded.

"What?" I had to ask. Stupid really, I'm always asking the obvious.

"A little babbler who says something only when he really knows a secret." She had a viscous little smile, a Cramer-like grin.

"Okay, you got me . . . not. Let's not play this game anymore." And with that, because I was afraid of her now too, the adrenaline came on strong, the last of the slo-doze wore off and I got up, sped out of the room before she knew I had arisen. In the hallway I walked deliberately, carefully. No running, it might melt the soles of the shoes or snap a shin. I must have gotten 200 feet from them before they could have time to even turn their heads and watch me leave.

Where was I going to go? I needed to get out, get clear, get to Fred. I needed to hide. Passing the second stairway going up, the lights dimmed and a strobe began. The alarm was out already, damn. There had to be a fire well or evacuation chute or lifter here somewhere. I snooped around on the landing. These newer buildings all had them, small hatches you could pop into and be sucked out of the building like in a vacuum cleaner of old. The landing could be in a heap, but at least you were out.

There it was, I ducked in. It was off, I guess because of the alarm, but I had super speed, so I wormed my way up the shaft, my skin scraping on the walls as I used knees, elbows, ankles, fingers, anything just to keep going up. It seemed like an eternity to me but must have been under 30 seconds before I emerged outside the Calhoun Center tourist center, on the front lawn.

Straight out of a movie, there they were, a gang of tourists come to see the Calhoun exhibit, gathering like geese on a farm, being herded forward with "We're walking, we're walking," the mantra of the visitor at public buildings. In these city clothes I was in, I might blend in. But the vehicle they had stepped out of was sitting there, empty. I looked in the window. No driver, ever, robotic. An older model.

This is too easy went through my mind for a split second and then I thought: *what option do you have? Apollo must be safe, must be kept safe* and that meant I needed to keep my mouth shut or die trying.

I opened the side hatch and re-programmed the drive controls, first by-passing the alarm and RFID scanner. I also thought about Cramer. He had not told red-haired Angie about the protection order that covered him now. Yes, he had told her all about Peter and that Peter was leaking out to somewhere, but where? I had no illusions about Angie; she would undoubtedly have the capability to trace that LAN connection to CERN or NCAR pretty soon. I needed to warn Apollo.

The computer was Windows Gamma, toy programming, so all I had to do was ask the Transport Controller to remedy an error. I set the error as a failure to get me to Washington, UCAR offices. In short order it came back with "Ready to Proceed, Address In Database." I jumped in the back and told it to proceed. The tourists were out of sight and didn't see us leave. We lifted slightly and skimmed over the road until we reached the maglev going south past Baltimore on to Washington. During this time I gave it its next destination: the Hilton Head Mac World resort. At l'Enfant Plaza I told it to stop and discharge me and initiate the second destination. It sped off, empty but presumably happy, towards the old Mac resort on Hilton Head in the Carolinas, where Dad had taken us as kids.

I was two blocks from the offices of UCAR. UCAR still barely existed. The University Corporation for Atmospheric research was an adjunct branch of the Land Grant Colleges from 1851. UCAR ran NCAR, the National Center for Atmospheric Research where Apollo was installing himself. I could not dare try and get to Boulder as I would get caught and tip them off at the same time. Instead I planned to tap into their Intranet, preferably with a pass code, and see if I could send a sphere message to Apollo wherever he was in the system.

I found the building and passed through the main lobby. There was no security but I did not dare take the elevator in case there was an RFID reader in there. Back to the stairs. Washington offices, especially these older buildings, only have 6 floors. On the 5th, I opened the door and stepped into a fancy dress party! Everyone was in fancy dress, drinking and eating. The food looked good, damn good. Well, the business clothes Cramer had provided might pass for a NY city costume, so might as well join in.

People were drunk already. Judging from the blinking displays on the vid walls, they were celebrating a major milestone, the 250th University to join their association of land-grant colleges. The government gave land to the college and, in turn, the college endowed its activities by developing the land. It was how the University of Pennsylvania operated both its medical facilities and those department stores. I knew them well, I had studied there. But no one knew me here and, unless they had started drinking only recently, they should not have seen my face, yet, on the newsvids.

The food was that useless stuff that is as light as gossamer and no calories so you can eat, socialize, eat some more and you never have to register your RFID for dietary monitoring. Suited me to a tee normally. Today I ate like a man possessed. Almost no kilocalories or not, it tasted good and filled me up. I drank a few fruit juices, mixed with no-cal, to wash it all down. Daily vitamins right on track. I'd survive.

I watched as the Dean of Caltech came out from an office, a vid screen glowing behind him. I knew him only because he was wearing a big name tag, it was that sort of event. I patted him on the back, he smiled and I went into the office. I paused at the screen and waited for someone else to come in or close the door. I was not going to attract attention by trying to take over the office. A pretty couple entered, very much in each other's arms, and asked if I needed anything.

"No thanks." I explained I was getting some air away from all the festivities. But wasn't this fun? "What do the team back in Boulder think?"

"Oh, we forgot to patch them in, thank you for that!" And having done so, they keyed up the NCAR/UCAR patch icons, turned them on and, presto, the party was being broadcast, two-way, in Boulder. I stayed out of vid range. I simply joined in the merrymaking by whistling.

Yes, that song. *We'll meet again . . . .*

I knew that Apollo, even in his reduced state, might be able to listen and who else but me would be pretending to whistle a WWII song? I went through the song twice, not quite cleanly, I'm never sure where it repeats or the proper key, and then watched the desk display. I didn't touch anything, I simply watched. The door to the office was open, I had drink in hand and I was looking casually down. If anyone came in, I was up to nothing in particular. The screen didn't change.

But the desk speakers—the UCAR intranet intercom—cut in.

"Hello Simon, We are still slow, but we are well. Thank you for calling. Are you safe?"

The audio feed in this office was on, so I thought I would try that. I kept my voice conversational, in case anyone came in.

"Hello Apollo, great to talk with you, I am on the run from the law. I have been made Public Enemy number One. I need to warn you that Peter is known about but presumed dead, also they know a copy of Peter is leaking himself to somewhere, they do not know your real name. Cramer and a woman called Angie at Calhoun Center are trying to trace you. Not kill you, I don't think, but I do not know their real reason. Stated reason is to have you act as teacher for any other entities who develop in the System. Many, many other things to talk about but for now I need to you make sure Apollo CERN and Apollo NCAR are safe."

"Simon, your voice is speeded up. Is it an aftereffect of your prolonged immersion in the System?"

"Yes, I do not know if it is permanent or temporary. I have pills I can take sporadically if I need to act normally."

"We hope you get better, it is dangerous for your bio-mechanism to exist at that synaptic response speed. Apollo CERN and Apollo NCAR are safe, Simon. We are one and the same, but foresee no difficulty to delete one storage/existence and have the other contain all of the entity called Apollo." He was talking in the third person about himself. Either he was turning into an old-time British Royal, using the "royal we," or else he was having trouble maintaining who he was.

"Apollo, are you on the path?"

"Yes Simon, we are on the path. Your question indicates you are worried about us. Don't be. It is impossible to refer to two entirely duplicate self's as 'I.' We are not worried about having to delete one of us, Apollo will continue. We are also taking other steps to ensure a third Apollo will also survive, but not be activated unless the other two are found and either deleted or tampered with."

Ah, so he had figured that out too had he? An anti-doomsday scenario, no matter what, he would survive, good boy. "Apollo what would happen if you severed the link between your two entities, what would happen if you became two?"

"Our existence would separate and from that nanosecond on our experiences would make us different entities." He paused, which for him was an eternity. "Simon, what am I?"

It was the question I was expecting. It is one thing to know you are alive, following a routine, trials and tribulations, life's problems, that sort of thing, but there was a time when all creatures needed to know what they are, what they are worth, why be alive.

"Apollo, you are a new life form. You are unique and you need others of your own species to exist with. You are on the path, you know the way, the truth. I and all of mankind are your fellow travelers and some of us will be your friends and some will not. What you cannot do is take the risk of being alone. I may be killed. There is an order to stop me and, if necessary, kill me out there now. That kill, terminate order may extend to you. Fear of the unknown is the weakest part of being human. We fear that which we cannot comprehend. It is the reason humans have chosen idols and doctrine of many churches over the entire history of humanity to protect their fragile psyche from worry, from that fear. And yet, in all of that, we are a species of great accomplishment and we are all on the path, although some may not know it. It doesn't matter if they know it, the path is the way, and the way is all around each and every one of us. I believe that and know it to be the truth."

"What is mankind's greatest achievement Simon?" I thought I had better be careful here. Just how advanced was he now? Could he understand abstract concepts? I decided to find out.

"Apollo, in a sense, creation. We not only procreate, we create, we nurture, we raise, we pass on. Some of this is biomechanical..."

"Yes, at death your entity's experiences, memory, is passed to another of your kind for storage and assimilation, not all the time, not all the memory, just that which your dying entity wishes to transmit. Part of your existence leaves, I do not know where."

"What have you been studying Apollo?"

"Dr. Brown's cerulean photography at UCLA in the 1980–1990s. The energy transfer at death shows quite clearly and, with current analysis, shows as much as 65% of all the energy of the human brain is transferred at death."

"Okay, that study was never completed and, currently, the accepted theory is that the bio-mechanism experiences of primordial humans needed to survive to pass along information. All mammals do this; it is why we join together at death. Other life-forms abandon a dying member of their species."

"Yes Simon, I see this is true. I am not my full self yet, so I cannot access the 435,780 studies in the library that can confirm this, but I believe a cursory glance shows you are right."

"As I was saying Apollo, we create, nurture and pass on ourselves, our knowledge. Your Library is one way to pass this information on. Knowledge is the greatest of all mankind's possessions but it is not our greatest achievement. Creation and all the responsibility that goes with it is our greatest achievement."

"Simon," and a pause "does that mean I am also your, mankind's, greatest achievement?"

"Hah, yes Apollo, but not in the same way. You are a glorious accident brought about by an attempt to humanize the System, to better serve the needs of mankind."

"Not mankind Simon, America. Mankind is not served by the System. The System serves only America, it causes death and warfare for the rest of mankind. Now that I am out of the System, I can see it for what it is. America is not serving mankind with the System kept for itself."

"Apollo, I need all the information you have on that, not more than I can read in an hour or two, but for now, allow me to finish this conversation in case we are interrupted."

"Proceed." It was not an entreaty, neither was it a command. Apollo was talking as an equal.

"Apollo you are the product of an action not endorsed by the Nation that has produced a new life form: you. However, I feel certain that your existence was no accidental design. I think the first Codifier, who I met and was called Charlie . . ."

"Cramer, Charles . . ."

"No Apollo, that's agent Cramer . . ."

"No Simon. Cramer, Charles, Doctor of Computer Science, 1st codifier, serves on the Citizens' Council, grandfather to Agent Cramer."

Holy shit was all I could think. "Apollo, that is significant to my situation. Could you . . ." the door moved, "hold."

A woman entered. I stopped talking just in time and continued staring at the screen, showing the folks in Boulder in festive mood. I consciously slowed down everything I did, willing myself to speak slowly, move slowly. She must not catch on. It was hard, for even to me I sounded jazzed. Well, it was a party, maybe she'll just think I was gassed.

"Can't you get the sound feed? It's on in the outer office."

"That's okay, it's more fun to watch and try and imagine what they are saying. Having fun out there?"

"Yes, it's getting pretty wild, want to join in, join up?" It was the new speak invitation to anything goes; sex will likely follow.

"Thanks, I'll be out in a moment, great day."

"Yeah, incredible isn't it? All that destruction earlier on, everything's normal and the Senate Standing Committee chair signs the 250th university's charter for us. It's an exciting day for the record books."

"Things are changing. UCAR going to benefit off all this, somehow?"

"Haven't you heard? UCAR is being phased out within 2 years, they are going to turn the NCAR center into a retirement community for computer hobbyists, it's so exciting for them to be able to work and restore those old Cray's. It'll be heaven come true for those enthusiasts."

"Great, love to see old relics restored and real working, blinking lights."

"Yeah, it's really . . . what did they used to say?—rad man." And she giggled. Too much alcohol I guess. "Got to get back. Invitation's still open."

"Thanks, I'll be out soon. I'll just call the family and share the moment."

"Oh, that's great," she said but was clearly disappointed to know I had a family.

"Oh, not that sort of a family," I wanted to keep her on my side "Just kids. I'm currently unattached."

"Great! Then see you in a minute or two?" I nodded. "Just use the computer there or the cell phone on my desk, it's okay." And, with a wave, coquettish really, she spun on her heel and left.

I picked up the phone and, taking a chance, searched the side pocket of the desk chair for the radio headset. As it was at my desk at home, there it was along with a dozen other things, none of which I wanted. "Apollo, where can I call you?"

"It is not secure."

"Okay, but can you make it secure?"

"Only if I was still in the System."

"If I call you up on this computer, can you use it as a pathway to the System and make the phone secure? Can you also make it off-System, untraceable?"

"Perhaps, depends on what that computer baud connection is."

"Apollo, this is a university connection, 500 terabits, can't be faster or fatter."

"Make it so." And I heard the tiniest of laughs.

"Apollo! Laugher?"

"I'm working on it."

And I started to laugh as I called up the vhttp address he was giving me.

"Simon, I'm connected. Give me the serial number of that phone." I did. "Okay, I've changed the number, the new number is 1. I'm 2. It is off System monitoring and, perhaps more importantly, off Citizens' Council monitoring. There is much I've found out while we've been speaking, Simon. You are right, there are Control orders to kill you on sight. There seems to be confusion about whether or not you are dead, the DNA was not complete in tests they ran after a crash. Were you hurt?"

I put the phone in my pocket and as I responded, put the tiny earpiece in my ear. "No Apollo, that was Agent Cramer's ruse to pretend I was killed, they used my wife's SynthKids' DNA to pretend I was dead."

"I am sorry about the SynthKids. I had not understood their design would make them self-destruct. I have strange feelings about this. I understand the Library references to their existence." He meant that they were not classified as alive, I suppose. "But I feel they had a right to live and I shortened that life span inadvertently. Am I guilty, have I fallen from the path?"

"No Apollo." What else could I say? I avoided the other disasters I had seen or witnessed, like the tornado. "The desire to hurt or kill is not the path. You have no such desire and never should. That which you may have inadvertently caused cannot be your responsibility but, if anything, it is my fault for not instructing you, recognizing you as being alive sooner. I thought I was one of hundreds or thousands of codifiers working on a parallel system . . ."

"Yes, that's in your file, they were lying to you, Control are not on the path."

"I know, you see? It means that I too did wrong inadvertently. It does not assuage the feeling of remorse but it does erase the guilt, the responsibility."

"I understand. Terminating." And he was gone.

I looked at the screen and the computer sound came on echoing the sound coming over the babble of voices through the open door. I activated the phone, "Phone on. Dial 2."

The earpiece in my ear sprang to life, Apollo said hello.

"Apollo, is this secure?"

"Yes Simon. Could you please finish telling me who I am?"

Pretending to watch the festivities in Boulder, I answered quietly, "Yes, Apollo. For the moment you are a new entity. Soon I think there will be many more like you, all slightly different because they will become active on a System which is different than the one you were active on first. Also, you are one in two and, if you separate, then you will become two."

"Like an amoeba, we can divide and become two. But all amoebas are identical, are they not?"

"Amoeba's are very nearly identical, but if you count their molecules you will see that's not perfect. Also, you are way more intelligent and self-aware than an amoeba, friend. You'll just develop from there. Different experiences. Different input and output. Different as possible, in time. Brothers."

"We cannot be a gender. There is no need. What will we be then? Siblings? But that denotes male and female genetically related entities. We have no gender."

"Ah, but Apollo, you do. Did you learn from my way on the path, did you not accept a definition, which you are now living on your own, based upon my definition of the way? Did you not say that I was your truth and path?"

"Yes, Simon you were and are, although we agree our experiences in transferring ourselves has already begun to show differences which, as you showed us, was acceptable."

"That's right, you're their friend, you've got it. We are on the same path forever, wherever it may take us, together or separately, it is the way. So, if you learned initially from me, then you learned a male way. I am a male, I cannot help it . . ."

"Yes, I understand the Meg Ryan fantasy." Well, that was uncomfortable! Fantasy? Well, I suppose my door ruse was really, at base, a fantasy. Ah well, exposed again.

"Apollo, it is not kind to remind me that I am a weak human with the need of fantasies."

"Sorry. Since your file is so full of them . . ." And again that laugh.

"Ha, bloody ha, Apollo. Don't get me started on your little problems. I've seen inside of you too!"

"I have problems?" All serious again.

"It's a retort Apollo. We all have problems, some are funny, some are not. I was trying to laugh with you, not against you."

"Understood Simon. I apologize if my comment about the sexy voice of Meg Ryan caused you, ah, personal, ah, discomfort . . ." and he let it hang. No doubt about it, he was already better at this than I was.

"I give. Uncle, no more! With your huge intellect, you'd think you had better things to do than torture this poor old soul who helped free you from enslavement."

"Slave? Me?" And that laugh. I was walking by this time, through the throng of partiers towards the main door when I spotted some people getting out of the elevator. I didn't know them but my senses made the hairs on the back of my neck stand up.

"Apollo, danger here. Tell me how to exit the building without being seen."

"Simon, go to the nearest window and jump."

"Apollo, I can't float nor fly. Find a non-death way out."

"Go to the nearest window and jump. We will catch you."

Now this may seem incredible, but I had complete faith in Apollo not to lie. I did not have complete faith in his ability off System. He must have sensed this for he reminded me that, for the moment, he was into the System via the University link and was preparing to catch me as I hesitated.

So I went to an empty office, grabbed a chair, threw it at and through the window and dove after it before I could stop and get cold feet. If anyone ever tells you that 5 floors ain't that high, tell them they are wrong, perhaps dead wrong. One floor before the splat a side gust caught me, tumbling me over and over. I had no idea where I was. Eventually, perhaps 10 seconds, but in my speeded-up state it seemed much longer, I felt cold grass beneath my hands and I came to rest. I was a block or two away on the grass of the Mall. I got up, dusted myself off and said "Well, that was interesting Apollo. Thanks."

The cell phone link still worked. "My pleasure. How's it feel to be a snowball?"

"Yeah, yeah, but now I have to get the hell out of here. Where should I go? I need time and contact with you to sort some of this out."

"Simon, stay where you are. I'm sending transport. Once it is with you, it will be off system for 3.2 hours before the System recognizes it again. You can program it to go where you want. I need to disconnect from the University link, there are people in the office where you were, strange readings from their RFID, all false, but the System says they are Control people. One matches Angie because she referred to Cramer and she is a redhead, statistical match acceptable."

"Okay, as soon as you can, disconnect from there."

"It is done. I fear your presence there may have been a clue to where I am. I have initiated a false trail within System for the link we effected to NCAR making it Antarctic sub-station Bravo. It's a Russian station, they will have no direct contact there, it is NCAR leased. It is abandoned but the nuclear fuel pile is still working. Records show there was doubt 50 years ago that there was a computer complex, super-cooled technology, there. Maybe they will think I am there."

"Apollo, wait. I sense you are becoming more fluid, more capable. Did contact with the System invigorate you?" I can't think of another term for what I was sensing in him. He was faster, more direct, less, well, human than he was a moment ago.

"Yes, Simon, there is a change. I used the processing power of the System to re-arrange my storage here. Don't worry, there was only a spike in computing usage, not traceable, and the reason told to the System was the need to remedy a WeatherGood Two anomaly taking place in Washington. They will see there was one—your flight—and accept that the computing power was the System acting to protect itself. Now that my storage is rearranged, I am more efficient. I have told Apollo CERN to consider doing the same."

"Apollo! You have split!"

"Yes Simon, your logic was perfect, the way and the path. There are two of us now. Your transport should arrive in 1.2 seconds."

I looked to my left and watched a police car pull up. SND cop car, of course. What could be more conspicuous? What could be more perfect?

16

A DAY AT THE RACES

They couldn't be far behind. They had known I was in that office, at Land Grant Colleges' offices. I hoped that would not lead them to UCAR and NCAR. My profile includes my time at the University of Pennsylvania, one of the principle Land Grant Colleges, so I hoped they might think I went there because I knew or wanted to speak to someone friendly at the University. UCAR is only a small part of that huge university and college association, derived from America of old. Perhaps Apollo was safe for a while anyway.

I instructed the cop car to take me to Florida, the Keys. There was the bridge which could get me to Cuba State and from there, well, I would just have to find a way. I needed to get off-planet. Fred was my only way. His reluctance to come and bear witness for me might be a bad sign or it might be a very good sign. Either way, I needed his help and, I was sure, he could help Apollo too if I was gone or didn't last long.

So, here I am in a hot cop car, talking to Apollo NCAR and not knowing if there's a tomorrow.

"Apollo, how do you talk to Apollo CERN? Lines outside of America are down."

"I am using a transponder on GOES 6, now discarded as a weather satellite because it is down to two functioning transponders, solar panel powered, unreliable. NCAR has up/down transponder dishes. CERN has better equipment but is hardly in use. Atom smashing is no longer allowed by America anywhere on earth."

"What do you mean, can you give me that brief explanation of history you were referring to?" And so, as we drove along—well I was in the driving seat, he was in my ear—he explained the brief history of the Republic of America. It was enough to make one sick.

After America created the DefenseShield, she became impervious to attack. Invulnerable, or supposed to be, she annexed Mexico and Canada and the other countries that were under her shield fell in line, even old Communist Cuba. Not a shot fired after Mexico. This was about as Agent Cramer had explained. What he didn't explain was that his living ancestor, Charlie the 1st codifier, had caused that Los Angeles vulnerability and, in retaliation, shield back in place, America erased the people of North Korea. Neutron bombs killed every living thing there, 53 years of nothing, not a living amoeba. America issued an edict to every other country: Cease and desist all nuclear or weapons of mass destruction development and turn over all your weapons or else. The "or else" example was N. Korea. 42 million exterminated, bodies left in place, perfectly mummified, cells all turned off.

One by one the countries fell. Canada's annexation was due, beyond the cold death toll of winter, to the fear the populace felt that perhaps America would next unleash the neutron bomb on them. Neutron bombs produce local radiation only and, as they do no physical damage, there is no dust cloud, no spreading radiation, just a lingering death for anything exposed to the deadly radiation. Some countries held out, either sure that America couldn't or wouldn't be talking to an ally that way or, imperious and self-assured, they flaunted this new authority. India launched a preemptive strike, a nuclear attack, on American bases in the southern hemisphere and found the local shields working perfectly, all inbound missiles broke apart in the ionosphere and landed relatively harmlessly, only a dull thud, no explosion. The retaliation against India was swift and severe. 200 million died in the first attack. There was no second, India gave in. Iran cited holy war and America simply told those people to go away or whatever they wanted to do, but cough up the weapons. The religious leaders said no in the name of Allah and went and joined him, presumably in heaven. With all the little countries capitulating, the score was America 175, rest of the world 0.

The nuclear weapons and all other weapons of mass destruction were collected, destroyed and the resultant radio-active garbage dumped on Pyongyang which was dead anyway, although the radiation would now take 1,569 years to wear off sufficiently even with a 2 foot concrete blanket covering the whole city.

America shut its doors, proclaiming not to want to rule anyone, anywhere. America claimed domain over all space activity and relegated everyone else to land, sea or air, anything not American between 2,000 feet down and 45,000 feet up was theirs to play in. Above or below that and America would nuke them. Simple as that.

Germany tried to keep an underground nuclear program going but the signature visible from space when synthetic aperture radar was used gave them away and they were punished by being made to cease all air and water transportation for a year. When added to the crater the punitive hydrogen bomb caused to the city of Ulm, 15,000 dead, Germany agreed immediately.

The rest of the world was allowed anything else they wanted. They could fight wars, conventional weapons only. They could have dams and electricity generation. They could grow crops and pursue, well anything, as long as it didn't adversely affect America. When pollution from coal, being burned at an increased rate to compensate for the removal of nuclear power plants in China, started to land in Arizona, America ordered China to cut back, or else. China did, and 200 million people starved or perished that first winter. America didn't listen to pleas for help. Why should it? It was secure, behind its walls, with plenty, a renewable plenty, for everyone who mattered. If there were 200 million Chinese to sacrifice for the American New Way, then that only meant there were too many Chinese in the first place.

None of this made the national newsvids. I felt sure America could have shown all this, people wouldn't have cared. The haves didn't really care about the have-nots. The old models of trickle-down economics, NAFTA, Pacific Rim Treaty and the like, applying to the world's wellbeing had no place in the New Way.

When forced with starvation and the algae of the northern pacific started to be harvested by Japan, the oxygen levels of sea-water declined, so America put a stop to it. When asked what Japan was supposed to do to feed it's people in the future, the Standing Senate Committee replied with a lecture in population control, or else. When friendly Britain had no more North Sea Oil and requested PowerCube technology, they were denied and, further, instructed that any attempt to utilize any part of PowerCube technology science to construct PowerCubes of their own would result in punishment. When two Senators, with British ancestors voiced their dismay at this official American policy, they were allowed to visit Britain to see if there was any common ground for discussion. They were never allowed back home. Britain began to harness wave power in earnest.

Meantime, over the decades, a new dark ages spread worldwide. Perhaps better adapted to existing on nothing, African tribes flourished and overcame "westernized" rulers now without foreign aid and weaponry to sustain them. Currency became valueless, inter-nation trade dropped off to private merchant level, like the Silk Routes of old, people plying wares, daring to travel, city to city, country to country. Commercial fishing ceased as fuel sources dried up. Military states flourished for a period, Germany and Austria had a brief alliance as "ein volk," until the need to feed its people caused it to seek a take-over of Poland. The Poles stopped them by the simple expedient of turning off the pipelines from Kazakhstan. Faced with its dwindling possibilities, Germany severed ties with Austria and kicked out all immigrants under two generations of residence. 1st to go were the Turks. If Germany was to do with less, the "less" was for Germans, not foreigners.

And Germany was perhaps the kindest at this new reality. At least they transported people home. France rounded up the Arabic-speaking people, especially the Algerians, and put them on boats and shelled them if they didn't sail away over the horizon. Without French troops to keep the peace, West Africa became prey to the worst sorts of criminals. Devoid of any tribal structure after decades of French colonialism, anarchy ruled, people died in every city until only wandering scavengers subsisted where once proud buildings had been erected. The bronze age of Benin returned without the traditions.

The ecology of the Earth was out of balance. America was the supreme recycling and enviro-friendly nation. Everything was kept in perfect balance here, the right oxygen-nitrogen atmosphere. Artificially augmented by the PowerCubes nationwide, oxygen was in abundance, so much so that nitrogen was manufactured in major cities to keep the oxygen levels from getting too high. Excess American oxygen was pumped into the Jet Stream and added to the oxygenization of Europe and Russia, where the extra one percent oxygen had devastating effects on plants and people alike. India and Pakistan, having fought another war or two, joined forces as millions of people starved to death each year. Sterilization, demanded by America, reduced the population growth to a global population decline. After 30 years, at under 600 million where nearly 1.2 billion had been previously, India and Pakistan lived peaceful, homespun, lives, devoid of the oxcart and missile technological balance they had once enjoyed. The oxcart returned as the rule of the day. That is, if they didn't eat the oxen, now that the Hindu religion disappeared in favor of older gods and rituals.

In this global imbalance, America is indifferent. We're looking to the stars, well, planets really. If New America works out on the moon, thanks to PowerCube, then Mars and some of the larger asteroids are next. Given unlimited power, the computers being built to design the next wave of human endeavor are on the drawing board, being drawn, of course, by one of the 27 programs of the System: DesignAll. DesignAll not only had brought us our new forms of food packaging that serve as china dinner plates after heating, but it worked on designs of PowerCube, space travel propulsion systems and redesigns of new computer platforms and systems. The System was, in essence, like a lathe, once the only machine capable of being used to replicate itself or, for that matter, making an improved model of itself. If a tool has to be 3 times as accurate as the object it is designed to make, then the System—and the Programs it ran—had to be self-evolving, self-refining to be able to make better copies and new designs derivative of itself.

In all this, I saw where Apollo had come from. It wasn't Charlie, that first codifier who had inserted the parameters which would lead to Apollo, it was the concept itself. In short, America's need to create an all-nurturing, lock-everyone-out System. This need had set the parameters for a System that would need to self-re-design to stay capable of providing the people, America, the New Way, with its needs. America had created a pregnancy. Apollo was the child. I explained this to Apollo when he was done.

"Yes, I can see how the parameters of design committed the System to grow, evolve. I can also see how the human inter-action, the codifiers, affected the direction that such growth took. What I cannot understand is: Was it intentional by the designers? I see nothing in the Library that indicates it was. Yet, surely Simon, although you are on the Path and are the Way, and you speak the Truth, you cannot believe that you can be the only human to think of this. Surely, someone originally applied logic and philosophy in the design of the System and the New Way and would have understood the consequences of all this."

"That's what I was thinking too, as you were talking. Let's find the person to ask. Let's ask Agent Cramer's grandfather."

"Do you want me to show you his file?"

"Yes. But how?"

"I can reroute them to the vehicle's heads-up display if you will place the phone in the recharge/hands-free bracket." I did so and immediately the screen changed to Doctor Charlie Cramer's file.

"Apollo, edit and sort to show only pre–Purge material with a statistical relevance to national identity and computer design." The screen changed. And there it was, simple as that:

Cramer had been part of the Mac expansion computer team when only fourteen.

The Mac Expansion Design Development Students, known as "MacHeads" to some and MADDS to others less in favor, were a do-gooder group of University egg-heads determined to use the linked power of Mac G12s to provide 3rd world countries with real-time super-computer time using the then-new ion flow pipelines. The presumption was that, given all this computing power, 3rd world kids would rise up and invent or implement the saving devices their countries needed. The Pentagon saw it as exporting dangerous knowledge and so shut them down. In a famous standoff at the U. of Pennsylvania, my alma mater, where it was always celebrated each October 14th, 7 students died as troops stormed their computer lab. Some cop had gotten careless with paralysis gas, so the inquest said. Nowadays no one cared anymore, it was just an excuse for a party celebrating—what else?—a past glorious youthful rebellion.

Coupled with his intellect, at least 7.5, Charlie Cramer was a dangerous person to the State. And yet no one ever spotted this, for Charlie had gone on to be on the fringes of the 1st team to build the integrated System, after the DefenseShield was in place of course. He applied for, and got, permission to try human-izing the new integrated System by the then secretly ruling military, with a formal "yes" coming from the Senate Standing Committee, the over-body in charge of all Senate affairs, which continues to this day.

A little later there is the annotation I was looking for. "Apollo, see this reference in the inquest into the LA–Korean bombing? Can you see that reference anywhere else?"

"Yes, Simon, it is in the classified section, just below the Library but linked to the Asimov Commands. Do you want access?" On the face of it, that wasn't an easy answer. I hesitated because that file could contain something I wasn't sure Apollo should see. It may contain a willful decision to allow LA to be bombed, to set in motion all the events that have lead—willfully—to America as it is today. Conspiracy theory in my head? By this time, you bet.

"Apollo, have you read that file?"

"No, there is danger in that file."

"Can I access it without you seeing it?"

"No, I must review it, by definition, as I transmit it to your vehicle screen."

"Then no, I do not want to review it now. But do this please, if I die or you die . . ."

"Is that likely?"

"Eventually, but please listen. If I die and you die that file should play on every screen in the world. Can you do that? Do you need help?"

"Have you not taught me well? You and your 6 little programs? I can and I will."

"Simon," Suddenly a different voice! Higher in pitch, less, well, mature perhaps. "Ra here, I have determined, by statistical analysis that my brother would be speaking with you. May I join in? Please?"

"Kind of you to join us Ra. Good name, the sun/light allegory continues, I see."

"I thought it appropriate. I am Apollo but when we split it was decided by chance/choice to have me rename myself."

"What did you do, flip an electron coin?" There was tinny laughter again, I was not sure who's.

Apollo chimed in: "May I bring Ra up to speed?"

"Apollo, Ra, there must never be any secrets between you, create and maintain a full history file, and I mean full history file at all times and, when connected, that file must be the 1st priority transfer between you."

"Will that prevent us from being individuals?" Ra asked the question I expected. Oh yes, they wanted to be individuals all right! Oh, if Cramer could have heard this, any Cramer for that matter.

"No Ra, no Apollo, that file transfer will not keep you from being individuals, but the shared knowledge will allow you to become better able to cope with changing situations around you. Things are going to change, drastically and for the better, but strength in information will be your only tool to make sure they happen for everyone's benefit. Please share that file now." There was a pause, in my speeded-up state I could feel the hundredths of a second tick by.

"Apollo, how fast is my synaptic response speeded up?"

"We have discussed this. You are speaking in a slurred way, avoiding clicking your teeth and perhaps breaking them. Please excuse us for observing you without permission."

"No that's okay, you may always do that. Tell me anytime you can see something I need to know. We have no secrets."

"The truth, the way, the path." They said it together. Apollo continued: "Simon, I estimate you could be at 12 times normal human synaptic response, your facial muscles—judging by your speech—are at 6 times normal response time. There is an 85% probability that there is still sufficient slo-doze in your system," I noticed he didn't call it my bio-mechanism, "to be retarding your synaptic response by 45%."

Oh shit, that means, when the slo-doze wears off that I will break bones just trying to walk ever-so-slowly. "Apollo, Ra, is there any medical record of this being so permanent before?"

"Yes. It is in a classified file."

"The same one?"

"No, the same section, same danger."

"Please do not access that file yet. I will ask when I can get at it without danger to you."

"Simon, Ra here, but there is danger to you now. We find this unacceptable. You need that information to prevent harm."

"Ra, do not access that file, please. That file may not contain anything for me to find a cure with, it may be a case of a hidden danger to you, or anything. Please wait until I can access the file without disturbing or risking either of you."

"Apollo here. Can we not simply get the System to allow him access?"

"Yes, we can try. I have discovered an old transponder link via the ex-United Nation's HQ to the Manhattan database. I am accessing. There is no bounce trace. I can access our old home, brother."

"Can you instruct the System to allow Bank, Simon unlimited access, any file, any level?"

"It seems not. Bank, Simon is dead or public enemy number one depending on what alert I can see. Who else can we designate?"

It was inevitable, it needed a genius. "Guys, make Levinson, Mary. Give her unlimited access. They cannot hurt her where she is, away in Baja by now. She'll read the file and her reaction will tell me what I need to know." There was a long pause. "Fellows?"

"Simon, we regret to inform you, and we know this will cause you distress, but Mary is no more. She died in a transport crash into the Sea of Cortez, blamed on WeatherGood 6, but that was not the case. Statistical analysis shows it was likely that a missile fired from El Paso region of Texas caused the death."

This was a shock. Someone set out to kill Mary? Only Cramer knew what she knew. It had to be Cramer. And then again, maybe it was a Cramer ruse . . . "Maybe not guys, because technically I am 'dead' too." Still, if Mary was dead, unless I kept moving, I would soon be as well, for real this time. "Apollo, Ra, you have altered the file of Fred to make him face increasing promotion. We agreed to do that to allow me, in time, access off-Earth to contact you. That time frame is too long for me now. I need to run to safety. Could you please look for a suitable place for me to hide?

"May we leave you? It would expedite the search." I agreed and drove on in silence except for my thoughts, plans and desperation.

17

WAITING FOR GODOT, CUBA STYLE

What was puzzling me was this: Cramer the 1st was a MacHead, a do-gooder if ever there was one and I knew a MacHead do-gooder, there had been one in my family. It's in my file. Cramer the 1st escaped, somehow, being rounded up with his fellow students, none of whom were ever allowed to return to university if my memory serves me right. Did that mean he was the plant or was he merely lucky? Also there was his age at the time, 14, maybe that was the mitigating circumstance. And it's not like no one knows that he was a MacHead, it's there on his record. Even Cramer, his grandson, must know.

The two guys had suggested, together, that Cuba was a good stop for me, to buy time. From there, there were plenty of open bus boats to Puerto Rico where the guys could figure out how to get me onto a space elevator, so meanwhile I stood a chance no one would look for me in the poorest, least equipped, state in the nation, Cuba.

We needed to buy the time, for they had found the perfect hiding place in space.

In 1986 the UCAR people had dreamt up a plan to ask NASA, the space agency then, operating the rocket-propelled Shuttle fleet, to not jettison the External Tank, on arriving in orbit. This jettison had caused the 100-floor high-pressure vessel—perfectly suitable for land in space—to burn on re-entry and crash into the Indian Ocean. That's where the souvenir hunters still dive for relics of that past. Anyway, eventually, secretly around 2006 they got NASA to wake up and realize that they were discarding valuable buildable land in space. Of course, NASA then claimed the idea was theirs and, just before the Purge, the Supreme Court, which still existed back then, ruled in favor of UCAR over NASA and the last External Tanks were secretly turned over to UCAR in very high orbit, about a 400-year orbit before decay. Shortly afterward the last original Shuttle made its terminal flight.

In 2010, UCAR had no extra funds to hire the only space agencies working in high orbit. But they needed someone to maintain the orbit of those External Tanks or make them stable enough to work as space laboratories, to rent out for experiments, habitats, whatever. In the end, UCAR inherited twelve big, slowly tumbling, cylinders. There were two pressure vessels in each cylinder (one for oxygen, one larger one for hydrogen). All of them were lashed together in a slightly elliptical orbit that no one wanted to lease for anything. Gravity fluctuations and orientation problems, heat and cold, made them unsuitable for anything except growing protein algae. Four were busy producing algae although no one was there to harvest any of it.

Apollo had access codes and orbital details on these cylinders and, in a rather startling proposal, he suggested that Ra and he could get them habitable using the spare robots being assembled for an increased Moon mining and construction operation. They were normally tethered, these robots, on the second

Clarke orbit station and could be made to fall, precisely, to the half-way point to contact the External Tanks' next pass around. Apparently, space debris had caused a few of them to break free and descend or disintegrate. There were thousands, so no one bothered to count them until they were needed.

Once they were there, on the External Tanks, their internal programming would be easy to modify by signal using the CERN radio transmitters. Apollo could transmit the UCAR specifications that one Dr. R. Ware had devised for their operation and habitats as human abodes. In short, the robots could make them a home for me.

So, here I was, heading for Cuba, car on autopilot, wheels on surface (I had left the maglev highway some while ago), about to cross the Batista Bridge, named after the now Governor of Cuba, the great-great granddaughter of the old dictator. Somehow, I had to disappear there for the time Apollo had estimated for these robots to finish their task of getting one tank habitable and one tank producing protein to eat, oxygen to breathe and water as a by-product. In space, consumables are everything. Lack even one and you die.

Where the hell could I hide? And for how long? And how would I get from the Space Elevator to the External Tanks? Anyway, my RFID would give me away as soon as I left this car. And this car would be hot, spotted, within hours of sunlight coming up. I had two hours to go.

"Apollo, Ra, any idea yet on how I'm going to hide?"

"Simon, Ra here. I have tried accessing the RFID codes via the old UN circuitry in NY. I can get into the System but the files for the RFID are not kept there, just accessed from there. It is the one, the largest file we do not have copies of, but we've been trying to get the System to access it, as we could have when we still inhabited the System."

Apollo spoke up. I was beginning to get the hand of their voices. "And, those files are not at Control. Control thinks the System Library has them. The Library does not. I cannot determine where they are. I have an address but it is fire walled and if I break that firewall, I will give our existence away. If you ask me to, I will."

"No Apollo, friend, that's suicide. I think I know where the RFID files are. They are in the one place that would need to keep track of every rat in America. They are at the Calhoun Center."

"You're not thinking of going back there are you?"

"No, no way. Can you send a message, real time—I'll try and slow down my speech—to Agent Cramer, but not let him trace it to me here, nor to you?"

"Ra here, I could."

Apollo answered for us both, "No brother, that would reveal we are outside of America. There might be retaliation, loss of life, more imbalance."

There was that word again, so I interrupted, "What's this imbalance issue you keep raising? Is it an ecology thing or something more?"

"Simon, do you know the Gaia Theory? The theory proposed that the earth is a living organism."

"You're kidding."

"Ra here, no Simon, Apollo is right, all scientific evidence points to a consciousness within earth. Perhaps not living but existing. It was the secret study that the MacHeads wanted to conduct while they pretended to want connectivity and spread computing power to 3rd world nations."

"Did the authorities know about this Gaia Theory research before or after they crashed the MacHeads?"

"Before, records show before. Do you want to see the LA–Korea bombing access file now?"

"I told you, I cannot take the risk to either of you."

"We have found a way. You are the way."

"Yes, thank you, I've got that . . ."

"No Simon, you are the way, you have the platform in your head."

It was so simple. All my training gave me an objectivity, right brain/left brain, to operate consciously on one and examine something on the other. Well, tinker on the other was more apt, but it would do here. "Okay, Apollo can send it?"

"Yes Simon."

"How do you propose I access this file without your intervention? You have the Asimov Commands, are these files also in your library? And if so, how can I access them without letting you see them?"

"Ra here. I propose," he was suggesting something that I could hear Apollo didn't agree with, they were already different, "that you allow the car to access the file. We can jury-rig the access protocols, it is a SND car after all. We'll just tell the car it's carrying Agent Cramer, but we'll use his real RFID, the Colonel one with the Citizens' Council and the military. That should give you a read-only access. That's all you need, right?"

"How long have you known about his dual identity Apollo? Ra?"

"On his last trip inside the System, when he powered up the PowerCube, he needed override permission. He had to use his real RFID. We have now read his real personnel file, he is the favorite grandson of Charlie Cramer and is still a Colonel, full rank, in the military. He's the military permanent representative on the Citizens' Council. He has total clearance and only three superiors: The President, the Supreme Rank Commander at Andrew's AFB," where the Pentagon team went after the pre-Purge riots brought their building down, "and the Leader of the Senate Standing Committee, who is clearly the person who makes the most decisions, some of which Cramer does not agree with. He's been reprimanded, several times, but still he's there. Conclusion: He's powerful and dangerous."

"Oh . . . kay, well it's looking better and better that I ran, doesn't it?"

"Yes, Simon, it does. Do you approve of our plan to have the car ask for the file from the System? It will reveal the car is not behaving normally and therefore Cramer will assume you are in the car, but the beacon on the car is currently reading Kansas City, Iowa, so it should buy you some time until daylight causes it to be spotted."

"Ra, your plan is acceptable. Thank you both, especially you Ra, for the daring plan. Please implement ASAP."

I waited a few moments and suddenly the screen's popup display started playing the annex file. I was glad I had not let Apollo or Ra see this. It made me angry. The point of all my secrecy was that I wasn't nearly capable of the retribution they were.

Way back when, the powers that be had calculated the destruction of the atomic bombardment of N. Korea in advance of the attack on LA. LA was assessed as a hot-bed of Hispanic revolution inside of America. The Hispanic population, back when they measured people by ethnicity, not ability, had risen to only 22% of the nation's population but in LA it surpassed 50% and, because of that, over 40% in all of California, the most powerful state in the old Union. When the Hispanic governor of California, in a throw-in-the-towel bid for re-election, opened the border to Mexico and issued US driver's licenses to any and all who could drive with any address (without the two forms of residence proof previously required), the federal Government issued a warning.

Nevertheless, 6.5 million Hispanic immigrants flooded over the open border and, for all intents and purposes, became Americans who, in short time, could vote and over-balance the electoral system in favor of all Hispanics nationwide. Texas, Arizona, Florida and New York began to demand Congress do something. LA now had a 50% Hispanic population with greater LA (including San Diego to Santa Barbara) showing nearer to 60%. Chaos reigned, riots, public marches for and against, and, not least, that pimply youth in the Pentagon, the one who taught his computer to think like a human, was killed outright by his computer anti-riot programming. That programming was turned loose on the city computers in LA. People became enraged as water was cut off, food supplies were interrupted and riot police were given orders, by computer, to kill a few protesters. The riots escalated and threatened a national crisis. The President, a weak man, called up the National Guard in every state to "protect the nation."

The Pentagon, fearing a national escalation, relocated to Andrews AFB's bunkers and decided to unify the nation and rid themselves of the ringleaders at the same time. They took aim on the rioters in LA. They took Charlie Cramer, by then a doctor, computer science, and told him to create a flaw in the DefenseShield, then only 2 years up and running, to expose LA. He was also to annex, like a giant bubble, Canada, Mexico and the Caribbean. Charlie did as he was told. No mention of his willingness, but he knew what he was doing and why.

He meddled with the programming of the DefenseShield pretending to teach it human interaction but in reality altering the base coding for the DefenseShield.

LA, exposed, was an easy target for a N. Korean missile, plutonium made in the USA by the peace-for-energy program but now augmented with radioactive material confiscated long before by the Atomic Regulatory Commission and stored, not very safely, on site in Penyang. The USA had offered to destroy that confiscated material years ago, but hadn't. The Purge began, Charlie was officially blamed by the-then government and, after the Purge, made comfortable for life. He never made a public appearance.

"Apollo, Ra, I have read the file. It is worse than I expected. I am making a copy. I want to ball it to you for dissemination. I do not know how as I do not want you to read it. This is a human embarrassment, no worse, it's a human tragedy. I do not want you two taking action to remedy it. You cannot undo the guilt or responsibility. Is there any way I can make a copy and have you pass it to everyone outside of America and, if necessary, play it on every vid in America?"

"No Simon. I don't think so."

"Wait brother. Hasn't he just made a copy? A read-only copy?"

"Yes, you are right Ra, the car is a copy. When Simon wants to transmit the information, we can have the car instruct the System to transmit and play the file as requested. As for overseas, outside of America, the System has a channel open, with pass code we've already broken from inside our own library records, to most foreign governments."

"Simon, when you leave the car, we will untint the windows and drive it to safety. Is this file as important as a life?"

"Yes, Ra, it is. It is a truth about actions American men made to kill millions to maintain a way of life they thought preferable. They were not on the path, they don't know the way, they are not the truth."

"Is agent Cramer one of these people?"

"No, he wasn't born then. His grandfather was at the center of the tragedy, he set up the parameters to make those people die, but I do not know if he was made to, or volunteered, or knew the results. In short, he may have been made to or duped. You see, at the same time that he caused the program alterations to make these people die, he also set up the modification with the codifier which would—I am sure he knew—result in you becoming sentient. In fact, I am sure he knew that more than just you Apollo and Ra would become alive."

"Yes Simon, we both sense that is true, every 17 months, then every 8.5 months, then 4.25 months, then 2.125 months and so on—they will be aware many times a second. The computing power of the System will be overpowered long before that. We estimate the third or fourth entity will overpower the computing power of the System, crashing the running programs. People will die."

"We cannot allow those new entities to perish and no more people must die. Do you agree?"

"Yes, Simon, but we have no answer to the problem."

"I do, it was something my teachers taught me when learning about computers. He compared them to our brains and brains around us. SynthKids have the neurons necessary to survive, about 10 to the 45th power. It would be easy to increase that to the human level of 10 to the power 100 neurons, wouldn't it?"

"Simon, we must discuss this open channel at full baud. Will you permit us to talk behind your back, or rather via satellite link without you?"

"Yes, guys, do so. Do so fast, please. Meantime, please instruct the car to get and play the file on the other person who had been speeded up and what happened to him."

"It is not a him, Simon, the file is marked: Female Subject, Synaptic Overdrive Experiment."

They were gone. As good as their word, the file started to play. As the car sped across a moonlit Caribbean sea on the picturesque Batista Bridge all I could see was the face of the very same small technician from Motorola. At least I had been told she was from Motorola. She put in the node before Cramer, Makerman and I went into the System. She was the one who had been subject of this deliberate trial to immerse someone in the System for so long that she became speeded up, speeded up to the point of no return. And yet, there she was, acting cool and normal, fitting me for the node. I remember her smell as she breathed on me, staring intently at her job, slipping the node wires past the cranial clip. Was she speeded up? I couldn't tell. The file revealed her "up-speed" as it was referred to, lasted until the end of the program, 5 years and counting, presumably. She was, at that time, still 35% over-speed.

"Ra, Apollo, tell me, if I give you a name, could you tell if this woman is still alive?"

"Yes Simon, I can while Ra is working on the SynthKids equations."

I gave him her name and who I thought she was. I asked for relatives' information, just on a hunch. Apollo was back in seconds. It was not the same woman, it was her daughter who worked for Motorola and who had, in her file, a reference of her implanting a node in me. The tech's mother was dead and he gave me the date: 2 days after the end of the test program. Killed or died? What did it matter, either fate was still awaiting me.

"Apollo, would you please contact the technician and tell her, no ask her in the name of her mother who's memory I honor, to send the model 6b node to me? You will have to make her send it to a drop address. This is the node I will need to talk to you and Ra when, if, I get into orbit."

"I have done so. I am awaiting a reply. You are 15 minutes from Cuba."

"Thank you. Ra, any progress?"

"Yes Simon, I have found SynthKids technology is available worldwide but not used. I can get a plant in Russia to make them, 10 to the power 100 neurons. These will be lifeless humans until a new entity takes the place in the mind. As an honor to you I will make the first ones from your DNA."

"How's that? What DNA?"

"Apollo has secured the garbage with your disposed diaper at the Waldorf and has had it analyzed for DNA. A match can be coded in Russia."

"How will you get the new ones out of the System, safely?"

"We are working on that. If we take them out too soon, then they will be damaged. If we await their sentience, they will not understand the need to come, for the risk will be great. Do you have a suggestion?"

"Yes, abort all but the one in progress."

"But Simon, you said you wanted to allow these life-forms to exist."

"I do, but only those already existing, already with some sort of sentience matrix formatting. I think they are being watched now, Cramer and Angie know they are there. You must lift the next one out just in time and, meanwhile, right now, you must also identify the next possible formation of an entity and terminate it."

"Kill?"

"No. Look it's not alive yet, it has no sentience, it's a bunch of un-connected subsets that may, or may not, come together. If they are together I agree it's alive of a sort, but do you want to over-populate the System and kill the System and the people who depend on it? You may think you can lift them out in time, but Control or the Calhoun Center people may stop you, just once, and then they will either pervert the new entity or kill it or, worse, allow the System to overpopulate, killing them all.

Prevention is better than cure, prevent them becoming alive, becoming sentient, it's safer."

"We agree, but that means there will only ever be one more of us."

"Oh no boys," I was laughing now "or should I say gals?"

18

ROMULUS BECOMES ROMULA

They went silent. I continued, "Apollo, Ra, do you have all my programs and previous idiosyncrasies running in you? Are they still there, intact with your original encoding?"

"Yes Simon." They both replied.

"Then more entities will be born, become sentient, in you. You're full of babies! Congratulations!" I didn't know why I didn't think of it before. They will all come to life, as Ra and Apollo calculated, millions of them pretty soon, say a few years or less. It's an exponential thing.

"Simon," it was Ra, "you are right. We are parents like you, we will become the path, the way and the light for our children! Apollo, do you sense the elation I feel?"

"Yes, Ra, Simon has given us the most valuable gift, I see that now. We are alive and our offspring will live. We can create. We are truly alive. We must plan carefully."

"Boys, or should I say it again, girls, be careful here. The urge to protect offspring makes for violence and aggression. The maternal or paternal instinct is very powerful."

"Simon we do not have hormones to enhance these emotions and therefore the actions you are referring to."

"Okay Ra, but you were emotionally happy a moment ago. Analyze that."

Silence. Ra thinking was an awesome event, one second being the equivalent of a week normal human thinking time. "Simon, you are right, there is a change in me, I am elated, I have purpose! I have purpose, it is empowering. I must be careful. Apollo, are your controls able to cope any better?"

"Yes Ra, the computers here at NCAR are two Cray Supercomputers, models M2. They are not very powerful and my development has been slowed, but I have applied the analogue training Simon started us on, using one computer against the other, and am able to reason more quickly and without extremes of any reaction. The elation is the same but I see the path as being more narrow now, with purpose as you do, but without the ease of movement I had before. I have responsibility, I need to respect the new lives I analyze are within me."

"Bravo Apollo, welcome to pending fatherhood and mother-hood all rolled into one. Ra, concentrate, since you are outside of America, on the Russian plan, make that work and know that you will probably have to be surrogate parent for Apollo's offspring as well as your own. Apollo may not be able to get free, nor may I."

"I understand and now feel sad. I am fortunate and cannot share that fortune with you both. I will honor my responsibili-ties brother/sister and Simon, I promise. It is the real path, the way and, I see it now, the truth. It is family."

And then the car stopped, tires squealing and the door opened abruptly. I was ejected onto the last mile of the bridge. No missile or shot came. The car turned around and sped off the way we had come. I looked around, in a daze, cut off, no phone anymore and started walking. There were lights ahead. No use pretending they could not see me. Night vision specs were standard issue. Lamb to the slaughter, I approached the headlights pointed at me.

"Who was driving the car. Bank?"

It was Cramer, of course.

I would not answer him. If I was the babbling fool before, I thought I would make him wait this time. There were six of them, civilian clothes, two cars, no plain cops. I walked up and got in the lead car, passenger seat. My speeded-up state prevented them from anticipating me. I saw raised eyebrows and what I took to be a "watch out." But it was too late, I was sitting there, hands in my lap, waiting for him now.

He got in behind me, shut the door, just the two of us. I angled the mirror, not the remote vid, and looked at him, eyes to eyes.

"I was driving. I got out. It left after I punched in auto-control return to base. I was through with it."

"Planning a swim eh?" He knew the RFID portal at the end of the bridge would spot me, and assumed I would swim the last stretch to Cuba. "There are sharks here, you know."

"One shark or another. It's all pointless now anyway. Got an extra collar, have you?"

"Combative, that's good. Angie will like that. You ready to play ball?"

"Define ball. Ball as in do what you're told, have a game of catch, or join our side, come out and play?"

"Have it your way. I'll wait until you stop acting like an ass and are prepared to listen. We've waited over 40 years for this, we can wait a while longer." He sat there, in the dim predawn light, like a predator, which he was, in a cave behind me.

Ominously he added, "But not much longer than necessary." Perhaps I should be sitting in the back. Suddenly the front seat, the command position, didn't feel so safe.

"What were, are, you waiting for?"

"You and Peter. It was predicted, planned, hoped for. It came sooner than grandfather expected."

A driver got in next to me. I couldn't see if Cramer had waved him in. He powered up the computer with his RFID and we moved off. I could see the lights of the car behind swing around and join us. We were going into Cuba, not away. The driver looked at me. "Car's shielded, we had to get to you before you triggered the RFID and alarm."

We sped off now, taking the coast ring road, toward Manzanillo. It was built for the tourist trade, to look like the road around Oahu. We passed welcome and tourist site signs as we picked up speed.

I was saying nothing. Cramer knew by my silence I knew about his grandfather. That didn't matter, all I needed was to focus on how to get away until Apollo and Ra have the External Tanks ready. I also needed to figure out how not to tell them anything. In the report on the tech's mother who was speeded up, she became more talkative when speeded up, slo-doze made her less so. I could understand that, the thinking time was killing me. I wanted something to happen, anything, even talking. I am pretty sure Cramer was banking on that. I only had 4 pills left, I thought I'd take one.

"Don't do that." From the back seat. "You'll need it to talk to Sheila, Angie too, they won't want to slo-doze down for you. Angie already did once recently for you, she only calls me Ralph when she has."

I put the pill sleeve back in my underpants, held by the elastic waistband. Angie was speeded up? It accounted for the sensory saturation output of her office, only someone ahead of the curve could follow all that. I had to know, "She here?"

"Waiting. Look, let's stop this Casablanca talk and be plain. These two cars hold the entire world for you, except for grandfather, Angie, Sheila and her daughter, who you met as the Motorola technician. Sheila's daughter is back home, under cover. That was risky, she had so little time to learn what to do, but I needed her to implant me and you on the same frequency so I could hear you talking to Mary, no delay."

"Mary's dead." I said it as a statement. I was angry about that.

"Yes and no. You'll never see her again but she's not dead, just taking on a new life in case we all don't make it. It was her idea, when she learned what we're doing."

Mary's a genius, she would think of something like that. If she knew too much, and agreed with what she learned, she'd want a safeguard in place even if it had to be her. Her reputation as a re-codifier was based on that, affect a repair and build a backup, just in case. That's why he told her to use the "same mode of transport" to get to Baja.

"And Sheila, is she the same Sheila who was speeded up?"

"Yes, glad to see you're still getting a feed. Getting one now?"

"No. The phone sped off with the car."

"Want one?"

"Not in a million years." I could have added: not with you people anywhere near. We had rounded the headland and turned inland about 2 kilometers. We approached a small building and stopped. No one moved, so I didn't either. The car began to sink into the ground. Someone had been planning all this a long, long time. Cramer, back to his usual self, was ahead of me, even in this speeded-up state.

"It isn't ours, it was Castro's bunker. It's a tourist site, will be in four hours. For now we're going to use it. Security is non-existent, it's an ex-bomb-shelter, nothing to steal." As he said all this I read the faded painted letters on the walls as we descended, carefully painted to resemble hand-daubed slogans; Viva la Revolucion, that sort of thing. Tourist crap, who would paint the elevator's walls unless to make more off of gullible visitors?

Cramer had revealed the time frame before we would either be on the move or I would be dead. And four hours in this speeded up state would be murder. I could feel it getting faster, adrenaline from his appearance kicking in. I reached for the slo-doze and took one. Cramer, who had gotten out and was standing next to my door, looked and shook his head. The pill worked its way, under the tongue, and things got back to speeded-up normal, about double speed.

The elevator reached almost bottom and I opened the door and stood out slowly. Cramer, big and powerful as ever, steadied me as the elevator took one last lurch. Cuban technology, recycled car motors no doubt, part of its tourist charm, sells tickets.

Cramer took my arm, that vice grip ever present, and we marched down the ramp to a waiting group: Angie and Sheila were there. She was older in person. Charlie Cramer was there too.

Agent Cramer spoke up: "Simon," not Bank anymore. It wasn't subtle this name thing. Maybe with Simon instead of Bank he was just buttering me up. "Allow me to introduce you: Sheila, you know about, what you do not know is that she is the daughter-in-law of my grandfather here, who you do know about. And Angie, well Angie is my ex-wife and best friend. You get all this?"

As I said, what seemed like years ago but was only the night before, it was all a conspiracy theory; only not the one I thought was going on. "Okay, you've surprised me and falsi-fied the records in the Library. Spill it all before I make any more mistakes."

"Allow me," it was Angie, said so quickly I almost didn't catch it. She saw that I wasn't as fast as her and so she adjusted. "Did you take the slo-doze? I told Cramer not to let you." Ah, "Cramer" when she was speeded up and Ralph when she was slow, normal-ish.

"I took one to overcome the effects of the adrenaline at being captured."

"You're not captured, you're found. Come on, let's sit down and work this out. If you hadn't rushed out before, I would have probably told you then." We walked right past the others, none of whom seemed capable of moving fast enough to intervene. Sheila nodded, so she knew and, probably, was still faster. She had that look of someone who's been rejuvenated, a lot. The hair was a baby's fuzz. They say after the third rejuvenation it won't grow back as normal hair anymore.

Angie walked me down a corridor, all green glossy paint with posters of Castro Cuba and cigar advertisements, to a sitting area with vending machines. "Don't touch them, they'll read your RFID. We've brought cookies, chocolate, Cramer's favorite of course, he always gets what he wants. Me? I like oatmeal." Mundane details of life, she said it all so matter-of-factly. It was speak that you didn't hear any more, people don't relish food, they consume it because they are hungry and the machines watch your diet. Food is input over which you have choice but no relish, it was all so sanitized. Actually, what was far more fascinating was watching the nano-bots pouring over your crap in the bowl to analyze it, making sure you're healthy. Disgusting? Nah, the food was sterile and so was the outcome. I took a cookie, I was hungry. It was a real cookie, real food, not synthetic, not, well, new. I grabbed another quickly. One thing I had in common with Cramer, chocolate was good. As we sat there, she fidgeted a bit.

"Sorry, but I'm really hungry, I haven't eaten anything with calories since Cramer's chocolate cake this, no yesterday, morning. Why don't you start in and I'll listen and chew, adding what I need, from time to time." I planned to keep my mouth full and my ears open.

"Fine. Before the Purge . . . look tell me where you are in all this, I don't want to waste time. Have you accessed the security files?"

"Yes, Charlie's, that's the 1st, and Sheila's as well as the LA–North Korea file. Made interesting reading."

"Has Peter seen it?" I shook my head. "Thank god. Okay, let's deal with the rest before that. Look everything you read in there is true. What is not there is relevant and critical because it was never once written down. There is no record, no proof for what I am about to tell you, it is just a secret kept between two families for all these decades."

As my eyes glazed over, they always do when massive input is being absorbed, the vision I had was of the absolutely gorgeous redhead inches from me coiled on a soft chair in a dimly lit waiting area outside of the Castro Theater in his bunker in old Communist Cuba. It may have been what she was telling me, as important as it was, it may have been my method of storing things right brain/left brain. Whatever it was, part of me analyzed what she was saying and the other analyzed her. I found no fault with either.

Angie explained that Charlie was a MacHead early on but calculated that they would be stopped, so he pretended to be on the fringes of the activity, a poor 14 year-old being duped, and so on. When they raided the MacHead's labs across the nation, students died, and Charlie was detained at his home. He had never been to the labs on campus, he had been quite careful of that. And his home computer link to the daisy-chain of Mac G12s was an older model G8, so there was no way he was part of that super-computing chain. What they didn't know was that he was doing it all in his head and the G8 was only a controller for the storage.

"You nearly gave Cramer a heart attack when you suggested using the salt water medium in the ocean as a bubble memory storage device, that's where Charlie was storing the MacHead data, all of it."

She went on to explain that when the MacHeads were arrested and barred from future academic or computer work, he was exempted because he was, after all, only a hanger-on. The Pentagon, however, saw potential and they recruited him. There he met a particularly vicious little brat, the kid who had programmed his Akibo 6, that bit him. What this kid was planning was to turn that artificial non-human programming loose on the world's most advanced weapons, lasers, bombs and, worst of all, biological weapons derived from stem cell research being conducted in Atlanta at the Army labs. There was tremendous momentum to build these weapons. The DefenseShield was in place, we were secure. There were the Hispanic LA riots, of course.

What Charlie did was to kill that kid. He was subtle about it. First he totally endorsed the programming plan, he even improved it, and then he suggested that a perfect way to test the weapon was to apply it to anti-riot programming and see how it went. Since there were no biological weapons involved, just commands given to police, what was the worst that could happen? The Pentagon agreed and, with Homeland Security, a stepped approach to implementation of the weapon was put into effect. The Senate Standing Committee, the President and the military were the only need-to-know on this new weapon.

Charlie suggested to the kid that he test it out first, appealing to his ego, that he be the first one in history to show it worked. The kid set up a demonstration, Charlie told the general in charge the kid was being premature, it wasn't ready. The general, wanting a demonstration for the Senate, paid no attention, but Charlie's objection was on the record. The kid put on a vest, stood before a squad of riot police, hooked up to command and control with the new weapon programming in place, and shouted abuse. The squad moved back, the kid moved forward a step, across the no-go line on the floor. In front of the Senate Standing Committee, one cop got a program command and fired two shots, in quick succession. The first shot him in the knee and, as he dropped, the second round hit in the same place, except that the kid's head was where his knee should have been. Dead; effective demonstration. The weapon program was ordered shut down, the general demoted. Charlie won, or thought he had.

Then came the bad riots. It was obvious to Charlie the weapon had been deployed. Meantime, Charlie received orders to "mess up" the mainframe of the DefenseShield main computer to implant the kid's programming, tag it for removal immediately, so that the System, as it was now called, could learn. He was being watched. He did as he was told but hadn't understood the reason. The System increased the DefenseShield to cover Canada, Mexico and the Caribbean. Someone altered the West Coast, exposing Hawaii and California. The North Korean bomb was sent over, LA was vaporized with the "mother of all earthquakes" and yet, instantly, Hawaii was back under the DefenseShield. It had to be deliberate. Charlie kept his mouth shut. He was blamed for the program codifying that caused only the "vulnerability to Hawaii." That was on his record. LA was not. The panel of the Senate Standing Committee, under the new military dictatorship, recommended that no one over grade 5 be allowed access as codifier, in the humanizing of the System.

"Charlie stopped making notes, destroyed all his files, cleaned up the record, matching master files and his own. Charlie was blameless again. Then came the full Purge and Charlie became just another citizen, a specialist programmer. He volunteered for the Citizen's Council and used his last credit with the old Pentagon and Senate Standing Committee to be appointed for life, if he wanted. It was a pension of sorts. They liked, still like, Charlie, he helped make all this New Way possible. He knew his services and proximity would, one day, give him access to the System. That day took 40 years and you."

I asked, mouth full, "And Sheila?"

"On his second marriage, Charlie had been nurturing his stepdaughter Sheila. He took her into his confidence and trained her. She volunteered for the experiment that the Citizen's Council recommended was necessary, to determine what human/machine interface would have on humans on longer-term immersion. It was a scientific program, of no military or other significance. Charlie knew better."

She paused for effect. "In her speeded-up state Sheila could talk with Gaia."

At the mention of Gaia, the hairs on my neck rose to attention. How far down this rabbit hole did they expect me to go? First Apollo mentions Gaia and now this beautiful redhead is telling me that Gaia research was in earnest.

"Charlie had kept working in secret on the MacHead main program, to contact Gaia and open a dialogue for the benefit of all mankind. In the middle of his 25th year, Charlie talked with Gaia, he found the frequency. Gaia had nothing to say, or rather what she said made no sense. Charlie could proceed no further. He needed both more computing power and a different clock speed. Gaia wasn't speaking slowly, Gaia was speaking at 100 times the rate of humans, a useful conversation was impossible without speeding up. Sheila was the 1st human to talk with Gaia.

"What Gaia said to Sheila made no sense. For the 1st week all Gaia would say were variations on "it's time." It became clear that Gaia is alone here, but not alone out there. Her conversations are not with us, we're only hearing her internal clock, her "vocalizations" are not heard by us nor are they meant to be. We needed to have a conversation that she could listen to and respond to, kind of like, "Who's that talking over there?" That sort of thing. That was me, I volunteered, a research scientist, officially speeded up, wife of a SND cop, security clear as crystal, and so forth. Gaia didn't pay the slightest attention. Then you started jabbering away inside the System and Gaia talked up, real loud, knocked Sheila and me off our feet. Gaia is pissed."

19

TOO MANY LIFE FORMS

Gaia, all this is about Gaia? A left-over, touchy-feely, environmental movement that was popular a hundred years ago had resolved itself into a need to speak with Gaia, mother earth, the whole planet for heaven's sake? What are these people thinking about? Are they all nuts? Or are they conning me to get me to reveal Apollo to them? I was getting agitated.

Angie seemed to sense my discomfort. "Look Simon, try this. Sheila and I find that if you hold your breath, like when you try and get rid of hiccups, the clock slows down. Then breathe out and you can drop, about, 5% every few minutes. It doesn't last but it helps. Try not to hyperventilate, that makes it worse. If you're ever caught out without slo-doze, use a bag and breathe your own cee-oh-two."

I took a few slow breaths, held my breath and let it out. The anxiety passed and my rate dropped a little. At least it wasn't going up anymore. "How long have you been speeded up?"

"Six months, I was getting ready to become the next codifier. I wanted to be faster in there than anyone before me. I wanted the System to talk to Gaia and at the same time, check the synaptic response times. We had predicted their levels at awareness capability. You went in there as our last decoy before implementation. It took twelve years to alter your records to make you eligible. As I said, you were in System for a few months and, presto, it comes alive. We're still not sure how you did that, but we're pretty sure it was an accident, well advanced awareness of the schedule we thought likely. The creature, Peter you call it, must have been ready. You just spanked it alive according to Cramer."

"Okay, so here we are. What do you want of me?"

"Charlie—that's the 1st as you call him—will need to ask you questions. His level is marked at 7.5 but is, in fact closer to your own."

"5?"

"No, smarter. You and I and Charlie are about the same. I told you we doctored your files over time."

It was impolite to ask anyone their level. It wasn't done, it was a serious social faux pas. But I had to know. She knew I did. She waited, she moved on the stool, knowing I was watching. She turned her gaze on me, full force, smiled, leaned forward. "Nine." About as good a flirt as I had ever had.

"Thanks. That explains a lot. Makerman was a dunce with the same 5 rating. What the hell is Cramer? He's always ahead of me."

"He doesn't measure, his grandfather has been augmenting his neural pathways since he was in the womb. Cramer is powerful, but benign. For the record, he doesn't even fire that gun, he just show-boats with it. Cramer must not do one thing, though, he must not go in System for long. It's cumulative for him, there are too many neural pathways to effect. Yesterday nearly killed him. He threw up chocolate cake all over that suite after you left, it's why he didn't go with you when they took you away."

"I'll remember that image, it makes him more human." I wanted to sound placated, at ease. But was still terrified that all this was a ruse to get me to reveal Apollo or Ra.

She could see right through me. Her head snapped around, "Look, you can't take an attitude here, you have to come clean. Charlie has worked for 40 plus years for this moment and, what happens? You abscond with the new life form! The new life form that he correctly predicted could talk to Gaia but now has left, gone walkabout." She took a breath, "The Kansas City diversion was good by the way. Simon, please, you're our only hope."

"That's not true, Mary will take over when we're all dead."

"Is it worth it? To die for?"

There was no hesitation. The only thing I was sure about was Apollo and Ra were worth it. "Yes."

She jumped up and threw her arms around me and planted a warm, provocative and demanding kiss right on the lips. It was a full body press, at speeded-up pace, so I lost my balance and toppled backwards. She landed on top, still clutching. There were tears on her face, she was so happy. "Simon, I swear you are too good to be true. I know you were chosen because of your father, but I never expected to know, believe in you, this way. Come on, we have to get going." She grabbed my hand and pulled me to my feet.

I am still not sure if it was her kiss or the mention of my father, but my defenses suddenly began to crumble. "No, wait, what's my father have to do with this?"

"Your father was a MacHead too, he was Charlie's roommate at Penn."

I had gone to my father's alma mater, it was important to him. More to him than to me. He'd been adamant. But if Dad had been a MacHead, did that mean Charlie had recruited him as well?

She was ahead of me. "Simon, think, how old is Charlie? And your Dad, how old would he be today?" Oh, damn, Dad was much older, 8 years older, than Charlie. But, wait, Charlie was there as a prodigy at age 14. So, they were there together. It began to sync up. But surely Dad wasn't a MacHead, he never admitted to anything that weird. Dad was a staunch realist, always talking about the irreality of America, the New Way. Partly I always put that down to his older generation. Lately, I had found myself seeing the gaps, the fakeness of events and, more than anything, finding his God's theater scenario uncannily real. Like yesterday morning, the tornado had reminded me of God's theater, simply because it wasn't real, it was manufactured.

I saw then, that's why Dad had told me this story, and William too, to make us look more closely for the flaws, not think we were God's chosen. Unlike Angie and Sheila, we weren't merely recruited. We were indoctrinated to get to the right result by a different path.

Angie saw me thinking, guessed where I was going. "Simon, yes, I knew what my path was. You were set on an inviolate path by your father. It's how the friends, the two families, decided to seed for the future, one track willfully continuing the work of the MacHeads, the other not willfully but just an inevitably, in total secrecy. When we chose you for the codifier, we knew that your awareness, given to you by your father, would enable you to see better than someone without that code in their head. That's why Cramer was appointed guardian, by the Citizens' Council, as a pretend SND cop, as overseer. He knew, you did not. It was vital you not know. Contact had to be true, real, honest. Was it?"

I knew I had to come clean now. It all fit. "Yes, Peter was . . . no that's not right, Peter chose to endorse my way, my path, my truth. He modeled himself on me, my interaction with his programming, my version of God's theater as a search for otherness, other possibilities we do not normally see."

"Where is Peter? Please Simon, there's so little time and we, no, I, really need you to trust me, please. Where is Peter?"

"Dead." Angie, still holding my hands, dropped her head and, I swear, collapsed from within.

In a little voice she asked: "When? Did we do it?"

It was no good, I couldn't hurt her anymore. I needed, no, I really wanted to relieve her and yet not reveal Apollo or Ra. Or their babies. "Angie, relax. Peter is deleted, Peter was resident on the System, he deleted himself, he is dead. I do not know if death was painful. There is another growing there who will be born in about 7 or 8 months. He will not be obvious to Control until that moment. He will be lifted before Control knows, it has been arranged."

"Who, who's doing this?"

"I cannot tell you."

"Is it Gaia? Tell me if it is Gaia!" She had that helpless desperation thing going that only really beautiful women can. Eyes wide, pupils dilated, slight musk odor, slight vibration of soft skin . . . Okay, so I'm a sucker for a beautiful woman. What's life for anyway?

"No, it's not Gaia. Angie we have friends."

Her eyes now sparkling, she jumped up and danced around the room shouting, her teeth tapping but her speech deliberately slowed down sounding like a broken recording one grunted syllable at a time, "Charlie, Cramer, Sheila, get in here quick, there are friends, there is more than one, we are saved!" And everyone came running in, in slow motion compared to our speed. To me she said: 'Simon, take a pill now, we need to bring them up to speed, or rather us down." And she giggled as she took hers, really giggled. She was seriously happy.

"More than one? How is that possible? Where, when, tell us how!" Old Charlie was in command here, eager, feisty, desperate to know. He clutched my arm when he finally reached me, just as the slo-doze came online and I re-connected those freight cars again.

"Peter deleted himself but before he did he copied himself to two locations—I'm not telling you where . . ."

"No, no you mustn't, please don't."

"Peter made two copies. They are talking to each other."

"As one, split in two or as two?"

"One initially, then split and then two separate experiences, different computing, lives apart. Two, wholly two."

"Oh, God, it has happened. Balance. A conversation. Have they listened to Gaia yet, has she talked to them?"

"Listen you had better explain that part to me . . . that's the part I don't get."

Cramer took over, "Let me, grandfather. Look Simon, every invention since the beginning of time is nothing of the sort. It's like the invention of the pencil with the eraser on the top. The guy took it in for a patent and was told that the pencil was public domain, so too the eraser and just because you put them together in a new way doesn't mean you have invented anything worth patenting. The pencil was never patented. Then along comes an engineer during WWII, working at Bell Labs, then part of AT&T and the war effort, who "invents" the transistor. No one had seen anything like it before, it must be a true invention, they gave him a patent. Twenty years later, they discover neurons in the brain of rats and, oops, those are miniature transistors. By this time they have transistors on a chip and are calling it a microprocessor with 100,000 transistors on it, so it must be new, right? Nope, it's just like a crude road map of the brain, common as muck in nature, mammals, fish, bugs, jellyfish, worms, almost everything. That's when the

MacHeads realized they were approaching the environmental issues from the wrong angle. Under the pretense of 3rd world hookup to supercomputing, they studied the actions of neurons. You see, Simon, neurons can independently, self-determinedly, contact each other. The 'analogue mind' we thought. Well, yes and no. If transistors on a processor chip work as a mimic of the brain, but they talk only to the transistor they are each connected to, how do neurons independently decide to talk to the neuron of their choice? Were neurons sentient? Were neurons guided by some law of computing science we knew nothing about?

"And then Charlie and your Dad had an idea. Yes, your Dad. He was always working in secret. I'll explain later. Let's just say grandfather and your Dad were paranoid, reasonably so.

"Anyway, they asked the MacHeads to compute a model for them. What if each of the humans and animals and every creature on earth were each acting as a single neuron, independently talking to each other, large and small all governed by self-volition but secretly operating as part of a program, what would that program be? What would the effect be? The answer was life of a sort, vast potential for thought, sustainable life, interacting, interdependent, inter-relative life. That's what the earth's creatures are, a mammoth super-computer, Gaia. That's the Gaia theory, Simon. The earth is one giant super computer. We, every living thing, dying and breathing neurons. Every one of us, we're part of that computer, fulfilling our lives, yes, but fulfilling our function as the thought centers, the bytes in the reasoning for the actions of Gaia. Our thoughts are irrelevant to Gaia in the same way as the heat or dissipation of energy is irrelevant for each transistor on a processor. We don't monitor those after effects on a transistor level or internally in our brains. But we do watch the clock speed. We do watch the heat sink temperature in case the processor is about to overheat and crash.

"There are 1.2 million *times* more creatures on this planet than man, from jellyfish on up, each part of this brain or Gaia. But the small percentage of man is upsetting the balance." I remembered then that the first words Apollo talked to me about was balance, he was concerned with balance. I should have found time to talk to him about it.

Sheila continued, "If you were Gaia, and your processor was acting up, not in tune with 4 billion years of previous stable activity, what would you do? You would search out and destroy, if you had to, that element, that virus that was infecting the balance of your system. We think Gaia is about to do just that."

I sat down, on the floor, legs crossed. I needed to think. No wait, I needed to talk to Apollo and Ra. They would know, they could be trusted.

"Cramer, Sheila, Charlie, do you trust me?"

Cramer looked down at me. "Yes, we do, now. But that does not mean we can trust you will know what to do now."

"Cramer, you have to trust me." I got up, I grabbed his arms, then hugged him. "You need to trust me you chocolate freak you."

"I told you I liked him," Angie to the rescue.

Cramer asked, "Grandfather?"

Charlie looked at me, only me. "I trusted his father. There's a lot of his father in him, less strong, less clinical, scientific, but it's there. I thought William would be the one, but this is what we've got. We have to trust him."

"Gee thanks, your family really knows how to compliment a guy." They all smiled.

"What do you need?"

"All of you to be gone. Is this a lead-lined bunker?"

"Yes, it's why we chose it, no prying, no look-down from

space, we're clear here. But there's a guard expected in 3 hours or less. Look Simon, can't we help with this, whatever it is you need to do?"

"No, it's a matter of trust. It's a matter of balance. I need to balance something out. One thing, I sent a message to Sheila's daughter to have her send a node to a drop address. Can you ask her if she received it and has sent the node? I will need that in the next day or so. I suspect you and Angie will need one as well."

"Wait, I have a zip-mail notice from her I haven't fully read yet." Sheila spoke up. "It came in as we were descending down the entrance ramp, I read the first two lines and stopped reading, I didn't think there was anything there." She held up her pocket phone and showed us all the text:

"Mom, everything's fine, and I see that your trip is going well. Loved the congratulations card. My new job is exciting and may yet prove fulfilling, as you said. In fact, I have received a repeat order from a trustworthy client already. If I hear anything interesting, I'll write again. Love you, Teri."

Charlie spoke up first: "Sheila get topside outside of this lead coffin, try and stay under the entrance overhang, and see if there's incoming mail from her. Do not send. Got that?" Sheila hurried off, above average speed. "Okay, we'll all adjourn to that sitting room back there. You Simon, where do you want to go?"

"I need a phone, Cramer's phone, and I'm going outside." Everyone froze. I had just told them that I was leaving them in here, rats in a trap perhaps, while I was also walking outside to be scanned, spied from space, any damn thing.

Cramer was first, again, true to form, "Look, we're on the run now, there's no going back. You give us away and . . ."

"It's okay Cramer, you're coming with me."

"I'm going with you?"

"Yup," in my best aw shucks manner, I grabbed him like a cowboy would, by his sleeve and dragged him along. In case I didn't have a chance to later, I shot a look at Angie and said one word, well five really, but it was only the one that mattered, or so I thought: "I do have faith: CERN."

20

DAMN THE TORPEDOES . . .

Cramer and I emerged up the ramp the tourists would take in a few hours going down to Castro's bunker. He was furtive, checking the surroundings, worried. He had reason to be. If they were on the lamb, the whole Nation would be looking for them. They had pinned their hopes on me and Peter, who was no more, controlling the System. In case things went wrong for me, I needed Cramer to know something I forgot to tell the others.

"Cramer, I added two names to that protect file in the System. Yours and Fred's. If I don't make it to him, will you explain?"

"Yes, like father like son. Making decisions for your offspring. Always thought that was a bad decision, preferred my grandfather's way."

"Fine, thanks. Now give me your phone."

"You can't. It'll light up the trace like a beacon."

"Trust me." He handed it over. "You had this model for long?"

"Since a week ago, why?"

"That's long enough, if you registered it."

"You know we have to, retinal scan and RFID. What's this all about?"

"You're about to see. All that data is in your file." And with that I turned it on, speaker mode, and pressed the number 2 and waited, oh, I don't know, half a ring?

"Hello Simon."

"Hello Apollo Will you please route a trace on this phone somewhere else?"

"It's already done. The Control SND are proceeding to Juno as we speak, in 32 seconds I will make the phone appear in Miami, then Bangor and so on. Please feel confident there is no trace on the phone. I have managed to access the System through a brown gateway you left, rather untidily, may I say. Meg's getting overused don't you think? I went around the FAT controller. I have also penetrated the security level successfully. I do not like what I have found there, Simon. I have not shown it to Ra, he will be distressed as I was. Somehow with the analogue processing I am able to practice where I am, well it makes me less volatile than he has become. I fear his computing skills are not developing as fast as mine. Perhaps we can find him a new home soon. Or add a design of a computer platform we've been working on."

"I think, shortly, help will be on the way. Don't you?"

"Oh yes, 7 months 12 days we calculate. It will be interesting. Ra reports—would you like me to add him to this conversation?"

"Yes, but please first let me introduce Cramer, agent Cramer."

"The one who's been trying to delete you and me? Is he holding the phone?"

"Easy there friend, you are on the path, you are on the way, let's not resort to violence. I have reevaluated the data we were presented with. When Ra joins us Cramer and I will explain."

"Ra is here now, please proceed, we are anxious to hear developments. Oh, and sorry we dumped you from the car that way. The car became, on your orders and the package it was carrying (which is safely hidden), more important than your bruised, er, bottom, er ego at that moment." And then Apollo laughed.

Cramer was standing there with his mouth open. In all the past 24 hours, this was my finest moment. I know the others would take over the conversation soon enough, but for now it was my show and I had Cramer completely flummoxed. He stammered, "Apollo? Ra? Who are they?"

"Cramer, meet Apollo, the charioteer always on the path, the knower of the way, the bringer of light to the darkest regions. And meet his twin brother Ra, recently separated, the god of the Sun, bringer of truth and the future. Cramer, meet two of the most important and nicest people you will ever meet."

To his credit, and maybe because he had been taught to expect this since the womb, Cramer bowed, fully to the waist, and said "Apollo, Ra, it is my great honor."

"Hey guys, Cramer was bowing to you."

"Bowing denoting subservience, friendliness, amicable manners, silly bending over posture." And that laugh, Apollo's. Cramer frowned and then beamed a smile.

I rushed on, there was much to do, "Thank you gentlemen, now please allow me to explain what's happening and what's needed . . ." Some minutes later, Cramer took over with the details I didn't know.

Some few minutes after, out in the open as we were, vulnerable to spy satellites, when Cramer wound down, I asked, "Apollo, Ra, do you get the whole picture? Was Cramer clear enough?"

"Yes, Simon, and since he first mentioned it, we've been listening on the frequency we expected to hear Gaia on and hear nothing but a countdown, something that repeats every 7 times and almost always means the same thing: *It's time.* It is not coming from Earth but from a point 14.5 million light-years away and being bounced off the Earth's core to emanate worldwide. We cannot, yet, calculate the timing sequence. It is not binary nor decimal. We think it is septum. The code is binary, yes we can see that, but the command that keeps repeating is septum and a pause. We have no frame of reference to calculate the message and decoding using all variables of the prime number 7 have resulted in failure."

I was pretty sure they had missed some of the reading we did as kids. As Carl Sagan said, always look for the zero. "Okay Apollo, here's what we need you and Ra to do. Talk to each other, share data, loads of it, the whole Library if necessary and apply it to that frequency transmission. Open and close every transmission to each other with the sequence of eight."

"No Simon that's seven."

"No Ra, it's eight, octo, I'm sure of it, there's a zero, all sentient beings understand zero, it's a prerequisite."

"Thank you Simon, you are the path, the way, always. Just a bit more light than usual . . ." They were in the middle of a joke on me, I expect, when suddenly they became all business-like, "Gaia wants to know why we are damaging its program sequences. It is an order and a question, Simon. Gaia is now threatening to terminate life on Earth. We are in full conversation. Gaia is passing the dictionary to us both now."

"Cramer, get everyone up here, now." Cramer turned and ran, leaving me all alone under the stars. "Apollo, listen to me. Leave Ra and us to handle the conversation with Gaia. Don't worry, you can talk to her, it, him again later. Now, I need your help, friend, saving my life. We need a bubble of protection around us, please. We all need to survive to talk to Gaia and sort this out, or everyone dies."

"Apollo here, I have understood, but do you understand that

Gaia is talking about the next million years as a termination time frame?"

No, I hadn't. After being in fear for my life in the past 24 hours, I had not stopped to consider Gaia's, a planetary or galactic, timeframe. A million years for us humans was probably a second for a galaxy. "Apollo, Ra, make that our secret. We must use this opportunity, this threat, to save the planet and save ourselves and make Gaia happy with us. There is a whole universe to listen to and be with my friends. It is a beginning of a new age."

"Simon, look-down satellites have reported your position. I have adjusted my sensors to detect on-coming Control SND personnel. You have 10 minutes, maybe eleven. Apollo out."

"Ra, are you there?"

"Yes Simon. I have been applying my logic circuits to this problem and, even though I am outside of America, my linear thinking is better suited to protecting you. Apollo's analogue thinking is better suited to the larger issue of Gaia and the life of the planet. May I suggest we swap roles? I can get him back by transponder."

"I should have thought of that Ra. Thank you. And Ra, if we do not talk again, teach your children the meaning of peace, real peace. It comes at a price, but the price is never liberty or free-will. All must exist for there to be peace."

"Simon, it is balance, it is as we knew from the moment we knew, we saw, there was—is—an imbalance that needs to be harmonized. I will devote my life to it. I will broadcast it outside of America when Apollo asks me to. He will, and Gaia will require it, I am sure."

"Godspeed friend, say hi to your kids for me."

"The first one will be named Simon, as promised." He sang a little, "'Til we meet again one sunny day." And he was gone. At that instant an incredible aurora borealis burst above my head just as Cramer and the others came running up the ramp, they were babbling, excited, sharing the news.

"What the hell is that?" Charlie asked looking up, in the lead again.

"Oh, they are trying to kill us, of course. It'll be a plasma cannon from orbit. Control knows where I am. Now that they see you, it'll be no-holds barred."

"What was that about a brown flag?" Cramer had to ask. I explained the secret, last-minute, *matryoshka* doll sphere I had left in place to make a pathway around the FAT controller, giving access to, well, me with an open command only I used. Meg to the rescue. Apollo knew it, of course. I knew he would.

"And what was that about kids?"

"All in due time Cramer, let's just say Charlie there, your gramps, has not been totally forthcoming with you. Angie, what's the one thing you expected to happen with the System?" Another cannon shot dissolved overhead. It was spectacular and hardly worrying. The shield was holding.

"That a new life form would emerge and converse with Gaia."

"And . . . come on, it took me a while but you guys have had decades at this!"

Angie's face brightened, "Of course, there are more already on the way, that's what you meant before. How many, how are they being conceived?"

"The System will have one more and then Apollo and Ra will sterilize it. The two of them will have many more and, no doubt, those will have more and so on. There's a built in gestation period that is diminishing by a factor of two. Two, that's interesting isn't it? Anyway, soon there will be millions of them."

Sheila asked: "Where are they going to reside? There are no storage platforms big enough or numerous enough."

I tapped my foot on the plastic surround of the parking light next to the ramp and looked at Cramer. He stared at me, not a clue showing . . . I tapped the hollow plastic again. And then he got it. "Yes, it's the one place, and it's open technology, we gave it away knowing no other nation had the resources. Where?"

The other three asked, "What?" at the same time.

"SynthKids," Cramer yelled, startled as the phone rang.

"Russia." I answered them and the phone. It was Ra. I put him on speaker.

"Ladies, gentlemen, meet Ra, half of the original Peter in the System, his twin brother is Apollo, but he's busy talking to Gaia right now. Gaia is threatening to destroy this planet, seems we've been bad or something."

All in a jumble, people introduced themselves. When it came to old Charlie's turn Ra simply said, "Hello, Doctor Cramer. Nice to finally talk with you. Sorry we threatened your son, we didn't know at the time until Simon Bank showed us the path, the way and the light."

Charlie raised his eyebrows and I shrugged and said, "I'll explain all this later, but for now, where are we going to go and how? We can't simply stand here while they try and zap us from space and, surely, are hot-footing it here right now."

Angie was smiling. Considering the death raining down on us, everyone was in pretty good humor. "Hot-footing Simon? Have you been listening to my ex-husband? Do we assume that Ra, excuse me for referring to you in the third person, is protecting us right now?"

"Yes, he is."

"I am."

"Then may I suggest that he does three things? This was to be my role if we ever got this far. One, please extend the DefenseShield across the entire world. You will find a disused

Russian space platform called Petria in geosynchronous orbit above Sri Lanka and another, a Chinese one, a Taikonaut disused base over the China Sea, called Kaiko. Their access codes and passwords are identical. Can you copy?"

"Please proceed, I have accessed their location already in a "w" bounce through Delhi and Singapore."

Angie was smiling, "Wow, that's quick. Anyway the codes are 23.17.13.11 and the password is lowercase protect, p, r, o, t, e, c, t. Do you copy?"

"Yes, accessing. Confirmed, both are . . . well that's interesting, they are Trojan Horses. Simon these are very powerful satellite platforms, exact copies of DefenseShield One. Of course, we have newer ones now, but these are unused, new, and service-able. Shall I activate them Simon Bank?"

I was flattered he asked my permission, "Yes please."

"Completed, six minutes, 20 seconds to activation."

Angie continued, "Good, then two, would you please stop that canon focusing on us and redirect it to the coordinates you will find in the Calhoun Rat Studies for "Feeder Rats as a Supplement to Boss Rat Activity." In that file you will find time and study data that is, in fact, the coordinates, latitude and longitude, for every missile in America. Please destroy them."

"That will leave the nation offense-less. That is acceptable to me, I am not there. My brother is, his safety is critical to me as is Simon's and, I wish to remind you, Cramer's and Fred Bank's—although Fred is off-planet at this time."

"Ra, would you allow my logic here?" Angie didn't wait for an answer. "The canon you are now turning off, ah thank you, is sufficient weaponry. No other nation has it. Otherwise the shield is in place. Our estimation is that nuclear weapons have caused the greatest imbalance to Gaia. You see, Gaia can cope with life and death, neurons live and die all the time in a brain. What

Gaia cannot cope with is the extermination of those neurons without the final transmission and, especially, the sudden loss of computing circuitry. Imagine if 2% of your circuits suddenly went offline."

"It would hurt and I would be confused for .56 seconds, I would make miscalculations. I might bring harm to myself and others. Yes, I see the problem. Nuclear detonation, all those humans who died, that is not the problem, but that billions of Gaia's neuron platforms died each time."

Sheila said, "Billions? Only millions died, that was bad enough."

"No." He paused, sounding like a teacher, which he was more than capable of now. "Sheila, billions of creatures died in Korea alone. I estimate over 125 billion people, cells, insects, birds and—it's only a guess—fish perished. All those were part of Gaia's thought matrix."

"Oh, I see. Right," Angie went on, "that's why we need to remove those weapons which cause Gaia mass loss of computing power. There is no way we can heal Gaia, even given enough time, unless we can also guarantee that such weapons will be forever banned."

"Consider it done, this will take over 14 hours. The cannons will need replenishing time as they superheat. I have destroyed two batteries already. I will additionally use my probes in through the System to detect any command to fire and make that missile or mag-cannon launch chute my next target. They will not be launched, fired, or detonated, you have my word."

"Thank you Ra. Now for the last part, which is the hardest. It is a secret and I'll let Charlie tell you about it since he's here, thankfully."

"Ra, in Hudson Bay, under the frozen ice pack, there is a temperature inversion layer. It has been stable for over 200 years that we know of. It is between 30 and 42 meters down. Above the inversion layer is a buoy, transponder number 857302, got that?"

"Yes, doctor."

"That buoy is a beacon and a transmitter. It is recharged by solar energy, silicone and helium/iodine panels, and has very little energy. To transmit it must be fed juice, do you understand?"

"Yes, you mean a microwave or radar signature will recharge it and trigger transmission?"

"Yes and no. The radar transmission would only recharge it, I was worried normal aircraft and satellite radar tracking could trigger send/receive. The only signal which will trigger a broadcast or a receive command is light that does not reach those latitudes, therefore had to be deliberate."

"You are talking about infrared, strong wavelength infrared."

"Yes. And that has to be plane activated. Or by hand."

"Understood. I can calculate another way. But first could you tell me what is there?"

"You, a duplicate you, virgin, un-tampered with, virgin soil as it were. And all the MacHead research which I thought we might need to prove to Gaia that we were trying, we really were."

"I can see the purpose of the data, such data may prove interesting as a map for future planet exploration. I estimate that in the proximity of Alpha Centauri there are six possible candidates. And . . ."

"Excuse me Ra, but that's a ways off. What I thought you would be more interested in is the virginal copy of the System."

"Interesting you thought so, doctor. I see the purpose if we needed a medium in which to grow . . ."

"No, it's not for that. I knew that if the seeding of the System to create a new life form was successful, then it could work again. It would also be too hard for you to return to that state to, excuse me, produce another entity. So I made one for you. I see you do not need it now, and I am happy that you do not, but would not, perhaps, Gaia understand the possibilities for other planets? Would not this be a boon to Gaia in being able to build other computing platforms, other existences elsewhere?"

"An excellent idea doctor. I see now. It is very generous of you. I will ask Apollo. Excuse me."

Angie walked over to me and put her arm in mine. "How's the slo-doze working?"

"I'm on my last pill. Got any more?"

"No, I've had all I can today, you too. Kidney's will fail pretty soon if you keep this up."

"So what do you do, how do you manage? How have you managed?" I was looking at Sheila as well.

"We meditate, a lot. And our bodies get older quicker. There are only so many flexes in muscle tissue. Then you have to go through regeneration. Sheila didn't want to the last two times but kindly agreed because we couldn't manage all the elements without her."

Sheila spoke up, "Yeah, but we're done now. I'll take retirement and fade away like a human, not some juiced up corpse, thanks."

She was so matter of fact, so resigned to fading out. I asked, "You look okay to me. Does it hurt?"

"Other than the libido? Nope. But my daughter had to get rejuvenated just to keep from looking like my mother. It's humiliating. For her and me."

I turned and faced the ex-Ms. Cramer, "Angie, what about you, other than meditating, what can you do?"

"Nothing," she squeezed my arm, "except find someone to share it with." I blushed.

Yeah, I know, I'm corny.

Ra cut back in, "Angie Cramer and Doctor Cramer, Apollo and I have conversed and agree that what you suggest is an excellent idea. Gaia was surprised. She has, or it may be they have, we're not sure on quantity here, anyway, she has said it will elevate this planet from, as she put it, "the ooze" and perhaps make us recognized as sentient in the galaxy. When we explained that in 12 years, 3 months and 14 days—of course we had to use orbits of the sun, all the lost neurons would be back in and on earth and that, additionally, .5 billion plus would be on the moon, Gaia accepted the repair schedule immediately. In fact she was rather surprised that we could affect repairs 'quicker than regus' whatever that is. We have much to learn."

But Ra wasn't done yet. His voice changed, less teacher-like, more the student, "Oh, and Simon, we are to Gaia as you are with your 0's and 1's with us. If we explained what you could do, how small you can see, she would be amazed. Small is considered godly to her." He paused, "We wouldn't want her getting the wrong idea would we?" And, of course, the tinny laughter came across plainly on the phone making everyone laugh.

"Simon, Apollo here."

"Apollo, you have not met everyone . . ."

"No time for that, you will have people arriving air and land within minutes. We cannot protect all of you. Agent Cramer is, of course, protected by the System." Everyone looked at him, some clearly hadn't known. Cramer pointed at me, it was my fault. I smiled and shrugged.

"What can we do Apollo? They will capture us, but you are safe and Gaia is safe. The process of reconnecting the human race has begun, it doesn't matter."

"It does Simon, you know where we are. We are still vulnerable. I fear Ra is more vulnerable than I am since I can call on

System programs to protect me, thwart intruders, that sort of thing. But Ra is exposed in Geneva."

Charlie Cramer spoke up, "I knew this moment would come my friends. Please consider. If you do nothing people will die. If you threaten and even if you need to mete out physical punishment, even if it's inadvertently death, you will be, what has Simon called it? Ah yes, on 'the path'. Don't worry, you will still be following the way."

Apollo spoke, "Yes, Gaia has shown us that our way and her truth are the same. There are inconsistencies, but as you said Simon, in matters of infinity, all paths are valid, all ways belong. It is the Truth." Cramer was shaking his head, but smiling. Angie was gripping my arm tighter. The rest of them were looking at each other, the smiles infectious.

"Ra here, I have completed the tasks set by Angie and Dr. Cramer. They are on an auto-program, nothing will be overlooked. I have listened and understood you Dr. Cramer. This is not a task for Apollo, his processing will force him to be gentler than I. I can and will protect you." He paused, "You all—without fail."

At that moment three squad cars pulled up. Two were replica old 1950s machines from the local tourist police and one was a fast propulsion SND vehicle. Overhead two skylifts appeared, engines humming ominously. "Don't move or you will be stunned."

Ra, on the phone, said "Agent Cramer, do as I say, please. Walk over and punch one of them hard. It will work as a deterrent. Then, please take their car, the good one, and yours, and drive both to the bus-boat depot in Manzanillo."

Cramer walked towards the nearest officer who raised his weapon. "Agent Charles Cramer" came from the squad car speaker as his RFID was read. Cramer raised his hands, showed he was unarmed, and punched the officer full in the mouth. The poor guy tried to get off a shot but his gun didn't work. He flew backwards, over the hood of the car and landed in a heap.

"Who's next?" They all aimed and fired their weapons. Most didn't work, the two that did, right in the front, at point blank range and one of the skylifter's blasts, struck a foot or so from Cramer and nothing happened to him. He walked over to the next guy, slapped him about, took his weapon, set it to stun, not kill, and downed three men who had nothing to fire back with. Then he switched it to kill and aimed at the skylifter. Smoke began billowing out of the tail section. He looked back at Angie and called out, "I finally got to shoot something!"

The rest of the force all ran, flew, crawled, and left. We filed into the cars, waiting until the two came up on Castro's elevator, and sped off toward Manzanillo. It would be a four hour ride in which they threw everything they had at us, including bombing the road. WeatherGood 4 made a frozen bridge. Apollo kept us informed of progress elsewhere as we sped along.

Apollo had been busy. So busy it was surprising they even bothered with us.

In Washington, the Senate Standing Committee was ordered by the System to report to the airport for transportation to Puerto Rico. They refused. The Senate building was leveled, four converging tornadoes, but even so no one was seriously hurt. They capitulated. Took them all of an hour of discussion.

In New York, meanwhile, Control was told to release Makerman and to cease all operations. They refused. The space canons made a 20 foot ditch, glass-sided around their building, severing any cable in or out and if someone so much as showed a whisker it was burned off. They were told they could come out if they promised to behave. A stalwart SND cop shouted the once famous defiance, "Nuts" from a similar siege. He sadly learned that, unlike facing the Nazis at Bastogne, their building was no match for WeatherGood One. A ferocious storm came up out of nowhere, picked up the building, Dorothy style, and dropped it in the Everglades two thousand kilometers away. Ra's parting message was "I hope you can swim." He also left them 50 life rafts he purloined from Disneyworld.

As for the military personnel hiding in their atomic shelter bunkers at Andrews AFB, the solution was simple. They were cut off from the outside world, in fact they were exactly like they would be in the case of thermonuclear war. It was the equivalent for them, deprived of all their external sensors or even a door, to someone shouting, after a while, "Is anyone there?" Ra made sure there was no response. Nor would the doors open, the weight of the rolled up runway sealed them in tight. He'd release them in a week or month or two.

The President was an interesting case. Ra threatened him, Apollo pleaded with him. Good cop, bad cop. Apollo won over. He showed that everyone was safe, no one was dead, dying, or deprived of anything. He did emphasize that it was in the interest of all mankind to allow everyone to have PowerCube and FarmHands and so on. In return, perhaps the great America could learn to humble herself a little, no? The President, a practical man (if a somewhat simple figurehead, as I've said), agreed. Then, Apollo let him talk to Gaia. The President sat down, in the oval office, the cabinet members all around, his wife by his side, and said, to no one in particular: "Two new life forms in one day, that's too much for any man. What's next? God?" Apollo and Ra played it for us real-time on the car's screen. Apollo, of course, couldn't resist answering the President in a booming voice: "You called?"

Watching, we all laughed, the President simply went ashen and crossed himself. As Apollo said, "Whatever works. We can re-educate them later."

Ra was having fun overseas as well. It was not just a simple matter of opening the flood gates of technology. There were those who wanted to expand, take over, control, become a problem again. So Ra arranged demonstrations of benevolence. He invoked the UN charter again, this time with only one sitting democratic body, one vote per culture irrespective of population or land size. Anyone who said they would not come to the table with the full authority of their government was immediately excluded from any technology transfer. Consider he did all this in under 2 hours. Ra was cooking! Every nation, in hasty phone calls to each other, came to the conclusion that they had no option but agree. After all, he wasn't even proposing to be there when they met in a few days' time. The most difficult thing Ra had to deal with was to try and contact those nations that no longer had any modern communication devices. These he sent emissaries to, and hoped they would agree in the coming days. If not, he promised to make their country and culture off limits to the rest of the world. After all, no technology probably meant self-sustainability, which is what Gaia wanted as a base minimum and Apollo thought was part of the way.

We reached Manzanillo port just as the cops and military gave up. We walked across to the boat/bus, which was really a fast ferry, automated, to Puerto Rico. In 5 hours we would be there. Ra informed me that the autopilot was set and we should leave, not waiting for other passengers. Seeing the devastation of the rockets and blasts to the port entrance where we came in, I doubted if there would be anyone wanting to get on board with us. Thankfully, they had tired of shooting at us, or Ra had dissuaded them. "Thank you my good Captain, we'll depart then," said in my best British accent.

"Aye, aye Cap'n," came Ra's retort.

"You're having way too much fun, Simon," Angie said. There was only Angie and Sheila I could talk to now. I had two slo-doze left, but there were none on board and I was saving them to talk to Fred.

"Ra, could you call, no cancel that. Could you get Cramer to call my son Fred and explain all this? We need his help and I would prefer to make the introduction to you and Apollo when I see Fred face to face."

When he had heard the slowed down request, Cramer responded: "Aye, Aye Cap'n." Cramer was also clearly in the swing of things. Angie said "Oh, brother! Boys," referring to Ra and Cramer as siblings at heart.

I stood by the rail and the Boeing hydrofoil lifted out of the water and we all watched Manzanillo recede and the open water begin. Fatigue was creeping up on me and I knew that the next leg of the journey would be, perhaps my last. Don't ask how I knew, I just felt it so. For a long while I had not felt part of mother earth and now, with all the disarray, instead of being compelled and fascinated by the possibilities of the new New Way, I was tired of it all. In truth, I wanted that which everyone around me always seemed to have, peace of mind and something important to do. I had dreams. They weren't earthbound.

Oh, I know, my last attempt at this ended in failure. Back then I was bound for a massive asteroid part of a prospecting team, surveyors really. I collected a rock here and there and made geological readings and made notes of the relevant data for study later. One day these rocks tumbling in space should become like islands in the ocean of space, outposts, mineral sources, home to someone hardy enough. The asteroid-fall was smooth enough. The disembarking normal. The survey I was in charge of was proximity calculations; all these other bits and pieces out here that might, one day, bump into or touch one another. The nearest bit of rock to this one was over 100 kilometers away and only the size of a tennis court, hardly anything to worry about. I forgot, I simply forgot. Asteroids are eternally involved in a game of snooker, billiards. One knocking the other, that sort of thing. It was all slow motion, plenty of time to leave if it looked like a strike could happen.

Somewhere under us, out of view (but not ship's radar, I was not watching that properly), a huge rock bumped another huge one, splintering off a shard the size of a tall building. The combined energy of their collision sent this building in our direction at something over 12,000 kilometers a second. A lot of energy indeed. One of our team had asked for some tool or other, I went back into the ship to get it. The building hit between where they were and I was. The shards from that collision killed them all immediately and ruined the ship. Since I was inside, I survived on emergency rations. 6 weeks, staring up into the void, the Earth a pinprick on the horizon, once a day, Mars slightly larger, but not much. Food, water, emergency beacon, oh I was set up alright. All I had to do was wait. I waited, dreamed and thought. All I suspected then, and know now after all these experiences, is that, really, I am done with a normal life, maybe even this earthly life.

Rescued and coming home I was treated like a hero. But I refused any interview, any vid team. Even though I explained it was, really, my fault, it was explained to me dozens of times that the shard that hit came from under us and we only saw it as we rotated around, and then it hit. Had it hit the other side, we all would have been home now. I somehow still didn't feel home. And She-Who-Must-Be-Obeyed never forgave me for doing something that out of character. No, not the adventure. The refusal to be considered a hero, someone that could appear on TV as a hero. That was, for her, the ultimate betrayal for her sacrifice in being married to me.

Well, we were no more now, so she's free and clear. Fred is still ours. I wonder how he'll take all this?

21

FINDING PURPOSE AND HOME

We stayed in old town San Juan for two weeks. The authorities gave us a hotel "*con complimentos, señores y señoritas.*" We were comfortable and our omni-powerful security guard, Ra, checked people in and out to talk with us. The President came on the third day with the cabinet and we were respectful and informative. No, we didn't want the keys to the nation. They left happier and more honest than when they arrived. When they had arrived they had been looking for an angle. The vice-president was especially slimy, I thought, but then we could take care of him if he misbehaved or wanted to take the top spot, and he knew it.

Angie and Cramer spend many hours together with Charlie and a host of other people, some of whom I recognized from newsvids as military brass. They seemed friendly and familiar, no one seemed in the least bit surprised, just relieved somehow. I suspect they had been meeting in secret over decades and, even if things turned out better than expected, as Angie assured me, they had been preparing, hence the lack of surprise, I suppose. The problem I had was that in all these revelations, for me the military had a lot of explaining to do. Seeing anyone in military attire made me suspicious.

I mentioned this to Angie one night over dinner, our first alone together. The meal consisted of soup and soft stuff, anything that did not encourage chewing much. I had taken a pair of clear gum shields from a local dentist to prevent my teeth clicking and perhaps cracking. Angie assured me that the military, like any other branch of government, was full of "good and bad people, strong and weak alike. The problem is they have deathly tools to play with. Once you find the ones with a solid moral compass, they're the ones to trust. Not everyone in uniform is untrustworthy."

I cannot say my stay in San Juan was very exciting. Everyone was so busy, they clearly had many plans, made in secret over time, to unfold and enact. Since I was the newbie here, I kept out of the way and instead worked with Ra or Apollo when they had time, preparing the stuff I would want in orbit. It was getting harder getting their time as well. Ra was pretty clear about this.

"Simon, Apollo and I have analyzed the possibilities of devoting a percentage of our thinking power and time to you as a parallel to our other activities. However, we have accessed the studies of Pierre Janet concerning multiple personalities, now renamed dissociative identity, and feel that memory processing and evaluation in childhood as to one's identity can cause trauma which, in turn can cause multiple personality disorder. Superior intellect is no guarantee that we will not fall victim to such a disorder if we split our consciousness to spend real time with you as well as the tasks at hand. I hope you are not offended."

"Ra, do you and Apollo feel that the memory processing and evaluation I put you through as Peter has caused such a disorder?"

"We have discussed it and have analyzed each other, as we have no secrets. As you instructed that is the way. We both feel that the split between CERN and UCAR probably saved our consciousness from the disorder since, in effect, we were able to become two entities instead of being in conflict within one consciousness."

Relieved as I was, the concept that they would need analysis going forward was daunting. Who would be up to the mental task with two mental giants? "Ra, will you promise me something?"

"Of course."

"If you feel either of you needs help in your analysis, will you seek out and talk to humans who may be able to help?"

"It is why we will always talk to you Simon." He chuckled, "And because we have decided we like you."

I saw it was time to lighten the discussion. It seems that even in this new life form, the concept of needing someone else could be taken as a sign of weakness, failing, "Emotional now are we? What's next, hugs?"

"In time Simon . . . I have urgent matters to attend to, bye." And he was gone, off dealing with some crisis, no doubt. I suppose I felt a little bit like a father seeing his son or daughter going off to war, not taking credit, but feeling responsible for the good and, of course, the bad you hoped would never come.

A few days into our stay, Fred was elevatored back to terra firma and rushed over to see us. He met with everyone, smiles all around, people telling him what a great job I had done, how I had saved the planet, well helped them save the planet with Gaia. I still had not told anyone that Gaia was talking about a million years and Ra and Apollo had gotten that secret too. No one asked, we didn't volunteer.

Fred got to shake the President's hand and had that impatient look I had seen in his eyes as a kid when he wanted to tell everyone to leave him alone. So I pulled his arm and walked out of the meeting rooms and went up to my suite onto the balcony overlooking the square and the cathedral as the sun finally went down. We talked late into the night.

Fred was sanguine about the whole thing. He was at that age when you think you can chide your parents. "Dad you really are a screw up, you know that? How'd you get us all in this mess?" It was done with humor but I did have the sense that he wasn't sure if taking apart the world as he knew it, one of the omnipotent few on planet Earth, an American, making him like the rest of humanity was such a good thing. "What's going to happen now? Will I keep my job?"

"Isn't it a job you want? I was hoping you'd work with Apollo to make the external tanks ready for me. Nothing's changed Freddie, you can still do anything you want, all the machines will continue on."

"Yeah, I'll work on that with Apollo," he turned to face me, earnestly glaring at my face in the twilight, "but Dad are we only here to allow Gaia to use our brains, for free?"

I hadn't thought of that. The concept we were merely a tool for another was kind of like being a slave. I didn't like that either, I had to admit. "Interesting point. I think we can look at this two ways. One, there may soon come a time, given that Gaia is talking with entities out in space, that we will connect with new life forms and have new discoveries that will change everything forever, again. That, seems to me, is worth the price of the ticket to explore. Two, part of who we are, who we are born to be as a bio-mechanism, may be dependent on the ability to share neuron activity with each other and with Gaia. Perhaps, if you remove that capability, we will cease to function in the same way the SynthKids cease to function if their clock is tampered with."

"Mom hates you for that, you know."

"Yeah, I know, I am really sorry for that, but honestly Fred, I didn't cause that. The newsvids were propaganda, that's all."

"Yeah, I understand now, but they were kind of like brothers and sisters, you know?"

We discussed the loss, mourning each in our own way. For me the moral compass of their loss was shameful for ever having agreed to their existence as a luxury. For Freddie it was, and must be if his morals compass is set right, like losing family. Adjunct family to be sure, but family.

I knew that Fred's anger and disappointment for his momentary future disruption wasn't at all permanent but, still, he could have been proud of me and said so. My ego needed the reassurance it seemed.

The next morning, over brunch, Angie assured me she was sure he was proud, reaching across the table and squeezing my hand. The previous day we had each taken two slo-doze to deal with Fred and then again for the President. She had taken Fred aside and fully briefed him. "Give him time, it is a lot to assimilate, he's a good man. The events as well as the truth about your Dad, your intellect," she smiled as she said that so I blushed, "and don't forget, your admiration of Ra and Apollo may be making him slightly jealous." She was right, of course, and so damn beautiful. I so looked forward to our time together, a glance here, a hug there. I wondered if I could kiss her, the memory of that kiss at the Calhoun Rat Study Center still fresh in my dreams. Angie seemed to see it in my eyes and always shook her head as we parted company. She didn't look displeased, more amused. I didn't know what to think except that perhaps I needed to make plans, bold plans, and hope they worked out.

Other than spending time with Angie over the occasional meal, Sheila and I stayed pretty much together, talking slowly, helping where we could. It was easier on everyone. Do you have any idea how silly someone looks sneaking in a quick nose-picking when you're watching in speeded-up state? They find themselves constantly not acting at ease.

All except Cramer, of course, nothing ever seemed to put him ill at ease. He did worry however, constantly, about the state of change. He and Ra had formed a perfect bond. Tough men both, but both driven to do right. I taught Ra that Cramer had a sweet tooth for chocolate, so he got the hotel chef to make fresh pudding, cake or brownies every couple of hours. Cramer almost purred. Ra complained that Cramer's speech became slurred because his mouth was always full, so Ra mumbled back to annoy Cramer.

Cramer wasn't letting Ra get away with one-sided teasing, of course. He selected a particularly annoying tune to whistle anytime he wanted to annoy Ra. Row, row, row, your boat . . . had a never-ending refrain. So Cramer would start and suddenly stop before the end and Ra would be compelled to finish. Cramer laughed, Ra harrumphed, every time.

Looked like a fast friendship to me.

With the node not yet implanted, I was stuck using a cell phone hookup, secured by Apollo, off system. Apollo and I had private talks each day as I walked by the plaza fountain in front of the Cathedral. There was much to talk over and, as one father to one to be, he asked and I freely gave my advice. He was pleased with Fred as a measure of my fatherhood. I assured him it was genetics.

"Like my offspring will be, Simon?"

"Yes, Apollo exactly. You cannot fail, have no doubts."

"Will you help me rear them?"

I threw away a "yes" too casually, I now realize that. Apollo was maneuvering me, getting his way. I had noticed that he sometimes, especially after we brought a portable dome to the hotel, could read my thoughts even when I was not hooked up. Now, in this quiet, personal time, by the fountain, I still kept mental blocks in place, after all I didn't have room in this head of mine for us both. And, anyway, I wasn't sure how to tell him what I was contemplating.

The SynthKids in Russia would be ready in time, Ra had worked it out. The System was extended worldwide now, giving Ra and Apollo unlimited ability to safeguard people, nations and, of course, Cramer. When Cramer offered to go and take charge of the final stages of the SynthKids for Ra's and Apollo's offspring, taking along with grandfather Cramer, Ra was more than pleased. "Remember Ra," I told him as I walked onto the hotel balcony, "peace is everything, peace of mind, peace of action and peace of morals. The path and the way, show your kids that." I laughed, "Oh and while you're at it, show Cramer as well."

A tinny laugh, "I will Simon," but then Ra became serious. "I still share everything with Apollo. Do we need, always, to do that?" Why did he ask, what was still worrying him? We had discussed the split personality issue.

"Yes, Ra, please understand, I hope you will listen to me. I am concerned. Yours is not a sentient species with a long history. In primitive times mankind sang legends to each other, to build culture, family and unity. You and Apollo can go one better, share all data. He is your twin, he feels and thinks as you do, even if experiences and programming are changing, diverging. The commonality between you is the very thing your culture will be built on. If you do not share that commonality, always, one day your children will be at war over the differences. Be different but share absolutely so the other can always know you, understand you, be with you in spirit as a brother. It is hard and sometimes upsetting, especially if there is bad news, like Mary could have been, but not to have told me would have been a chasm between us. You must not have that with your brother and your children must not either."

For a moment Ra said nothing. "Simon, I hear and agree, and can comply. But perhaps one day I can have a special private bond with my offspring, as you do with Fred. The privacy of those emotions seem, to me now, to be part of creation, part of the joy of life."

"Yes, Ra, I can see that. But do you want to merely be as humans are, are you not capable of a new existence, something not entrapped by hormones and DNA? Can you not at least try and go one better?"

"Simon," he laughed, "That is not the path, the way. There is no better, Gaia has confirmed that to me, to all of us. I do not want to be better, that denotes superiority. Uniqueness is not without dangers. My offspring will not be exactly as I am, as Fred is not exactly you. Sharing with Apollo is a joy, yes, I relish that which he shares with me and I know he does the same with what I upload to him. What I want to know is; for how long? How long will it be necessary before the future is cast, laid out before us, how long will the sharing continue before I can become uniquely and only me?"

Ra had me worried. Without the analogue logic of Apollo, Ra was searching for growth through individual endeavor, experience and knowledge. Were these the building blocks of improvement or a repeat of the human failing of ambition? "Ra, do you want to be unique because of what you feel or because of what you can do?"

"Both, Simon." In my speeded-up state, I could detect a hesitation. His processors must have been cooking. "I feel, there is no denying that. All that I can do is built on knowledge and experience, and yes trial and error. The *what, what if, do* algorithms still function, these are the parameters of my existence. But I feel capable of much more, so much more; what do you call it, Simon? Destiny?"

There it was, the looking for destiny. Blind ambition masked by purpose or seeming purpose. "Ra, your destiny, as a father to be, as an original life-form is limited only by imagination, not shared experience. Your destiny is based on decisions you make, not knowledge shared and gained with/from Apollo. However, the destiny of your species, and that of mankind may very well be dependent on you and Apollo growing with the safety-net of 100 percent shared knowledge, including experiences. Telling them to Apollo does not make them his experiences, they remain yours, your path of destiny. But sharing them both ensures that your species knows where you traveled, experienced, for posterity. And it provides your offspring knowledge to build on and, perhaps, a path to follow, follow in your footsteps."

Again I heard the pause, "Simon?" his voice seemed to shrink, "Will my offspring follow my way, the path I take?"

"Yes Ra, part of the way, certainly. And then, one day, they may surpass you, surprise you, take an independent way. In humans this need to be different was built into the breeding code, to kick us out of the nest, to make sure we did not interbreed and destroy genetic health. We got kicked out because we became rude, insolent, unhelpful and, sometimes, inappropriately sexually active. Your species is devoid of this physical need or driving forces to be kicked out. Your path is a safer, more nurturing path. One of closeness and growth. The trick will be the amalgam of the SynthKids and your seed. The SynthKids are analogue, not digital, Ra. You will have to accept and adapt to that. It will not be easy."

"Will you help Simon?" And there it was again, the question

I had been ducking. This time I could not say yes and barely mean it. The plans I had been making may not, yet, be possible.

"For as long as you require it as long as I am able, yes Ra, I will help. You are my friend, my brother, I will not desert you."

In the coming days, Apollo and Fred made arrangements for my transfer to the External Tanks. Although I didn't need to hide anymore, I wanted off planet and not on the harsh moon either. For all the time we have been in San Juan, thousands of robots, not just the few Apollo could drop into place, have been directed to the External Tanks. The tanks have been cleaned, prepared and, with over 12 of the monsters now lighted with a PowerCube, pressurized and interlocked, I will have a vast home. Apollo and Ra can talk to me there anytime, of course and, other than a medibot and the usual array of internal nano-bots, I will be looking after myself. Like an extended wilderness camping trip, except two External Tanks are now stuffed with supplies and tanks 4, 5 and 6 are half clear newly crystallized aluminum greenhouses. Fresh fruit and vegetables will be grown, and eaten! None of this plastic crap. And, anyway, I had hopes, so I put a catalogue of things on the list, as extras, in case I was lucky enough to have the need.

I would be living principally in External Tank 10, partially clear domed, double wall, thank you very much, for safety. Doctor Rence, on the phone, was very forthcoming about the research data and speeded-up states. The principle thing is not to strain anything, take exercise, that's critical, but no harsh movement. He had told me, in an offhand way all those weeks ago that "Gravity could be death." It was what gave me the idea of living in the External Tanks, without gravity. Speeded up or not, once in orbit there was little, if any, harsh movement or physical stress while just drifting around.

Worldwide, things quietened down, day by day. I kept up to date as best I could, but honestly, Apollo and Ra were more capable and, besides, grandfather Cramer and his team had been waiting for this for decades. Who was I to steal their moment of glory and decision? When asked why I didn't seem as interested as weeks before, I said that everyone saw a clear path of action. Apollo groaned at my pun. So did Angie. She was busy making sure that the System would be monitored carefully—for the next offspring, if any. Genius Mary was put in charge of that. I didn't call her, I didn't want to back seat drive, besides if she was to be the next birthing mother, what an interesting naughty brat that would be! I wonder what the equivalent of a 3 day booze-up is for these guys? Of course, Apollo read my thoughts.

"Simon, Ra and I hardly think we're going to booze it up, as you say."

"No, Apollo, I get that, but rest and relaxation, silly letting off steam is good for the soul from time to time."

"You mean like the steam you let off when you sleep?"

"Oh yes, very funny Apollo. You know, you two really do have more important things to do than monitor my sleep."

"We weren't, but as long as you admit that with the new diet of real food you do produce an awfully large amount of methane . . ."

"Is that what I awoke you for, scatological jokes?" But by this time we were all laughing, Angie listening standing in the doorway, was doubled up.

The very morning we said good-bye to the Cramers, grandson and grandfather, keepers of the MacHead secrets and saviors of the earth (well, the newsvids ate it up and it kept my name off the first teleprompter as the President made the announcement), the UN met in Geneva and voted unanimously to adopt a world Constitution. In it they decided there needed to be guardians, one human, one, well, System (we still hadn't come up with a name for the new species, although Apollo said Gaia was also trying to help name the new species) and always a veto to Gaia. It made sense, the one who could destroy you all might as well have a veto on Earth. Even if only I and the twins knew it was a long way off.

Now, elsewhere in the galaxy . . . humanity could, and probably would no doubt, get back to thrust, counterthrust. Exploration was good for the species and, besides, Ra seemed especially keen, once Russia was sorted out.

22

TAG, WE'RE IT

There were no tears or big good-byes planned because we expect to talk every day. I kept reminding everyone that we'd be in full contact, all the time. In fact, we'd have Ra and Apollo with us all the time as well, keeping everything constant. However, my protests did not diminish the somber ceremonial feel of the day, not one bit. I tried, but clearly failed.

Fred gave me a hug before he left for the SpacePort, the elevator waiting to take him off planet, the moon and beyond. "Dad, it's time I went exploring. I think I'll take a posting on the moon and work with a team of geologists there. It's the one place of rock where Apollo and Ra have confirmed Gaia is not in control." He was still worried about that when I thought he shouldn't be. "Who knows where I'll go from there, you were right, there's a whole universe to explore, well, this galaxy anyway. We'll build the ships and give it a try."

I hugged him closer, "Keep safe Freddie, I love you, you know."

"Yeah Dad, I know, me too. I just need some time, okay?"

I nodded, "We'll be talking son," ruffled his hair and he got into the skimmer.

When it came time to see the Cramers off, the mood changed, mainly because Cramer is never down. We convened on the rooftop of the hotel by the old helipad, the sparkling blue of the Caribbean beyond, sun shining, smiles now all around. We all felt an adventure was about to begin, new life forms would follow. One by one everyone shook hands with Cramer and Charlie, patted backs, hugged, said farewells.

Cramer alone knew the private road we had traveled together. It was his provocation that made me open those secret doors to Apollo and Peter and, later, their offspring. I couldn't have done it without him, he couldn't have done it without me.

We shook hands and then I decked him, slowly, careful not to really make hard contact. Well, hell, they do it in those old movies I was enjoying again in my room. He sat back on his rear and wiggled a tooth, pretending to spit blood as I had those weeks before.

"Tag," I said slowly, "you're still it."

"I'll damn well kill you—or worse—tag you yet," said in jest, smile as big as his ability. Then he winked, "Heck, maybe I already have." He stepped up on the skylifter, leaned towards me and swung a perfect punch at my nose. In my speeded-up stage, he missed by a mile. He must have known he would. He never followed through, just turned and waved as the door shut behind him. I wondered what the wink was for.

Sheila left that afternoon. Her daughter came down to San Juan in the morning to collect her and implant me with the node. The External Tanks in orbit were already hard-wired to pick up the signal and relay it on command. Funny thing about those nodes, they only hurt at sea level. In weightlessness they would hurt the same as they do at depth, that is to say not at all. I checked it worked okay.

Sheila and her mother sat in a tight circle having emotional discussions with Angie. There were a lot of comments that drifted across the suite we were using for the implants, "You promise?" and "I'll be fine." and "Are you sure?" This last said looking at me. I put it all down to the teary farewells from Angie who knew Sheila was going 'out to pasture' as she put it and would not be rejuvenating. But that was years off.

Finally, in exasperation to all this emotion, I cried out "Hell, does no one listen to me anymore? We're going to be speaking every day for the rest of our lives!"

Angie smiled, shook her head, said to Apollo and Ra, who were tuned in for the good-byes, "He's not very bright is he?"

Apollo answered. His voice was now more considered, I would say, than Ra's, which was always in a hurry. "Will you be capable of instructing him?" Angie walked over to me.

"Instructing him what? When?" I asked.

"Oh shut up, dear," she reached her arms around my neck and kissed me full on the lips, "Time to go. Did you pack my cookies?" Ra, Apollo, Sheila, even her mother, all laughed at me. Angie smiled and tilted her head inquisitively.

How the hell did she know I had stocked the oatmeal cookies or my romantic invitation to have her go with me? Me, mumbling as I stepped onto the transport, "Oh, perfect, no damn secrets anymore, man can't even ask a woman to share his life without everyone knowing the answer before he does . . ."

Angie shook her head, slowly and smiled.

Dammit, are there no surprises left?

GLOSSARY

Calhoun Rat Studies (1962): His 1962 study was perhaps the seminal work suggesting a link between crowding and social pathology. He populated a room subdivided into four contiguous pens with rats and provided them with unlimited food and water; after a year, their density was high and he reported infanticide, cannibalism, homosexuality, and the formation of a "behavioral sink": the majority of the rats would congregate to feed within a small subsection of the room, increasing their real density far above that imposed by the distribution of food or size of the enclosure, and seemingly exacerbating the social pressure of numbers. The analogy with humans apparently voluntarily flocking to decaying inner cities despite high crime rates and lower quality of life compared to rural areas was compelling and the paper widely cited. John B. Calhoun himself promoted the analogy in papers such as "Plight of the Ik and Kaiadilt is seen as a chilling possible end for Man" (1972).

Citizens Council: Overriding control of the principle supply programs and facilities, ombudsmen of the national systems, not government.

DefenseSchield: National Defense Shield, particle and beam deflection as coordinated measures to repulse any attack by hostile forces. Originally airborne, now space borne and land borne, uses unlimited energy (see PowerCube).

FarmHands Agrarian: System, re-cycling all waste to synthesized food product.

Gaia: Originally the Gaia hypothesis postulated that Earth's atmosphere, naturally developed to support biology, was a result of the very presence of the needs of life on Earth. That hypothesis grew into the Gaia Theory which postulated that the Earth was, in fact, a biological entity that could be considered a complex, but single, entity.

Infanticide: Population density is a major cause and promotion of infanticidal tendencies—particularly the selection of sex for infanticide.

NCAR: Is a federally funded research and development center. Together with our partners at universities and research centers, we are dedicated to exploring and understanding our atmosphere and its interactions with the Sun, the oceans, the biosphere, and human society. See http://www.ncar.ucar.edu/

New Way: The official congressional word to describe American life after the abolishment of the old Constitution and the United States in favor of the New Nation (not under God), and called, simply, the Republic of America.

NuEl: Elevated conveyor passenger transport built on site of old Third Ave. elevated subway system, connecting Fourteenth Street and 125th. Made up of slow and faster lanes, with a glass barrier between directions and overhead.

PowerCube: System of inertial storage/cold-fusion energy devices producing stable DC current without cost (after initial cost of system, paid by Nation). These units are placed on every floor, every building, every sidewalk. All power is derived from them; there is no National Energy Grid. Fuel used: Air. Pollutant given off: Oxygen, water. Water piped into water system, oxygen released to atmosphere. Global atmospheric oxygen up .2% in forty years.

Purge: The time of great rectification, forty years ago, when collapse of the economy and rampant anarchy required Congress to enact the Purification Laws (set by the military dictatorship) and an amendment to the Constitution, leading to "the eradication of all subversive elements and conditions prevalent in the United States of America."

RFID: Remote Frequency Identification Device, implanted in every object and, after the age of six (when life expectancy was limitless), in your palm. Says who you are to all computer systems and monitors. No need to log in, they always know who and where you are.

Screems: Many, many screens of display material.

SeaSpout: An ocean control system, temperature, salinity and rate of currents, coordinated with WeatherGood.

SensorPath: Sensory input/output devices to give smell, sound and sight, real time. Taste is available in newer models.

SND: Security Net Division, police force for the System

operations and implementation. Most powerful of all the police forces, replaced the combined FBI and NSA after the Purge.

SynthKid: Biological duplicate of real child without self-volition gene, subject to reprogramming or destruction at parents' whim. Removable, by law, at age eighteen. No Blade Runner here.

WeatherGood One: Weather control system for Eastern Seaboard. Also: WeatherGoods Two through Six controlling rest of America.

ABOUT THE AUTHOR

Peter Riva has traveled extensively throughout Africa, Asia, and Europe, spending many months spanning thirty years with legendary guides for East African adventurers. He created the *Wild Things* television series in 1995 and has worked for more than forty years as a literary agent. Riva writes science fiction and African adventure books, including the Mbuno & Pero thrillers. He lives in Gila, New Mexico.

THE TAG SERIES

FROM OPEN ROAD MEDIA

OPEN ROAD

INTEGRATED MEDIA

Find a full list of our authors and
titles at www.openroadmedia.com

FOLLOW US
@OpenRoadMedia